# MURDER
# WITH
# LOVE

# MURDER
# WITH
# LOVE

A Luis Mendoza Mystery

# DELL
# SHANNON

William Morrow & Company, Inc., New York

*Omnia vincit amor: et nos cedamus amori.*
Love carries all before him: we too must
yield to Love.

—Virgil, *Eclogues, X, 69*

—But what a mischievous devil Love is!
—Samuel Butler, *Notebooks*

## AUTHOR'S NOTE

Obviously, for the purposes of this mystery series, the recent earthquake in Southern California had to be postdated to August. With the earth still quivering three days later (when this book got under way) it seemed ungracious not to acknowledge that the Earth Shaker had been at work in Mendoza's territory. We really do know the actual date was February!

# MURDER
# WITH
# LOVE

Mendoza drifted into the Homicide Bureau about three o'clock of a hot Friday afternoon: hotter than they usually got in early August. The air conditioning was not on, and Sergeant Lake looked stickily uncomfortable at his desk by the switchboard.

"So you finally show up," he said. "They haven't got around to us yet."

"So I see," said Mendoza. Beyond the anteroom, across the big communal detective office, all but two of the tall windows were missing all their glass. "And I'm entitled to half a day off for once. Anything new gone down?"

Sergeant Lake opened his mouth and suddenly the building shook a little and swayed. "Damn it, they say we'll be getting these aftershocks for a month," said Lake uneasily. "And I don't feel just so happy sitting here this high up all day."

"Well, the building hasn't fallen down yet, Jimmy."

"Higgins went out on a new body, but it didn't sound like much of anything—another heart attack, probably. The autopsy report came in on that bum—you don't have to ask what it says. Matt and Jase are out looking for possibles on the heist, and I don't know where everybody else is."

Mendoza went into his office, yawning. As he sat down in his desk chair, the building moved slightly again and the desk slithered an inch or so away from him. "Damnation," he said mildly.

The men at Central Homicide, LAPD, had been busy at the usual humdrum routine up to last Monday; there hadn't been anything big or very baffling on hand, just the tedious routine of clearing up after violent death. They'd had the heist job, a bar over on Fourth, the bartender shot; and the inevitable suicide, and the old wino over on the Row dead in an alley, and they had just cleaned up a hit-run. They had all gone home on Monday night, and the night watch had gone home by five-fifty Tuesday morning, and like ninety-five percent of the residents of L.A. County, were asleep in bed when a major earthquake occurred to Southern California. Later scientific estimates placed its epicenter out east of Newhall, but earthquakes are unpredictable in effect, and downtown L.A. being on a direct north-south line with the epicenter, destruction hit there too. A good many windows in the Police Building had been smashed, a few sidewalks buckled, a number of streets had been a shambles of broken glass from storefront windows, and over on Skid Row the old Midnight Mission, sheltering its usual collection of derelicts, had collapsed in rubble. Oddly enough there'd been only one casualty there: everybody had got out but one man when the roof fell in. The autopsy report was on Mendoza's desk now; he didn't look at it. He yawned again and lit a cigarette.

Out in the valley, of course, there had been devastation and disaster, and for forty-eight hours nearly every law man in the county had forgotten his regular job to help out on all that had to be done, from directing traffic down here to helping evacuate nearly a hundred thousand people from their homes to picking up looters in evacuated areas to ferrying people to the nearest civil-defense centers. But now things were getting cleaned up. The engineers had drained the reservoir and the dam was under repair, so all the evacuees had gone back home yesterday. The searchers had found the last of the bodies in the rubble of the two hospitals which had collapsed, and it was going to be a good long time before those freeways were in use again, where the overpasses had fallen down. Things were getting back to normal. Only, as usual after a major quake, they were getting the aftershocks, some of them registering respectably on the Richter scale, and the experts said they might go on for weeks.

Mendoza, finding himself tossed unceremoniously out of bed in Tuesday's pre-dawn, and hearing Alison's exclamation as she picked herself up from the other side of the bed, had been much occupied since; with things getting cleared up, he had taken most of today off. In fact, this was the first time he'd been to the office since Monday night—all hands had been needed in the disaster areas. Fortunately Hollywood was not in line with the quake's epicenter, and the house on Rayo Grande Avenue had only lost a few dishes and glassware.

Hackett came in looking hot and tired. "Jimmy said you'd finally shown up. Well, I don't blame you for taking some time off. They haven't got round to our windows yet, I see." Men had come on Wednesday and carefully cleared away the shards of glass still in the frames, but they were probably replacing the windows one floor at a time; and this was a big building. "And do you know what I just saw in the *Herald?* Talk about insult to injury—the specialists are now saying that because this one was on the San Gabriel fault, there's still pressure building on the San Andreas and we could have another big one any time. My God."

"Yes, I saw that—encouraging," said Mendoza absently.

"And we'll never get anybody for that heist job. No special M.O., it might have been any pro hood in town."

"Also encouraging." But the only homicides occurring since Tuesday morning had been natural deaths—heart attacks, and one heat prostration.

At least they had Nick Galeano back with them, just this week, from his little siege in the hospital after he'd been shot up by a kid high on the acid.

Higgins wandered in and said, "Welcome back. Not that I blame you for taking some time off, Luis." He pulled his tie loose, got out a cigarette; he and Hackett together made the office suddenly smaller. "The new one's just more paper work—another coronary, looks like, and probably brought on by fright at these damn aftershocks. And do you know what those damn-fool experts are saying now? In the *Herald—*"

"We saw it," said Hackett. "Spreading alarm and despondency, if you ask me. Not, for God's sake, that anybody in my family is worried— Mark got quite a kick out of it, first one for

13

him, and Angel just says, Fate. What is to be will be. Well, I suppose she's right at that."

"And Mary says the same thing," said Higgins gloomily. "Steve and Laura got a charge out of it too—their first one. And we didn't get any damage, but—" He massaged his prominent jaw. Mendoza and Hackett regarded him with idle amusement. Higgins the longtime bachelor, falling for Bert Dwyer's widow, had now some hostages to fortune to worry about: Bert's good kids, and the new baby due in October.

"God," said Hackett, "I wish it'd either cool off or our windows would get put back." It was obviously useless to pipe refrigerated air conditioning to offices minus windows. "We don't usually get it quite so bad in August—"

"I'll tell you something funny, Art," said Higgins. "It's always hot when we get a quake. Hotter than usual. I wonder if there's any connection."

"Well, one of the experts up at the planetarium—on TV last night—seems to think it's a matter of the sun and moon being in direct alignment. There was an eclipse on Monday night, you know—"

Matt Piggott and Jason Grace came in and Grace said, "Have a nice morning off? Not that I blame you. We might as well throw that heist job in Pending, we'll never land on anybody with enough evidence." His chocolate-brown face, moustache as neatly narrow as Mendoza's, wore a pensive look.

"I said so," said Hackett.

"And aside from the paper work on the other bodies, business slow," said Piggott. "Everybody so scared by the quake they're sitting quiet at home, maybe."

"Waiting for the next one," agreed Grace. He lit a cigarette and strolled over to the windows, and Hackett told him nervously to stay away from there.

"One of these aftershocks could send you right out. I wish to God there *was* some legwork to do, I'd just as soon be on the street as up this high—"

"Fate," said Mendoza. "Trust your guardian angel, Art."

"And you can laugh," said Piggott, "but there are, you know.

14

The guardian angels. Look at Higgins—and Tom, come to that." They thought about that; maybe there were. Higgins getting away from those three escaped cons, back in April, without a scratch; and Tom Landers' strange ordeal last June, when he'd got mistakenly identified as a pro hood. But Landers' guardian angel, you could say, had been pretty, trim, smart (in both senses) Policewoman O'Neill down in R. and I.

"How's Tom doing with that cute blonde?" wondered Hackett. "Anybody heard lately?" It was Landers' day off today.

"He's not," said Grace sadly. "His mind's made up all right, but she's a very sensible sort of girl, that one. Says they haven't known each other long enough to be sure. But she's still dating him, so maybe he'll get her to marry him eventually."

The inside phone rang and Mendoza picked it up. "Yes, Jimmy?"

"Things starting to move again," said Lake. "Shooting at a travel agency over on Spring."

"Right." Mendoza passed that on. "You can toss for it."

"I'll go," said Hackett at once. "I feel safer on terra firma." He got up.

Grace grinned. "In earthquake country—like the old joke says —there are times when the terra just isn't so firma."

"That does it," said Higgins. "I'll go too, with the third-rate vaudeville jokes floating around. And I don't like these damn windows any more than you, Art."

They left Mendoza yawning again. "And the elevators," said Hackett as he punched the button. "They can get jammed—"

It was the Acme Travel Agency, We Send You Better, and a little crowd had collected in the street outside, where the black-and-white was parked at the curb. Hackett and Higgins shouldered through the crowd to find another small gathering inside the building. Off to one side, one uniformed man was riding herd on half a dozen people and his partner was standing over two people sitting in a couple of the chairs lined at one side of the long counter—a sullen-faced dark young man and a sobbing

15

blonde. There was a body on the floor on this side of the counter, with the colorful travel posters above it.

The second uniformed man came forward. "Very glad to see you, sir. Quite a little party here, by what we gather. It was the owner called us—Mr. Haskell—" He nodded at a scared-looking middle-aged man over there with three women, another man. "Seems this guy just walked in and started shooting. Here's his gun." He handed Higgins a big revolver. It was a Colt .45, empty now.

Hackett bent over the body. Another young man, a good-looking man, fair, well-dressed in a light-gray suit, white shirt, dark tie. He'd been hit in the body, at least a couple of slugs, maybe more, and he'd bled a good deal onto the patterned vinyl flooring.

"He just—he just walked in and started shooting—" The middle-aged man came forward hesitantly. "You more police? He—that one—" he nodded at the corpse, "he'd just come in, with the lady, his name was Gorton, he said they wanted plane reservations for Rome, and I was just— When this other one came in and just started shooting—no reason at all—and Ruby screamed, that's Ruby, she works here of course, I ought to say I own the business, it's my own business, my wife and I—only Marge went to the bank, thank God she wasn't here when— And he just started shooting, and—"

"All right," said Hackett, and stood up.

"There's an ambulance on the way, sir," said the other uniformed man. "All these people say they witnessed it, so we held 'em for you."

"So who's the marksman?" asked Higgins genially. The sullen young man didn't look up at him.

"Goddamn little bitch," he said. "It was her I ought to've shot. Her too. Just bad luck I didn't get her too." He was also a fairly good-looking fellow, dark and tall, with a pugnacious jaw, and well dressed. "Damn little bitch—and my *partner*—my good old friend and partner! Rome, yet. With *my* wife—on *his* vacation! For God's sake, I ought to've—"

"So, what's your name?" asked Higgins.

16

"Oh, for God's sake. William J. Campden. He's Dick Gorton. For God's sake—Campden and Gorton, such buddy-buddy partners—for God's sake, in college together, and—"

The blonde emerged from her handkerchief, where she sat sobbing, and she was a very pretty blonde even with her eye makeup smeared over one cheek and her eyes red. She was, in fact, quite a dish for any male who appreciated the obvious. She had big brown eyes and a nice slim rounded figure, and her long flaxen hair waved shimmering past her bare shoulders, and she was wearing a very abbreviated white sundress and spike-heeled white sandals; her toenails were painted blood-red. She sobbed and hiccuped and said, "You big bastard! Killing Dicky! You weren't ever going to know anything *about* it—it didn't matter— you were supposed to think I was visiting Mother in Colorado Springs just like I told you! You wouldn't have known anything about—and you didn't need to *kill* him! You didn't—"

"So it's Fate," said Campden bitterly. "I just happen to leave the office early and stroll up to Benny's bar for a drink. Just in time to see my dear little girl-wife and my buddy-buddy partner —who I thought was up at Tahoe, where he said he was going— all cozily going into a travel agency arm in arm. *Rome* yet, the man says. My God. I wouldn't have known— Oh, you are a prize, Sandra. You really are."

"Well, you *wouldn't* have! And you didn't need to—"

"Mr. Campden, if you'd just—"

"Oh, hell," said Campden. He looked up at Hackett and Higgins. "It was just damn bad luck I had the gun on me. Or Fate. We keep it at the office, I was taking it home to oil it. And I've got a temper that goes off—as you could maybe guess." He sighed a long deep sigh. "So—he's dead. She's the one I should have— Little bitch Sandra. And me the innocent husband, never suspecting a thing."

"We weren't g-going till next month, he said Rome in September was w-wonderful—but I was so scared about the earthquake so he asked for his vacation early—and you had to see us, just an accident really— Oh, Dicky!"

"All right, Mr. Campden, up," said Hackett. "I have to explain all your rights to you," and he started to go through that ritual. Higgins was calling up more cars, to ferry the witnesses in to make statements.

The Central beat was getting back to normal after the earthquake: the irrational, the wanton, the senseless crime and violence.

By the time they got all the witnesses back to the office, Palliser had come in, so he and Grace and Piggott shared the job of getting the statements down with Hackett and Higgins. It turned out that Campden was a lawyer; he and Gorton had shared offices on Spring Street. Now it would be up to the D.A. what he wanted to call this, manslaughter or murder second or whatever.

They were still busy on that when Lake put through a call from Wilcox Street.

"Mendoza?" Sergeant Barth of that station in the middle of Hollywood. "We've got a thing here we want you on from the start. Whether you're busy down there or not."

"Not very, for once. What's up?"

"Well, it could be quite a thing—I'd just like the experts on it, Mendoza." Barth sounded abrupt and worried. "It's La Presa Drive up above the boulevard. Bring a lab team, hah? Right now."

"¿Cómo? Something important?"

"To us, yes," said Barth. "One of ours. Patrolman on our beat. No, he's not dead, but his chances don't look so good."

"¡Cómo! I'm on my way." Mendoza reached for his hat and started out. "Jimmy, I want a lab truck to meet me at this address." He passed it over. "Pronto. Seems business is picking up."

It was still very hot on the street, in late afternoon. The Ferrari's steering wheel was nearly too hot to touch. But at least the freeways downtown hadn't collapsed, and he made good time up to Hollywood.

La Presa Drive . . . Luis Mendoza had been a cop on this force for twenty-four years and had ridden a squad car awhile;

18

he knew his city in and out. This was a quiet little backwater with some of the oldest streets, the oldest houses, in the hills above Hollywood. There were new, smartly fashionable areas up here but this wasn't one of them. The winding narrow streets off Outpost Drive had a faded gentility; the houses on them had once, thirty years ago, been substantial upper-class houses, many of them large, but time had run by and the moneyed people, the elite of Hollywood, had moved to newer fashionable residential areas.

When he found the house, around many curves of the narrow street, there were three cars parked in front, one a black-and-white. As he parked the Ferrari, the big mobile lab truck pulled up behind him and Scarne and Duke got out of the front seat, with Marx and Horder climbing out the back.

It was a big old frame house, perhaps forty years old. Like most of the houses up here, it didn't have much yard around it: these were small lots carved from the hillside. It was painted white, it was two-storied, with a strip of lawn and a front porch. The front door was open and as Mendoza stepped to the porch Sergeant Barth appeared there—stocky, middle-aged, worried-looking.

"Mendoza, glad to see you. Now we've got a very funny thing here indeed. You'll want to talk to his wife, of course—she's at the hospital, naturally, went along in the ambulance—as long as there's any *chance*—but it didn't look too good. Well." Barth passed a hand across his face. "He's a good man, Mendoza. One of our bright young men. Kind to end up downtown as captain—a career man. Patrick Henry Logan."

"So what happened?" Mendoza glanced around the living room. It was large and rectangular, dim because the house faced north, and rather sparsely furnished: a long Naugahyde-covered couch, a few chairs, a long coffee table, plain beige drapes and carpet. Another plainclothesman and a uniformed man were bending over chalk marks at the other end of the room. A door there gave a glimpse into a den or dining room, to the right; to his left here, the square entrance hall had stairs leading up.

"There's no sense to it," said Barth angrily. "Look, Mendoza,

19

he's a good man. He's got four years' service with us and he's passed the detective exam already. He'd be up for promotion when there was a hole left. He's twenty-six, married three years —his wife's name's Sally, she works part time at a dress shop down on Sunset. They haven't any family yet, and there's house payments, I suppose, car payments— *I* don't know. What I do know, I've talked to some of the other men he worked with, and there isn't anything showing—Logan and his wife get on fine, her father was a cop too, retired captain out of Hollenbeck—and Logan wouldn't, for God's sake, have any enemies—a very easygoing guy, doesn't get into arguments with people, very clean record with us—an ordinary fellow—well, not ordinary, an ambitious career man—but you see what I mean. There's just no reason—"

"All right, I've got Logan. What happened to him? And what do you want here, the full treatment?"

"But absolutely," said Barth. "For a start, this room, the den and the kitchen." Mendoza nodded at the lab men, who started unpacking their bags silently. "So, his wife doesn't work Fridays. He's on the swing watch, due in for briefing at three-thirty, start the tour at four. Riding a one-man car in central Hollywood. He'd have left home about three, to get down to the station and change into uniform. His wife said good-bye to him about a quarter of three when she went out to do some marketing. They've both got cars, yes. She came home about three-forty-five and found him. Up there." The chalk marks on the carpet were at the end of the room, just under a window; also bloodstains—quite a little blood had been spilled on the carpet, there and over by the door into the den.

"The call went down at three-forty-nine, Sergeant," said the uniformed man. "And I'll back that up, my God— Pat's a very mild guy, easygoing all right, nobody could have any reason to—"

"She called the ambulance, and us," said Barth. "Whoever it was, Mendoza, and whatever the hell it was, he'd been all but beaten to death. I don't know whether any weapon was used, there could have been—the interns said it was touch and go, and

20

if there was any chance they had to get him in fast—one artery pumping blood—multiple skull-fractures, I'd guess, and probably internal injuries—"

"*Dios.*" Mendoza got out a cigarette and looked at it. "A career man, you said. So Logan is not just the average five-nine, a hundred and fifty or better."

"That's the damn point," said Barth, "or one of them. He's not. He's six-one, a hundred and eighty-five, and he's in top condition. He knows judo. Last week he ran into a pro heavyweight up on Fairfax and brought him in alone—hell, the man was drunk but still—"

"Mmh, yes," said Mendoza. "Yes. And he's an easygoing fellow who hasn't any enemies, as far as anybody knows. His wife— Well, of course you haven't had a chance really to question her yet."

"Not really, no. But she told us that. Nobody with any reason to—I only talked to her a minute or so, she naturally wanted to go with him in the ambulance, but she's a cop's daughter and a cop's wife, Mendoza, a level-headed girl—a nice girl—upset as all hell, you can see she's in love with him—and she'd know. Wouldn't she? About anybody with any reason to—"

"Mmh, yes," said Mendoza again. "But we all know, depressingly often there's no reason behind the violence. Some people don't need reasons. *¿Cómo no?* See what the lab can pick up. At least we can narrow down the time—between two-forty-five and three-forty-five. Did any of the neighbors see anything, a car or— Mmh, indeed, six-one, a hundred and— You know, Barth, that says to me that it could have been more than one X. Jumping him. Because—" He looked around the room, where Marx and Horder were efficiently dusting every surface for latent prints and Scarne was taking photographs—"Logan would have put up a fight, just attacked by one man—even unexpectedly. There'd have been more mess in here, furniture knocked over, and so on."

"That just occurred to me before you got here," said Barth. "But for God's sake *why?* Who? Why Logan? Because it looks as if it was a personal grudge of some kind, beating him up like that, and there'd be no reason—"

"Reasons and reasons," said Mendoza absently. "Some people don't need much reason. I suppose the wife hasn't had a chance to look around for anything missing."

"Burglars?" said Barth incredulously. "At three o'clock in the afternoon? Up here? And beating him nearly to death?"

"*Posible*. If only just. In any case, we want her to look. And there won't be much traffic up here at any time of day. We ask the neighbors whether they saw a car, anybody on foot, anybody near this house. A car is more likely. We can, of course, look at his reports over the last couple of weeks, what and who he ran across on the job—" Mendoza met Barth's disgusted expression and grinned sardonically.

"I thought you were supposed to be an expert. For God's sake, Mendoza! A uniformed man riding a quiet beat in Hollywood?"

"*Inverosímil*, yes—very unlikely. Not one of us who hasn't heard it—I'll get you, cop—but threatened men live long, so they say. But just now and then it does happen. We'll look and ask. But first we ask the neighbors—any of them who were home. There might be a shortcut here."

Owing to the winding street, not many near neighbors on La Presa Drive would have been in a position to observe anything near the Logan house; and only three of them had been at home at the crucial time. Any car passing up the street could have been heading for Castilian Way, or Oporto Place, other little streets farther up. What they got really didn't take them much further.

Mrs. Richard Fitch, who lived a block down from the Logans on La Presa, but in the nearest house to theirs—these were short blocks—was much shocked to hear about Patrick Henry Logan. She had been working in her front yard from about three to three-thirty, she said, and only one car had passed her going up the hill, and that car she knew. It was a red Mustang owned by young Jim Brinkman—the Brinkmans lived up on Oporto Place, her son Bob went to school with Jim.

Mr. Fred Nicholson, retired stockbroker, lived on Castilian Way, at the corner where La Presa crossed it. All he could tell them was that some time that afternoon a car had passed his house, "Like a bat outta hell," said Mr. Nicholson. "One o' these souped-up jalopies, sounded like—no, I didn't see it, and I couldn't tell-you what time it was exactly, somewhere around three, I guess. I was out in the kitchen getting a can of beer out of the refrigerator—my God, we don't usually get this kind of heat in August—and it *could* have turned on La Presa but I just couldn't say." Mr. Nicholson was a widower and lived alone. "Like people said to me"—he was garrulous, pleased to have visitors—"after Agnes died, I ought to sell the house, get an apartment—but it's been home for thirty years, I know it's too big for a man alone, but it's home—where Agnes and I lived thirty years. I stayed on. And tell you one thing, never so much as a crack in the plaster last Tuesday, it's a hell of a lot better built than these jerry-built new apartments. . . . Logan? No, I don't know him—I'm sorry, I wish I could help you more, but—"

Mrs. Claudia Franks answered Mendoza somewhat distraitly. She lived in a pink stucco house across the street and down the hill from the Logans. She was a big blonde woman in her forties, corseted and very neat in a tailored navy dress, discreet makeup, and she looked at the badge and said to Mendoza, *"Police?* But what on earth— Well, I'm expecting an important telephone call, if it won't take much time—of course I want to cooperate with— What? A car? Well, yes, I've been home most of the afternoon, mostly in the living room here, but I don't— Yes, I did hear a couple of cars go by. It's pretty quiet up here as a rule, you notice— But of course I didn't go to look out, why should I? Well, yes, one of the cars was kind of loud, like one of those little four-cylinder things, but I didn't see it. Why?"

"Do you know the Logans, across the street?"

"Why, of course," she said. "Such nice young people, and Mr. Logan—" A phone shrilled somewhere and she said, "Oh, that'll be—I'm sorry, you'll have to excuse me—" And she shut the door precipitately.

And of course that told them nothing. Nothing at all. A noisy car heading up (possibly) La Presa Drive. Young Jim Brinkman. Well, talk to him, but—

When Mendoza started home at six-thirty, Patrolman Logan was still alive—but only just, in Intensive Care at the Hollywood Receiving Hospital.

What had happened to him, and why?

Mendoza came out of the garage; at this time of year it was still light, and a vigilant voice assailed him from the alder tree. *Coroo, coroo—YAWK!—Yankee Doodle came to town!* That damned mockingbird—and Alison said it was nesting again.

He came in the back door to find his household looking much as usual. Their shaggy dog Cedric was slurping water from his bowl, and Mrs. MacTaggart was busy over the stove, while all four cats—Bast, Sheba, Nefertite and El Señor—were weaving round her legs reminding her that this was their usual dinnertime if anybody remembered. Alison, red hair in disarray, was supervising the twins' supper.

"Honestly!" she said, as the twins erupted at him shouting. "Johnny—Terry—¡bastante! Come back here and finish your pudding— Honestly, Luis, it is maddening. I got a man to come and look at the driveway—" The driveway, last Tuesday morning, had sustained a large crack down its middle. "But he can't come to fix it until next week."

"As long as it gets fixed eventually," said Mendoza, kissing her. "Things getting settled down to routine again—we've got a new one. A peculiar new one . . . *Pues sí*, Terry, I'll read to you —let me catch my breath, *niños!* And come to think—"

"And of all things," said Alison, "those experts are saying now that this quake was on the San Gabriel fault so the San Andreas is still under pressure and another one could happen any—"

"I saw it, I saw it," said Mendoza. "So encouraging, yes."

# 2

On Saturday morning when Mendoza called the hospital, Logan was still hanging on, still unconscious. Mendoza and Hackett went over there at nine o'clock; the wife was still there, and they wanted some opinions from the doctors too.

"I don't know why he's still with us," the chief surgeon told them. "We're not saying yet he'll make it. There were four skull-fractures, one arm and shoulder broken, stab wounds in the chest, and a femoral artery severed—we've been pumping blood into him since he was brought in."

"God," said Hackett. "Stabbed—any other weapon used, you think?"

"Probably. Nobody made those dents in his skull with a fist. He's got a very sound constitution, of course. My God, who'd do such a thing?—some personal grudge, was it?"

"Anybody's guess," said Mendoza, "so far."

Sally Logan was sitting where she'd been all night, in a little waiting room at the end of that floor. She'd be a pretty girl ordinarily, dark-brown hair, blue eyes, a nice figure; but her eyes were red and she looked very tired and her plain blue cotton dress was rumpled. There was a man with her, a man perhaps sixty, burly, with curly gray hair and a weatherbeaten face. He eyed Mendoza and Hackett and said, "They got Central on it right off. Just as well. I'm Royce—at Hollenbeck up to last year." Sally Logan's father. "What the *hell*—I just don't understand it, who'd want to hurt Pat?" He looked very angry.

Sally Logan told them wearily that Pat's parents lived in

25

Pittsburgh; she'd wired them and they were flying out. "Now, Mrs. Logan," said Mendoza, "we don't like to bother you at a time like this, but there are questions we've got to ask—"

"Sure there are," said Royce. "Trouble is, there aren't any answers. No enemies. Nobody with any grudge on him. No recent trouble of any kind. Pat—"

She sat up and looked at the men from Homicide. "That's right. There's nothing I can tell you," she said steadily. "Nobody who could have any reason to want to hurt Pat. It's c-crazy. Hurt him like *that*. I'd know if there was, and there just wasn't . . . I'm sorry, I'll try to— Yes, he'd tell me about anything like that, we always tell each other everything. Anything different, or funny, that happened on his tour, you know, or— But he hadn't been on regular tour until—day before yesterday. Tuesday and Wednesday he'd got sent out to Valley, the civil-defense people—"

"You're doing no good sitting here, Sally," said Royce roughly. "I've told you. When you've answered all the questions, you're going home to bed. We'll hear any news fast enough."

"We'd like you to look through the house, Mrs. Logan, check to see if anything's missing."

Royce glanced at Mendoza. "Berserk burglar? Doped up? That's possible, I suppose."

"There wouldn't be anything—valuable—to steal," she said. "Pat might have had ten or twelve dollars on him, not any more. Yes, I see. All right. But just for *that*, to—"

Mendoza shrugged at Royce, who got up and urged her to her feet. Pat Logan had had nine-eighty-seven on him, still in his billfold when they undressed him at the hospital. Barth had checked at Wilcox Street: Pat Logan's uniform and regulation Police Positive .38 were just where they should be, in his locker there.

"So?" said Hackett when Royce had led the girl out.

"It looks as if we'll need the crystal ball for this one, Arturo." Mendoza lit a cigarette. "Just a peculiar thing with no shape to it."

26

"I wonder about that Jim Brinkman Mrs. Fitch mentioned. You never know where a lead will show."

"*De veras.* I'm still thinking, especially after what we heard from the doctor, a couple of X's. To do such a job on him, and he was hardly a helpless victim—he'd have put up a fight, and he doesn't seem to have." Logan's right knuckles grazed and bloody, that was all. One of the first blows knocking him out?

"I'd buy that," agreed Hackett. "In fact I'd say it's obvious." He slid his bulk into the Ferrari behind Mendoza. "I wonder—"

"Inspiration struck you?"

"I don't know," said Hackett. "I'll think about it before I say."

Downtown everybody was in except Lake; it was his day off, and Rory Farrell was sitting on the switchboard.

There'd been a new body—just a kid, said Glasser, over the report: with the kit on him, all the equipment for mainlining the H. Piggott had gone out with him on it, and said now, "Back to Sodom and Gomorrah, I swear. He couldn't have been eighteen —these idiotic kids conned that there's no harm in it—the devil getting around these days."

Nothing else had turned up. They had got the statements from Campden, Mrs. Campden and six other witnesses to the shooting yesterday and there wasn't any more to do on that until Campden came up for arraignment. Palliser, Grace and Landers were just sitting around, listening with interest to the details on Logan. They agreed, more than one X. But who, and why?

"And Echo answers," said Mendoza. "Where's George?"

"Down the hall after coffee. I guess," said Grace, "everybody is still staying home waiting for the next quake."

As if it had been awaiting the word, the building moved uneasily, and the floor was momentarily unsolid under their feet. "The Lord," said Piggott gloomily, "bringing down destruction, and I'm just surprised it wasn't sooner and more."

"I don't *like* these damn aftershocks," said Glasser.

Higgins came in looking annoyed. "These damned aftershocks," he said. "I spilled half my coffee just then." He drank from the paper cup. "What'd you get at the hospital?"

Hackett started to tell him. There was no sign of any work done on the windows yet, and the hot morning sun struck through brightly: the office was already stifling.

"Lieutenant," said Farrell, looking in. "New one. Sheridan Hotel up on Grand."

"So, I'm the lieutenant—let some of my minions go and look at it," said Mendoza. Patrick Henry Logan, that good career cop—

Landers and Palliser went out to look at it. Tom Landers was feeling a little moody these days. He'd finally met the right girl, his very smart Policewoman Phil O'Neill—Phillipa Rosemary, only not, as she said, for an LAPD officer—but little blonde Phil O'Neill had a great deal of common sense. Hadn't known each other long enough, she said briskly and sensibly. And she'd got to know his family up in Fresno when she was playing his guardian angel last June, and there was his sister Jean deviling at him, when are you and Phil getting married—and his darling Phil acting so damned *sensible*—

Well, she went out with him, and by God eventually he'd get her, Landers vowed to himself.

"Business picking up a little," he said as they got into Palliser's Rambler.

"Maybe. I hope not too hot and heavy," said Palliser. "I've got a muscle pulled or something in my shoulder—" He felt it. "They had me using a shovel over at the Mission most of Tuesday."

"That was a mess. Lucky only the one casualty. It'll seem funny to have it gone."

"We'll lose some city landmarks after this one, all right." The oldest houses in Los Angeles, over on Olvera Street, had sustained heavy damage; anybody's guess if they could be restored.

The Sheridan Hotel was not the classiest hostelry in town. It was an old tan-brick building, and as soon as they entered the lobby they both noticed the ugly gaping cracks in the wall above the counter.

"She ain't gonna fall down right this minute," said the man behind the counter. "Patch it up a little, she'll be O.K. She come through the 'thirty-three one too. You more cops? Thought so. It's upstairs, second floor. Maid went in and found him. Seems he's registered here all right, but—"

"What's the room number?"

"Two-twenty."

They climbed uncarpeted worn stairs and found the room. A uniformed man was standing in front of the door with a frightened-looking Negro girl. "I'm Warner, sir. Miss Millie Weekes—she found him."

"Oh, my Lord!" she said. "I didn't know anybody had that room again—I just went in to check on the towels—oh, my Lord!"

"Little party here last night," said the patrolman. "I would guess."

They went in. This was an old hotel, the rooms shabby and cheap. The furniture was old and sparse—a double bed, a small chest of drawers, a rickety straight chair. Palliser and Landers looked around the room, looked at the corpse, and made some immediate educated guesses at what had gone on here.

The body was a man's body, a man not young, a big man with muscled shoulders and an incipient paunch. He was lying on his back on this side of the bed, and he was wearing only gray trousers and an old-fashioned sleeveless undershirt. There were bruises and blood on him, and also marks on his bare throat. He was cold. There were a few indications of a struggle: the worn rug scuffled up in one place, the lamp on the chest knocked over.

On the bedside table was a bottle of cheap Scotch three-quarters empty, and a glass. On the chest, a paper cup with a few drops of Scotch left in it. There was a package of paper cups on the bed. Ashtrays full of ashes and dead butts: in one, a crumpled pack that had held Lucky Strikes. Palliser turned over the ashes in the other tray with a ballpoint pen and said, "Detectives they call us. Sometimes we hardly need to be, Tom." The cigarette stubs in that ashtray were all stained with pink lipstick.

"And," said Landers, looking at that, "this kind of hotel, the very superficial cleaning—whatever the lab may pick up here could be useless. On the other hand, you could say not much finesse, if that's the word."

There was an old leather billfold lying on the bed beside the paper cups. Palliser flicked it open with the pen—the shiny worn leather might yield some nice latents—and there was a little folder of plastic slots for I.D. cards, photos. The first slot held a California driver's license for Christopher W. Hauck of an address on Melbourne Avenue in Hollywood. It was a four-year license, which said he had a clean record as a driver. He'd been forty-six when it was renewed last year.

They told Warner to stay on it, told the maid they'd want a statement from her, and went back downstairs. Landers called the office for a lab team. They questioned the clerk.

"Like I said, he was registered. Last night—I'd never laid eyes on him." He showed them the entry in the registry. A nearly illiterate hand had filled it in: *Mr. & Mrs. C. W. Hauck.*

"Oh, yes," said Palliser. "You didn't sign him in?"

"Nope. I go off at five. It'd have been Jim Glidden, he's the night clerk."

"Where'd we find him, you know?"

"Home asleep, I guess, this hour. Sure, his address'll be here somewhere—" The clerk found it: Judson Street over in Boyle Heights. They waited for the ambulance, the lab men, turned them loose on the room, and took the maid back to the office to get a statement.

When they came out to the street again, Landers to head for Boyle Heights and Palliser to Hollywood, there was a lone picket strolling up and down in front of the building. He had a long white beard and threadbare clothes, and his homemade sign proclaimed THE END OF THE WORLD IS NEAR—REPENT!

"I wonder if Matt's seen that," said Landers, and Palliser laughed.

"And I might add that we wouldn't have laughed at it at six A.M. last Tuesday."

"No," said Landers. That was a fact. And things were pretty

30

much cleaned up down here now—except for all those empty windows in the Police Building—the glass swept from the sidewalks, the crumpled old Mission posted with *Unsafe* signs and awaiting the bulldozers; but out in the valley the engineers were still working to repair that dam, and it would be some time before work started on the freeways.

Jim Glidden finally answered his doorbell after Landers had leaned on it steadily for five minutes. It was an old apartment house in this down-at-heel section of the city, and Landers fully expected Glidden to be elderly and down-at-heel too, so he was a little surprised when Glidden did open the door—a fellow in his early twenties, slim and fair-haired and healthy-looking. He was yawning, tying an old terry bathrobe over pajamas.

"What the hell?" he said to Landers. "Don't tell me I got out of bed for a Fuller Brush man? What? A cop? A *cop?*" He stared at the badge. "You don't look old enough."

Landers was nearly resigned to hearing that; but Phil had reassured him that he'd aged at least five years over that queer affair last June. "It's for real," he said equably. "Like to ask you some questions, if you're the Jim Glidden who's night clerk at the Sheridan Hotel."

"That's me. Come in." He was still yawning. "I know it's not the Beverly Hilton—"

"Detective Landers."

"Sure. Sit down. But they do say, beggars can't be choosers," said Glidden. The apartment living room was rather bare of furniture but looked neat and clean; there was a bookcase full of books on one wall. Landers sat down on the couch and Glidden on a chair opposite.

"You aren't exactly what I expected," said Landers. "Not a very lucrative job. A dead-end job."

"But a night job," said Glidden, "where I can usually snatch a few hours sleep. I'm studying for the Bar, but it's a long haul and I'm earning my own way. Dad died last year, my mother works uptown, and the hotel job's very handy for my purposes, see what I mean."

31

"Oh," said Landers. "Well, last night a Christopher Hauck registered at the hotel. When, and who was with him?"

"And I am not exactly an idiot," said Glidden, cocking his head at him. "Yes. The manager laid that on the line when he hired me, and it wasn't any business of mine whether I liked it or not. It's a convenient job for me, as I say, and what the hell could I do about it anyway? I will say it wasn't just so often it happened—we get a lot of small-time salesmen, that kind of thing, people without much money but straight clients. Once in a while that—the obvious john with the girl-friend, but the manager says their money's as good as anybody's." He shrugged.

"So, Hauck? A girl with him?"

Glidden grinned. "The other way round, I'd say. He'd had a few but he wasn't high, he knew what he was doing. I'd never seen either of them before. The girl—" He thought. "About twenty-five, five-four, good figure, bleached blonde, she had on a dress that was just barely there—skirt up to her thighs, and a lot of costume jewelry. Yes, I'd know her again. Neither of them had any luggage, of course."

"That's very helpful, Mr. Glidden. We'll be asking you for a formal statement."

"Sure. Why? I mean, what happened to bring the cops around? Did he end up murdering her or something?" asked Glidden curiously.

Landers grinned at him. "The other way round, I'd say," he said dryly.

The address on Melbourne Avenue turned out to be a comfortable-looking old California bungalow on a quiet street. The woman who opened the door to Palliser was middle-aged, plump, comfortable-looking like her house, with gray hair and rimless glasses.

"Does Mr. Christopher Hauck live here?" Palliser brought out the badge. "I'm afraid—"

Her face changed. "Something's happened to him," she said quietly, "hasn't it? Come in. I'm his sister—I'm Reba Roberts.

32

Yes, Chris lives here with me—I'm a widow, never had any family, and when Joe died we thought it was only sensible Chris should— Something's happened to him, hasn't it?" She sat down on the edge of a chair, staring at Palliser.

"I'm afraid so, Mrs. Roberts." He broke the news as tactfully as possible, making no implications, but the crude facts could hardly be glossed over.

"And I might have *known*," she said sorrowfully, angrily, harshly, cutting across his words. "I might have *expected* it. Chris running around after *women* all the time—and a man his age ought to have known better, but the ones like Chris don't change. Don't seem to learn anything. But to die like *that*—" She gave an involuntary sob and Palliser asked if he could get her a glass of water. "Thank you, sir—the kitchen—"

She sipped the water and wiped her eyes with a clean handkerchief. "It's a shock—of course it's a shock, did you say Sergeant? Police coming to tell me— Well, he was my brother, we grew up together, I can't but say he was a good brother to me—Joe didn't leave much, but Chris always made good money and he was generous, I've got to say. He helped out on the expenses, I don't know how I'd have managed to pay off the house, it hadn't been for Chris— What? He's a—he was a construction worker, Sergeant—a master carpenter, a good workman—he always made good money. He was good to me. But you couldn't talk to him—he never married, and he was always chasing round after—you know—loose women. Like that. I can't deny it. Like he was still just a young blade, know what I mean. I couldn't talk to him—he'd just laugh and say he's footloose and fancy-free, you're only young once and better love it up while you can. He always said it that way—better love it up while—"

"Would he have had much cash on him, Mrs. Roberts?"

"Probably," she said. "He liked to carry a good roll. He'd've got his paycheck yesterday—over four hundred dollars, two weeks' pay. He might have had it all on him, times he'd take it all in cash. . . . But to die like *that*—some little floozy he'd just picked up— Well, I suppose it's just as well we haven't any family to feel the disgrace, Sergeant. . . . I suppose I can't —make any arrangements—right away?"

"We'll let you know," Palliser told her gently.

So Chris Hauck, who should have known better at his age, had just been asking for it, he reflected on his way back downtown. Carrying the roll, picking up the floozy. But no floozy had beaten and/or strangled Hauck, obviously. Hauck, still loving it up. Asking for what he'd got.

The bearded picket was still in front of the building.

Mendoza, leaving Hackett typing a report, went up to Oporto Place to see Jim Brinkman. It was absolutely nothing, of course —only you never did know where a lead would turn up.

He didn't turn up any lead from Jim Brinkman.

Jim Brinkman was home alone in the old stucco house on the winding hillside street. He had just finished his first term at L.A.C.C., and during vacation was tutoring in math to get his grades up, he told Mendoza. He was an upright-looking young fellow, in contrast to the long-haired louts wandering around town in the dirty clothes. He was middle-sized, stocky, dark, and polite to a lieutenant of police, if bewildered.

He'd come home about three yesterday afternoon, sure, he said. From his math lesson. Straight home. And his mother had been home, she could say. They didn't know the Logans at all. And he didn't recall passing any other car on the way up the hill here—up Outpost he'd come, and then up La Presa to Oporto. It was a quiet neighborhood, not much traffic.

Mendoza came back to the Ferrari and said, "*¡Mil rayos!*" That had been an exercise in futility, as he might have known it would be. He went back to La Presa Drive and parked, and tried Mrs. Franks's pink stucco house; there were questions she hadn't been asked yet. But nobody answered the door: the pink stucco house was empty.

Frustrated, he drove back downtown and noticed the picket for the first time. He wondered if Matt had seen that yet. Upstairs, he found Palliser and Landers talking about the new body with Farrell, and heard the details on that one.

34

"Asking for it," said Palliser. "Loving it up, my God. But at least somewhere to go on this one."

"You hope," said Mendoza. He got the lab on the phone. "That hotel room—have you got anything useful?"

"You boys are always in such a hurry," sighed Duke. "I couldn't tell you yet. We picked up a lot of latents—a few good ones, more bad. It'll take a little work to raise any on that paper cup but we hope to eventually. And weed out any belonging to the corpse, yes. And analyze the lipstick. We're on it, Lieutenant, but we don't produce instantly. Tomorrow, maybe something definite." And that was what they always got from the lab.

"I wonder," said Mendoza, "if Matt's seen that picket downstairs." Palliser and Landers laughed.

"Yes, he did," said Farrell seriously. "And all he said was that children and fools speak the truth. And for God's sake, Lieutenant, will you stay away from those damn windows! One of these damn aftershocks could—"

A new call from Traffic at four-thirty turned out to be the inevitable accident. Higgins went out on it, and looked at it sadly. There was a sign posted prominently on the building—an old stucco apartment house on Temple—*Unsafe for occupancy.* The quake hadn't knocked it down but it was all ready to go. And Alfredo Reyes, entering the building, had put his foot through a rotten stair-board and brought down a wall on his head. Alfredo, who had been nineteen, had left a friend outside, who explained it all tearfully to Higgins and the patrolmen.

"Yessir, we see the sign—but it's Alfredo's old grandma, she lived here but they make ever'body leave—after the earthquake, see?—but it's her little bird, little canary—she was scared then, forgot it, but she wants her little bird—poor little bird, Alfredo just wanted get it for his grandma, she loves the little bird—"

Higgins felt depressed, taking the names, the address. He went back to the office and typed up the report and started home. As he turned into the drive of the house on Silver Lake Boulevard, his spirits rose a little. At least the house hadn't got one crack in its plaster, last Tuesday, and his family would be here to welcome him—the good kids Steve and Laura, his as well as Bert's now, and his lovely Mary, and the little Scottie Brucie.

They were. And to his question Mary's gray eyes laughed. "I'm fine, idiot. Only getting awfully tired of feeling like a pup tent, this far along. Well, I *do*. And looking like a horse—"

"You look," said Higgins fondly, "just fine."

Hackett went home and told Angel about Patrick Henry Logan. "A miracle he's still alive. And no rhyme or reason to it, you can see."

"There must be—you'll find it," said Angel encouragingly. "Dinner in twenty minutes—have you weighed today, Art?"

"I was two pounds down." Hackett fought a perennial battle against his metabolism and Angel's cooking. And four-year-old Mark and his darling Sheila belatedly discovered he was home. . . . Hostages to fortune, he thought, and him with all the seniority built up in earthquake-prone L.A.— But there were all those people who went right back up Mount Vesuvius to rebuild after an eruption—

Palliser went home and just grunted when Roberta told him she'd got the teaching job starting in September. He didn't so much approve of her going back to work, even for a year, to help with the house payments. "Don't go all *male* on me," she said. "You know it will be a help, John."

"Now, Robin. You know how I feel, that's all."

And quite without planning to, Matt Piggott surprised himself by proposing to Prudence Russell that night, and she said yes. His vacation was scheduled for next month. . . .

And Jason Grace went home to his Virginia and she told him the test had been negative again. They'd been hoping to start a family ever since they'd been married, but no luck. . . . "Don't fuss about it, honey," said Grace.

"Well, I can't help it, Jase."

.    .    .

36

"Now settle down, you two," said Alison firmly to the twins. "Yes, yes, *los cuentos*—your father'll read you—*the stories*," she added suddenly. "English, the stories. Spanish, *los cuentos. ¿Comprenden?* Oh, damn."

Mendoza laughed. "You get A for effort, *cara*."

"But we've got to get them—untangled, Luis," said Alison, smoothing her red hair. "They haven't a notion of any difference between, and when they start school—"

"A couple of years yet, after all. *Pues sí,* I've got to agree with you, but—"

"If you'd just think what you're saying," said Alison, and to the solemn twins pajamaed and powdered ready for bed, *"Pues sí*—But yes. Two ways to say it, you see? Spanish—English."

*"El cuento* all about *el lobo*—he eat her all down!" said Miss Teresa with ghoulish satisfaction.

"The wolf," said Alison. "And it's eat her all up, Terry—"

"Down. *El lobo* with *dientes muy grandes!*"

"No *el lobo!*" shouted Master John. *"La bruja* burn up in *la estufa!*"

Mendoza rocked with laughter. "It is not funny," said Alison crossly. "We said we'd have to try—the English only, until they grasp the difference—"

The cats were elsewhere, napping after dinner. The shaggy dog Cedric was very much present, listening interestedly.

"And if you ask me," said Mendoza, "not that I go along with the head doctors, but this sudden thirst for blood—"

"Eat her all down," said Terry pleasedly.

*"La bruja* burn up *muy mucho,"* contributed Johnny.

"Very much," said Alison. "Very much, Johnny. Oh, for heaven's sake, Luis! That's silly—"

In pursuit of broadening the twins' literary horizon, last month, from Mother Goose and *Just So Stories*, she had unearthed a battered copy of Grimm from their heterogeneous collection of books, and that had been an instant hit.

"But don't they say, *achara*," Mrs. MacTaggart had worried, "all those terrible ogres and killing, not right to frighten the mites so—"

"Nonsense," Alison had said robustly. "After all, Máiri, generations of children have been brought up on Grimm and Andersen and turned into quite normal adults—besides, don't they say too, relieving frustrations—"

And the wolf gobbling up Grandmother had been much appreciated, as well as the witch burned in the oven, but as to reaching any understanding about the difference between English and Spanish—well, the twins were not quite three, of course.

But something, as Alison said, had to be done.

"The wolf," said Alison now. "English, Johnny. *The wolf.*"

"He ate her all down," said Terry bloodthirstily, and giggled.

"All up, Terry."

"*La bruja—la bruja* all burn up—"

"The witch," said Alison. "English. The witch. Two ways to—"

Mendoza said, "*¿Donde irá a parar todo esto?* Talk about dilemmas, my love—"

"And you are being no help at all! Honestly!" said Alison. "Honestly! Now, Johnny, say it after me. The wolf. That's English. *El lobo.* That's Spanish. Two different—"

"Read about *la bruja*," demanded Johnny, thrusting Grimm at Mendoza. "She got all burned down in *la estufa*—"

"Burned up, Johnny."

"You are," said Mendoza, "fighting a losing battle, *cara.*"

"Oh, for heaven's *sake!*" said Alison. "I'm just trying to—"

On Sunday morning, somewhat to the surprise of the doctors, Patrolman Patrick Henry Logan was still alive, and his pulse was just a trifle stronger. They weren't saying yet that he'd make it, but the odds had shortened a little. If by the grace of God he should make it, he could provide answers for all the questions eventually. But the doctors weren't being definite yet.

Just as they were thinking of lunch, the lab sent up a report: the lab usually got something for them in time, and it had turned up another X for them now.

"But they are so stupid," said Palliser. "The little pros at the bottom. I do get tired. That Hauck was asking for it—begging for it."

The lab had identified some latent prints from the used paper cup. They were in L.A.'s records. They belonged to one Linda Schnell, who had quite a little pedigree—soliciting, shoplifting, prostitution. She was Caucasian, twenty-seven, blonde and blue, five-four, a hundred and twenty, appendectomy scar, old record of V.D. at General Hospital; she'd been picked up last about four months ago, on a charge of shoplifting, thirty days in—the address then had been on First Street.

She wasn't there now.

"Nobody that size accounted for Hauck," said Landers.

"So she's got a boy-friend," said Mendoza. "Put out an A.P.B. on her, Tom." The continuous thankless dirty job—

## 3

Nobody who knew George Higgins would have called him a sentimental man, but his rough-hewn exterior concealed a warm heart, and he had, late yesterday afternoon, called the Humane Society about that canary. The canary belonging to Alfredo Reyes's grandmother. He'd just got back to the office on Sunday after lunch when he got a call from a cheerful-sounding Mr. Ryan.

"Just thought you'd like to know we rescued that canary, Sergeant. Oh, yes, it was all right—hungry and thirsty, but it's perked up now."

So that had turned out all right—only not for Alfredo Reyes. Higgins put the phone down just as Sergeant Lake looked in and said tersely, "Call from Traffic. They've just found another body on Main."

Higgins swore; more paper work; and he and Grace were the only ones in, so they both went over.

This half-block of building, once small shops, along that stretch of Main, had been scheduled for demolition before the earthquake; the quake had done half the job. It had been a four-story building, and most of the roof was still there but inside ceilings had crumbled, floors given way, and part of the front wall had collapsed. The hard-hatted city engineer said to them, "Everybody knew the building was vacant—condemned six months ago. So nobody had a look around here until now." This afternoon, inspecting city property reckoned unsafe, they had; and there was another body. Half buried in the rubble of a fallen ceiling, inside one of the former shops.

"I suppose," said the other city workman, "he could have been a bum sneaked in here to sleep."

That, when they took a look at him, was probably what he had been. He was an elderly man, and his clothes were old and shabby. He had two dimes in one jacket pocket, and a broken wine bottle in the other: it had originally contained cheap muscatel.

Both Higgins and Grace could guess he'd never be identified. Just another derelict. The city would bury him and that would be that. Since Tuesday the known death toll from the quake had crept up day by day as more bodies were found; this would add one more.

They saw the body off for the morgue and went back to the office; Grace typed the report. No work was getting done on the windows on this floor yet, but they had noticed a crew working on those on the first floor. Eventually they might get back their air conditioning.

There had been an accident up on Olive, said Lake, with one D.O.A.—Piggott and Glasser had gone to cover that.

"Where's the boss?"

"Up at Wilcox Street."

Mendoza and Hackett were up at Wilcox Street to talk to some of Pat Logan's fellow officers before they went on shift. Mendoza had asked Barth to bring them in early, but he didn't know what they could tell him, and they weren't telling him anything new at all.

"There just couldn't be any reason for anyone holding a grudge on Pat—" That was the consensus. It seemed that Bill Roth and Mike Gomez knew Logan somewhat better than the others; they'd all been in the same class at the Police Academy four years ago, and at Wilcox Street since.

"He's an easygoing guy," said Gomez. "Well, hell, excuse me, Lieutenant, but you know all the tests a man has to pass before he can even apply for the job, on this force. We like to think, the real pros—us. There just couldn't be anything on the job behind this, Lieutenant. Have you heard how he's doing?"

"They're not ringing any bells yet," said Mendoza.

"I'd go along with Mike," said Roth. "But what else could have triggered it? The only thing I could figure, some hothead high on something, but—"

"But," said Mendoza, irritably rubbing his moustache the wrong way. It was a large But. None of the men could offer them anything more: Logan was a good cop, he and his wife got on fine, he liked his job, he was a likable, easygoing fellow.

"So, something right outside?" said Hackett on the way back downtown. "That crossed my mind, Luis. A thing like this so often at random—just chance that it was Logan. A couple of junkies hunting anything pawnable to support the habit—and running wild when they didn't find much loot."

"No," said Mendoza. "The house wasn't ransacked, Art. All right, it says nothing that that's an older neighborhood, not wealthy homes up there—the punks turn up anywhere. But he still had his billfold on him. Nobody had searched the house. They—I think it's got to be they—just came in and went to work on Logan. The front door was probably unlocked, that time of day—he'd have been just about to leave the house, probably, the time margin what it is. His car was still in the garage. Keys in his pocket."

"So what other answer is there?"

"I don't know," said Mendoza. "Damn it, it's just shapeless— it shouldn't have happened, there's no reason for it to have happened, only it did. I want to see his wife again, and by then the lab should be able to tell us if they picked up anything useful at the house. And if they haven't, I'll be damned if I can see where else to look, Art."

At the office, he called the hospital. Logan was still unconscious, but it began to look as if he might make it.

Landers and Palliser had gone down to R. and I. to have a look for known associates of Linda Schnell. They ran into brisk, neat Phil O'Neill, trim in her navy uniform: she was busy at one of the computers, but flicked a warm smile in Landers' direction. Waiting for the right cards to emerge from the slots in answer to their questions, Palliser said he could wish Landers good luck there. "A very smart blonde, Tom."

"And very damn practical," said Landers. "But I'll get her— eventually, I swear."

The computer turned up some names from their records— Angie Black, Julia Kurtz, Marian Henry. They looked, and their pedigrees read about the same as Linda's: the same charges, the fines, the thirty-day and sixty-day sentences. These were the drifters, the irresponsible, lazy ones who always lived hand to mouth, and used sex to earn money because it was an easy way. These days, a lot of them would be on welfare, but even the increased largesse the welfare board handed out now wouldn't buy all the liquor they wanted, all the fancy clothes— other things.

One of those women, Marian Henry, was in the county jail now on a thirty-day sentence for shoplifting. They drove out North Broadway to see her.

In jail, of course, she was clean and neat, and they wouldn't let her plaster on the makeup. She looked sullen and sorry for herself, in the plain tan dress, county issue to prisoners: she was a small dark woman in the mid-twenties, with heavy-lidded dark eyes. She said she didn't have any yen to talk to cops.

"You know Linda Schnell," said Palliser economically. "Know her pretty well, don't you?"

"And so what if I do? Can I have a cigarette?"

Landers gave her one, lit it. They were talking to her in one of the interrogation rooms; she slouched over to a straight chair. "Know where she's living now?"

"Why? You want her for something?"

"We'd like to talk to her," said Landers.

"So go find her. I'm not about to help the fuzz."

"Who's she been going around with lately, Marian?" They had a few names also from the computer, men Linda had lived with off and on—boy-friends. And the boy-friends had showed up in Records too, inevitably. Leo Farber: burglary, theft from the person. B.-and-E. Ray Wengel: burglary, narco possession, pimping. Harry Fordick: armed assault, assault with intent twice. And they had looked at the disposition of all those cases with resignation and frustration. The softheaded judges, the damn court decisions so careful of the criminal's rights while ignoring those of the upright citizenry to be safe in their homes. None of those men had served over six months in jail, on any one count.

"What about it, Marian?" asked Landers.

She shrugged at him. "I mind my own business. I wouldn't know. Linda's a pal of mine, I'm not about to help you pin anything on her."

"You might be doing her a favor by telling us about her boyfriends, Marian," said Palliser. "By what we can guess, at least one of them is a killer. He killed a man last Friday night—a john Linda'd picked up."

Her eyes narrowed on him. "Don't con me, cop. Linda wouldn't take up with nobody like—"

"So maybe she didn't know he was. Has she picked up a new boy-friend lately?"

She hesitated, looking from one to the other of them, her mouth tightening. "That's a come-on, you're tryin'a scare me some way. Linda—"

"Gospel truth, Marian. Anybody who kills once can kill twice. And it was a very messy kill, wasn't it, Tom? Fellow beaten and strangled, looked like—"

There was a long silence. "I haven't seen her in a while," said Marian Henry finally. "I been here four weeks today, and I hadn't seen her, maybe a week before I got picked up."

"So, five weeks back, Marian—Linda had a new boy-friend?"

"She—no," she muttered unwillingly. "No, she knew him before somewheres—hadn't run into him in a long time, she said. She said he was a very nice guy, a real fun guy, she said."

"Oh, she did. And so what's his name?"

She put out her cigarette in the glass ashtray. "Foster. Foster Sterry. I never seen him, that's all I know."

"So I guess you can congratulate me," said Piggott, pushing the button for their floor.

"Congratulations, Matt," said Glasser. "That's good news. Time you settled down, acquired a family."

"And see who's talking."

"Well, I just never seem to meet a girl I'd want to settle down with. Maybe some day."

"We figured on getting married next month, when my vacation—"

"Good," said Glasser. "She sounds like a nice girl, Matt. Prudence. I like old-fashioned names like that."

The elevator landed and they walked down the hall. Two uniformed men were waiting for them at the door of the Homicide Bureau, with the three witnesses brought up from the scene to make statements. It had been a simple traffic accident, both drivers somewhat at fault, but the paper work went on forever. "If you'd just come in here, Mr. Hulbert," said Glasser, "I'll get your statement down for you to sign—"

Piggott was taking the two women into another room. Piggott, that rather lonely man, the upright fundamentalist, deserved a pretty, nice wife, and good luck to him.

Landers and Palliser went back to R. and I. to look for Foster Sterry. He wasn't there. At least by that name. No computer knew Foster Sterry.

"Computers," said Palliser, "are fallible. Sometimes the old-fashioned routine still pays off."

Landers translated that. "Put the word out to the pigeons that we're looking for him. And with the A.P.B. on Linda, it could be when we find her we'll find him."

They had shoved that heist job in Pending. There had never been any solid leads on it, anything like usable evidence. Now, it was dead. Now they had other things to do. They separated and went wandering around the Row, the streets around there, putting out the word that the cops were interested in one Foster Sterry. Half an hour's work, half a dozen men passed the word —the grapevine would take it from there.

Palliser ran into one of their more reliable informants coming out of a bar on Fourth Street—Joe Perez. Joe owned a hole-in-the-wall hamburger joint on Second; he had a small pedigree of petty offenses, not much.

"Foster Sterry?" he said, wrinkling his brow. "Don't ring no bells, Sergeant. I'll ask around. What I can tell you is about this bookie, see. Just showed up last week, started operations outta a pool hall just down from my place. I can put the finger on him for sure, Sergeant—"

Palliser took the name, the address. A lot of the unthinking citizenry might think that set of laws was unrealistic, and so it looked to be: legal to place a bet inside the track, illegal outside; legal to play draw poker only in towns where gambling was permitted (which meant, here, Gardena); illegal anywhere else. Some people would always like to gamble, and there'd always be gamblers to oblige them. What the citizenry didn't realize was that legal gambling was always linked up with the more unsavory things—the syndicate dealing in women, in pornography, in narcotics, the rackets generally.

Palliser went back to headquarters and passed on that information to Lieutenant Perce Andrews in Vice.

By three-thirty Mendoza and Hackett were up on La Presa Drive again. They found Royce there with Sally Logan, and a nice-looking older couple introduced as Logan's parents. They had all been about to leave for the hospital.

The men from Homicide listened to the expected repeated questions. Why did it have to be Pat? Why had it happened to Pat? They'd like to know too. Royce, the longtime cop, stood by jangling coins in his pocket restlessly.

"The doctor called a little while ago, they seem to think Pat's a little better—"

"Yes, we heard, Mrs. Logan, that's good news. We're all pulling for him to make it, you know," said Hackett. "Did you have a look around here for anything missing, anything—"

"That's just impossible," said Sally Logan. "No, of course there isn't. Dad and I both think there must have been more than one, because you could see there was hardly any struggle, and Pat would have— But there's nothing gone, and—"

46

Hackett followed Mendoza's glance round the living room, and sighed. A transistor radio sitting on the coffee table. A TV on its own wheeled stand in the corner. Possibly another radio in the kitchen. There probably wouldn't be much jewelry here, a young couple still with house payments, car payments, all the rest; but Sally Logan's mother was apparently dead, she might have a few pieces of jewelry from her. There would be clothes, the odds and ends pawnable. If the X's here had been a pair with the habit to support (the habit also increasing the likelihood of that savage random attack) there would have been things missing. The house would have been ransacked. Logan's money would have been taken.

And all that Royce would have seen, too. He was worried about Logan, evidently fond of his son-in-law; but he gave them a sardonic grin and said, "Just nowhere to go, is there? It couldn't be a personal motive, and it doesn't seem to have been even the random thing, the senseless thing we've all seen too damn often."

"Well, we haven't had a lab report yet. Could be they've picked up something to offer us a lead," said Mendoza.

"Always possible. Occasionally those boys pull rabbits out of hats. Let's hope they can here."

"Oh, there was one thing I remembered," said Sally suddenly. "After you talked to me before, Lieutenant—at the hospital. Of course it couldn't be anything to do with Pat's getting—but," and she attempted a stiff little smile, "I know cops, all right—you always want every last little detail."

"What's this, Sally? You remembered something that might—"

"It couldn't possibly tie in anywhere, Dad. But I suppose you'd better hear about it, Lieutenant. You see, we don't know too many neighbors up here—we're both busy, and it isn't a neighborhood where people—fraternize, which is all right with me—but of course we do know some people by name, and of course some of them know that Pat's on the force. Well, the Stanceys up the hill, and Mrs. Franks, and some others—you're friendly, say Hello, and Nice day, and like that. But anyway, what I'm getting to is that last Wednesday—yes, it was Wednesday, because they'd called Pat to come in early, everything was still in a mess out in the valley, the civil-defense people rushing around and all those people to be evacuated—they said to come in at noon. So it was about nine o'clock that morning, just after the office called, that Mrs. Franks came. I'd never exchanged more than six words with her before. Pat was upstairs shaving—"

"Mrs. Franks. That's the fat blonde across the street?" asked Royce.

"That's right. And I was just leaving the house myself," said Sally, "you know I work all day Wednesdays, so I didn't know anything about it until Pat got home that night—he told me then. He—"

"What did she want, Mrs. Logan?" asked Mendoza interestedly.

"Well, she didn't say much to me. She said she understood Pat was a police officer, and she was terribly worried about something and maybe he could give her some advice. I thought it was a little funny," said Sally, "but when Pat told me about it later, I—the poor woman. And rather a silly sort of woman, but you can't help feeling sorry for her—"

"He talked to her then?"

She nodded. "I went up and told him, and he was a little surprised too. I mean, she's an older woman and— But he said—he said—" Sally put a hand to her throat. "He'd just finished shaving, he was wiping his face—and his hair all on end—he just w-winked at me and said, went to show how the neighbors must appreciate the superior wisdom of cops—and he'd be right down—"

"But you weren't there when he talked to her, hon?"

"No, I said I left—I was late. I asked her to sit down, said Pat would come in a minute. I didn't hear about it until that night."

She faced them, a little bewildered, in the living room of the pink stucco house. She was not a very intelligent woman, or a very sophisticated woman: five minutes' conversation told Mendoza and Hackett that. She was, however, an honest woman, if shallow and sentimental, and she said, "But I don't understand

48

why you're asking about it. What happened to Mr. Logan—just terrible, but it wasn't anything to do with us. With Donny. Mr. Logan—there's so much violence going on now, isn't there? People say, all the terrible TV programs. His wife's very pretty, and he was so kind and good. It was all perfectly awful and I've been terribly upset about it, but of course as Dr. Hopewell said it's best to *know*, and I never would have if it hadn't been for Mr. Logan. He was so kind, taking time to explain, you know."

"Explain what, Mrs. Franks? Why did you want to see Mr. Logan that day?" asked Mendoza.

"Why, it was Donny," she said. "My boy Donny." The living room of the pink stucco house told them, possibly, all they needed to know about Claudia Franks. It was painted pink too, with ruffle-bordered rose-colored drapes, fussy Victorian love seats and a French gilt desk, framed flower prints on the walls. "I've tried to make it up to Donny, for not having a daddy, you know. His daddy died when Donny was only two—this awful leukemia he had, just a young man. Of course he left me well enough off, I don't mean millions but comfortable, and I've tried to make it up to Donny. Anything he wanted—and he's always been a good boy—but—" A slight gasp— "I—I'd been worried about him. Just lately. I know a lot of young people get into trouble these days—you read in the papers—and these terrible drugs all around—Donny has his own car, of course—"

"How old is he, Mrs. Franks?" asked Hackett.

"Eighteen. He's just eighteen. And just lately I'd been worried—he'd be away till all hours and I wouldn't know where—and not answering when I asked, and sometimes he was so strange, not like himself—and cross— He—he—swore at me sometimes. You read in the papers how even good young people, from good families, get to taking these drugs—and I was frightened," she said. "I was frightened. He wasn't acting right. I didn't know what to do."

"And you thought of—mmh—Mr. Logan." Mendoza had made a steeple of his long hands; he watched her.

"Well, you see, I suddenly thought—a police officer would know more about that sort of thing. I was a little embarrassed—

but a police officer, well, it's rather like a—a doctor, isn't it, and then I thought too, a man—sometimes mothers don't understand boys that age, however much they *love* them—but— And he was very kind," said Mrs. Franks. "So kind and helpful. He listened to me, and he asked me some questions—about how Donny'd been acting, you know. He explained there were symptoms that'd show, he said—was Donny very moody lately, and was he eating right, and did he wear sunglasses, and were his eyes blistered-looking, a lot of things like that— And it didn't seem possible but he said— My Donny!" She put a crumpled handkerchief to her mouth. "It was just how Donny had been acting—"

"He told you the boy was probably taking drugs?"

She nodded. "He asked—if we had a—a family doctor. Of course I've gone to Dr. Hopewell for years, and he took care of Donny since he was a baby—not that he was ever sick much, a big strong boy he's always been— Anyway, Mr. Logan said I should get him to examine Donny, and find out—and there were clinics and hospitals where—maybe they could cure him, if he was—"

Which had been quite proper advice from Patrolman Pat Logan. "He also told you something else," said Mendoza.

"Yes, he did. He said if—if we found out that Donny had been taking drugs, we—the doctor—ought to inform the police. But I don't know if Dr. Hopewell—"

"Mmh. You called the doctor," said Mendoza. And what did this rigmarole say? Wednesday: the day after the earthquake: two days before Logan was attacked. . . .

"Well, I was terribly upset—I'd been afraid, but what Mr. Logan said—about *symptoms,* and Donny acting just like he said— Yes, I called Dr. Hopewell. He doesn't have office hours on Wednesdays, I called him at home, we've gone to him a long time and I thought—in an emergency— And he did. He came right away."

"What time was that?"

"When I got back from talking to Mr. Logan. He said he had to be on duty at noon—it was about ten to eleven when I got home—"

Patrolman Logan, diverted from regular duty that hot Wednesday, working overtime helping out the civil-defense crews still digging out the bodies, helping evacuate the thousands of people in the path of that dam threatening to give way. "Yes?"

"Because Donny was there then," she said. "Just lately I never knew when he would be. Or where he was. I—I only found out in May he hadn't been going to school. And he'd gone out that morning before I got up. In his car somewhere. But he came home—it was funny, as if it was meant—just before I did. He was up in his room playing records—this terrible music the young people seem to like—not what I call music, but— And Dr. Hopewell said to keep him there, he'd come right away—and I don't know how I could have stopped him, Donny I mean, if he'd wanted to leave, but he was still up there playing records when the doctor came, and it was just terrible—" Suddenly she began to cry in an indecisive sort of way. "Calling me names and swearing—but I know it wasn't the real Donny, these awful drugs—Dr. Hopewell said—I was so thankful he was there to manage everything— And he had a terrible time with Donny, he called an ambulance and they had to—had to—he was fighting all of them—"

"I think we'd like to have a talk with Dr. Hopewell," said Mendoza gently. "Where do we find him, Mrs. Franks?"

They found Dr. Oliver Hopewell, irritated at being invaded by cops on Sunday, at home: a neat expensive modern house in Westwood. Dr. Hopewell was, probably, a very competent general practitioner with a good practice, and he recognized the necessity of cooperating with the police; he concealed annoyance and answered them readily.

"Of course the woman's a fool," he said brutally. "Indulged the boy every way, never attempted to discipline him, and there's a substantial income, I gather. Not that I know much about the boy—never much wrong with him physically—but, given our present social culture as we might say, maybe this was expectable." Dr. Hopewell was fiftyish, with a nakedly bald head and an unexpected little white beard like a billy goat's. He hunched his shoulders. "A scene, yes. I could see the boy was high on something—I called an ambulance in a hurry. I couldn't have handled him alone. As it was, we had a time getting him to the hospital—naturally I didn't dare risk giving him morphine or anything else until I knew what he had inside already. It turned out to be the Blue Angels. In the vernacular."

"Sodium amytal," said Hackett.

"But it could have been anything—as I needn't tell you. From speed to heroin to any of the barbiturates. My God, these *kids!*" said Hopewell. "Anything."

"We know. So?" said Mendoza.

Hopewell spread his hands. "What can I do? I didn't get much out of him. I might guess he's been the whole route, from the pot to H to the acid—oh, I know the jargon!" He laughed mirthlessly. "And I also know—as you gentlemen do—that it's largely futile, once they're hooked, to try for the permanent cure. But we have to try. Make the gesture. And Mrs. Franks, God knows, has the money for the deluxe attempt. I've got him in the Spencer-Evers Clinic in Huntington Beach. They deal exclusively with the addicts—on a private basis—and they're very good." He shrugged again. "I wouldn't take a bet on Don Franks, but for whatever good it'll do, they'll try."

"No, Doctor, neither would I," said Mendoza. "But didn't it occur to you that the local police might be interested in Don Franks? That—"

Hopewell stared at him. "Why? Oh—he hadn't any narcotics on him, Lieutenant. Naturally I made sure of that, and I searched his room at the house. That was after the ambulance came and the attendants had him under restraint. He was absolutely clean."

"And high on the Blue Angels," said Hackett. "Then."

"Naturally if I'd found any narcotics on him I'd have—"

"You might have assumed," said Mendoza, "that a user could give us the names of any suppliers. You should have contacted the precinct—"

"My God, Lieutenant," said Hopewell, "give you a few more names to chase up? With all of it, any of it, available almost anywhere—the suppliers on every high-school campus in town? I don't remember who said it— 'To understand the twentieth century is to come to grips with madness.' *I* don't know the answer. I can only try to help where I can."

"*Ya lo creo,*" said Mendoza. "And this was on Wednesday."

"That's right. Why? Well, I got there—to the Franks's house —about noon. Devil of a nuisance, of course, my day off—and by the time I'd seen him and called the ambulance and we got him under control, and I looked over his room, well, call it twelve-forty. I saw him checked in at the clinic at one-thirty. It's a good one, as I say, they try—"

"He's been there ever since," said Mendoza.

"Yes, of course. I said they specialize. The addicts of all kinds. The patients are very strictly supervised, yes."

Mendoza looked at Hackett. This unexpected new evidence, turning up the only smell they'd had of somebody who might harbor some grudge, some grievance, on Patrolman Logan. The apprehension and incarceration of yet another punk j.d. on dope. Would Don Franks have known that it was Logan, the cop just happening to live across the street, who had confirmed Mrs. Franks's fears and brought in the doctor? Probably—that would have come out in the little scene when the doctor first appeared. And the dope—of any variety—so often did spark off the senseless violence.

But Don Franks had been locked up at this clinic for addicts since Wednesday afternoon.

Their shapeless little mystery was still shapeless.

**4**

Mendoza eased the Ferrari up the drive, carefully straddling the
rather sizable crack opened by the earthquake, and into the
garage alongside Alison's Facel-Vega. At this time of year it was
still light at nearly seven o'clock, and most of his household
was in the back yard. Bast and Sheba were sensibly sheltering
on the back step; Nefertite was digging a hasty hole behind the
chrysanthemums; and El Señor, uttering curses at the top of his
half-Siamese voice, was making a run for the back porch while
the mockingbird dive-bombed him.

The twins were shouting. *"El pájaro* bite Señor—Daddy, see
*el pájaro—"*

*"YAWK!"* screamed the mockingbird, and got in a second
hard peck on El Señor's rump before he bolted into the house
by the cat door there.

"He's afraid El Señor steal *los niños* out of nest—Mama said—"

"Yes, yes, I see *el pájaro—*I don't know whether there are *los
niños* in the nest, Terry—all right, Johnny, *los cuentos* before
bed—"

*"El lobo* eat Grandmother all down," said Terry reminiscently.

Alison came out to rescue him. *"¡Bastante! El pájaro*'s gone
home, you two come in now. Tough day, *amante?"*

The shaggy dog Cedric went on barking furiously at the alder
tree, whither the mockingbird had vanished.

"You've given up on the untangling?" inquired Mendoza.

"No, of course we can't. But it'll have to be done like regular
lessons, you know, the deliberate effort made at it. Half an hour

mornings and afternoons—like that. And how long do mocking-bird eggs take to hatch?"

"I haven't the slightest idea. You said that creature's nesting again—the way he's attacking the cats—"

"Máiri doesn't know either. But I'm afraid there is a nestful of *los niños,* all right."

"I said we'd be stuck with him for life," said Mendoza. "And if you're conducting lessons, while you're at it you might try to teach him the other half of 'Yankee Doodle.'"

"Which is a thought," said Alison. She shooed the twins and Cedric into the kitchen, the other three cats preceding them. "I'll finish dinner, Máiri, you get these two settled down. Yes, yes, monsters, your father'll read to you—half an hour, mind, that's all—"

Johnny suddenly seized hold of Mendoza's trousers and began shouting at the top of his voice, "Rumple-rumple-rumple! *El villano* steal *el niño!* Rumple-rumple-rumple—"

"Now what in the name of guidness," said Mrs. MacTaggart, and gave him a vigorous spank on the bottom. He turned an angelic smile on her.

"We just got," said Alison, "to Rumpelstiltskin, Máiri. While you were at the market. . . . If you want a drink before coping with the monsters, Luis—"

"On general principles only." El Señor understood English and landed on the counter with a plaintive demand for his share; Mendoza poured him an ounce of rye in a saucer and their alcoholic cat lapped eagerly. Mendoza swallowed half his own drink and watched Alison meditatively as she got a big bowl of salad from the refrigerator. He was pleased she'd cut her hair; after six months of coping with it shoulder length, she'd had it cut again in the short feathery cut and looked like the Alison he had first known. The Alison who had, after too many years as the lone wolf, at last captured Luis Rodolfo Vicente Mendoza into the domestic scene—and who but a red-haired Scots-Irish girl could have done that?

"Out of the way," she said, coming past with the bowl.

"Who or what," asked Mendoza, "is Rumpelstiltskin?"

Alison stared at him. "You never had Grimm's fairy stories read to you?"

"Why?" he asked reasonably. "My grandmother'd probably never heard of them. Ask me anything about the pantheon of Aztec gods, but—"

"Well, maybe you'll improve your education along with the offspring's. Suppose you get out of my way and do so. With any luck they'll settle down in half an hour and we can have a peaceful meal."

Mendoza laughed, finishing the rye. *"¡Más vale así!* You reassure me, *gatita. Muy mucho,* as Johnny would say."

"Reassure you?"

"Because I was doing some thinking on the way home," said Mendoza. "About mother love."

"Prompted by what?"

"Mmh—this and that. Chiefly, I think, that. It's like apple pie and—and the circus and Disneyland," said Mendoza. "Nobody could possibly be against it. But, *Dios,* what havoc it can cause on occasion. The—mmh—wrong kind of mother love."

"You can explain it over dinner, please—I'm busy."

"I'm going," said Mendoza meekly and, pausing to hang up his jacket on the way, went to read Grimm to the twin monsters.


"What the hell kind of wild-goose chase are we on?" asked Higgins at nine o'clock on Monday morning. "This kid couldn't possibly have had anything to do with beating up Logan—he's been locked up since Wednesday afternoon."

"That's what I said," said Hackett, "until Luis pointed out that this whole Franks rigmarole was the only unusual thing showing up in Logan's immediate past." He was taking the Barracuda up the winding road carefully.

"Well, but I wonder just how unusual that was, Art—the citizen asking for advice. It's a funny thing, but even back when I was in uniform, you got it—the honest citizen taking it for granted that a trained cop would know what to advise—the boy getting into bad company, the girl taking up with a punk, Uncle

Bill's taste for whiskey. And I'd think these days, with most people aware of the rise of crime and—"

"We can ask his wife if it had ever happened before—if it happened often. But the fact is, it is the only different thing that happened to him this last week, and we'll just look round it a little in case it could give us a lead."

"Oh, I see that, sure. I wonder if the lab turned up anything at the house."

"Any luck, we'll get a report today."

They found Mrs. Claudia Franks in a pink housecoat having breakfast. "I don't have to get up early," she said apologetically, "so I don't. I suppose I should. But it doesn't seem— And I've been so worried about Donny." She undoubtedly had been: the only thing in life she had to spend affection on, which she'd done not wisely but too well. "Dr. Hopewell said I shouldn't go out there—to that hospital— If I could just see him, know he was all right—but Dr. Hopewell said—"

They showed her the search warrant: always better to do the thing the legal way. She was surprised. "Oh, you can look anywhere you like, of course—but what did you think might be— Oh, do you think he had some of these awful drugs here? Oh—"

It was a big house for two people: three bedrooms upstairs, a big den and dining room on the ground floor. Don Franks's room was the right front one. Hackett and Higgins stood and looked around it for a minute before they made a move, and each knew what the other was thinking, and there wasn't any need to put it in words.

When Art Hackett was eighteen, his father had been making a fairly good salary at an office job in Pasadena, the main office of a market chain. They had an old but comfortable house in an oldish part of town; Hackett had his own room, but things had been a little tight that year because it was his sister Elise's third year in college, and even though she worked summers to help— He'd had a modest allowance, but since he was twelve he'd also held jobs, the paper route, cutting neighbors' lawns, the odd jobs to pick up extra money.

And when George Higgins was eighteen, he hadn't had it so

good as that. His mother had died when he was twelve, and that year he graduated from high school, down in Santa Monica, his father had been killed in an accident. Higgins also had had the paper route, the odd jobs; and his father had had just about enough in the bank to pay for a funeral. Higgins had gone to work then as a common laborer, the only job he could get, at seventy per week.

She'd come panting up the stairs after them. "Oh, have you found anything? Is there—"

"Not yet, ma'am," said Higgins. "Could you tell us how much money Don might have, ordinarily? Did he have a part-time job, or—"

"Oh, no—nothing like that. He didn't need to— Of course he has his allowance, he has his car to run, and if he took a girl out— What? Fifty dollars a week, I—everything so high now— and if he needed any more he knew he just had to ask—I—"

Hackett got rid of her politely; she trailed down the hall looking back. Higgins shut the door. "My God," he said simply. "Two hundred per, just for existing. Just for taking up space."

It was a good-sized room, and expensively equipped. Transistor radio, a portable TV, stereo phonograph, a large collection of L.P. records in a rack. A mahogany bedroom set, old-fashioned and solid. A complete lavatory and wardrobe off the bedroom.

They started to look around. "What are we looking for?" asked Higgins. "Just the pills? But when he had that much for certain, he could buy a fix of any kind whenever he felt like it—"

"But they do like to be sure of the fix when the yen hits them," said Hackett, and added, "Well, well." Higgins came to look. In the top drawer of the bureau, under a pile of handkerchiefs, a new gun—a brand-spanking-new Smith and Wesson .38 revolver. "That cost something," said Hackett.

"Especially for Donny." Seeing that Don Franks was a minor and wouldn't be eligible for a gun permit, buying that under the counter he had paid something for it. And under which counter had he bought it?

They went on looking. They unmade the bed and turned the

58

mattress over. They looked under the carpet, behind pictures and back of drawers. It wasn't until they got to the lavatory that they came across anything else.

There, in the stall shower, one of the square tiles moved under Higgins' hand. He got out his knife, pried at the edges; it yielded and he lifted it clean out. Something came with it. The underflooring had been cut out just below it, a space just enough smaller than the eight-inch-square tile that it fit into it solidly; and firmly lashed to the underside of the tile with electrician's tape was a length of heavy twine. At the end of that, as Higgins lifted the tile all the way out, was a sizable plastic bag tied on the other end of the twine.

"I think we just hit a jackpot," said Hackett. "Gimme—let's see." They started to empty the bag carefully on the lavatory floor.

Most of the expectable lot was represented—it was, as Hackett said, a mixed bag. Quite a collection of the pills—the uppers and downers, barbiturates, bennies, the crystals, the Blue Angels and Red Devils and Yellow Submarines—several decks of H, and of course a separate plastic bag full of marijuana.

Hackett and Higgins looked at each other. "Did you say a jackpot, Art?"

"I think," said Hackett, "we'd like to know the names of some of Don's pals, George. If she knows any."

"I'd take no bets on that." They started to pack it all back into the bag.

She didn't. She looked at them anxiously and said, "Well, a boy Donny's age, they're growing up, you know, they don't like families prying and asking questions, and you've got to remember that— I saw an article in a magazine once, about letting young people alone, respect their privacy—and besides Don doesn't like being asked things, where he's going or who with— I know he used to be good friends with Bob Vandermeier—the Vandermeiers lived just down the hill when Don was in junior high and he and Bob—"

"You don't know whether they're still friends?"

"No, I—well, it's not as if I didn't encourage him to bring his

59

friends here, I did—we've got the nice sheltered patio and a bar-
becue and all—but he never seemed to want to. Not since he'd
been in high school—had his car—well, you know boys that age.
They're always coming and going. He—I didn't ask him any
more," she said nervously. "That—that was one of the things
that frightened me, you know. I tried to raise him to have some
manners—but just lately, he—well, I don't know where he
learned some of the language, and sw-swearing at me—just because—just because I *cared* about him, wanted to know where—
worried about him—"

"What's the answer, Art?" asked Higgins in the Barracuda.
"The hell of it is, you know, she just wouldn't believe you if you
told her it's mostly her fault."

"I wonder if that's too easy an answer. Sure, not a good idea—
anything Donny wants—the car—what was the car, I wonder—"

"I had a look in the garage while you were extricating us all
polite. I don't somehow think Mrs. Franks drives a Mercedes
sports model."

"No. But there are people who've survived the overindulgent
raising and not gone off the rails. But it's not our job to philoso-
phize, George."

"I'm speculating," said Higgins, "on something else. That's
quite a cache of stuff he had stored away. I wonder what Luis
got from the doctors at that clinic."

He and Hackett had worked together a long time, and they
were basically the same kind of men; but also they were both
experienced cops, and sometimes the shortcuts presented themselves to the experienced eye. They didn't have to spell out what
was going through both their minds.

What Mendoza, going down to Huntington Beach to that
private clinic, had got was just a little more suggestive.

He had called the hospital before he left the office. "We're
just cautiously saying we think he'll make it, Lieutenant," said
the doctor. "A minor miracle. His pulse is much stronger and
it's possible he'll regain consciousness some time today or to-

morrow. Of course the big question is, the extent of any brain damage."

Mendoza thought back to the time when Art Hackett had lain in a coma with the doctors saying the same thing. And Art had come through all right, which didn't say that Pat Logan would, and he knew what Sally Logan and the rest of them were feeling. *Pares o nones,* odds or evens—how the cards fell in the deal, he thought.

And of course Luis Mendoza had been brought up to believe that Something was in charge of affairs—and all of a sudden, now, dimly he wondered if Something was. When he came to think, the unexpected good luck (the guardian angels?) they'd been having lately—George getting away from those ugly thugs with a whole skin—and Landers getting taken off the hook by the belated discovery of the real X—

It was the way the cards fell. *Pares o nones.* . . .

They didn't let him in to talk to Don Franks. They had a rule of absolute isolation. But a scholarly-looking Dr. Faulkner talked to him readily about the case.

"I doubt very much whether he's really hooked, Lieutenant. No needle marks on him. No telling if he's tried the acid, but my guess would be—and I've seen too many addicts, more than I like to think about—my guess would be that he's experimented around with the pills, just for kicks, and that's about the extent of it. I haven't got him to talk much—beyond the usual complaints, complete with the obscenities, about the damn interfering fuzz, and Mama, and the doctor—"

*"Así, así,"* said Mendoza. "A free country, and everybody entitled to do his own thing and make his own decisions—nobody has a right to interfere with the beautiful souls seeking peace and love—"

"Oh, please, Lieutenant. Yes. But I did get one rather interesting thing out of him." The doctor adjusted his glasses. "We were running some tests, and I commented on the absence of needle marks—this was the first I'd noticed it—and he said, The H? Man, not him, he knew what that stuff could do to you. And then he shut up."

*"Interesante,"* said Mendoza. "In fact, you don't think he'd qualify as an addict? To anything?"

Faulkner said cautiously, "Well, you never can be sure, when they've gone so far as to experiment with any of it. But I don't think he's hooked on anything now, no. Once the sodium amytal was out of him he snapped back to normal—er—physically."

"Yes," said Mendoza. Physically. Most of the motive behind any addiction was not physical. A lot of reasons, or sometimes only one.

"So, have we got the other half of the story?" said Hackett.

"Very possibly." Mendoza straightened the desk blotter, brushed ashes off the polished wood; he sat back and lit a cigarette. It was very hot in the office; both Hackett and Higgins had pulled their ties loose. Some time the repair crews would get up as far as Homicide, to put glass back in their windows, and the air conditioning would get turned on. Some time.

Mendoza had passed on Faulkner's opinion to his two senior sergeants, and heard what they had to tell him. The office was quiet—doors open to the central corridor—except for the sporadic typing where Detective Jason Grace wrote a report in the big communal office across the hall. Palliser and Landers were out hunting known associates of Linda Schnell, and evidently Piggott and Glasser were out on something too.

"But it doesn't add up to anything for us," said Hackett. He readjusted his bulk in the chair beside Mendoza's desk and it creaked protestingly. Higgins had hoisted one hip to a corner of the desk.

*"Qué contrariedad,"* murmured Mendoza. "What a disappointment for us."

Hackett looked at him suspiciously. "Well, it seems to me as if we'd been ferreting out a little suggestive evidence to hand over to Callaghan up in Narco. What led us to Don Franks?— Mrs. Franks's little heart-to-heart with Patrolman Pat Logan, last Wednesday morning—"

"Indubitably."

62

"—And aside from the fact that we've agreed it was a couple of X's who beat up Logan—how is he, have you heard?"

"They're saying he'll make it. No guarantee on the amount of brain damage. Same like you that time. But maybe his guardian angel is doing overtime."

"Thank God for that— A couple of X's who beat up Logan, neither of them could have been Don Franks, who's been incarcerated at that clinic since Wednesday afternoon. It was Friday Logan got jumped."

"All on the nose," nodded Mendoza. "The only reason we went looking at Don Franks—what, George?"

"Well, my God, he was the only one who showed who might have had a little grudge on Logan. Logan kindly explaining the symptoms of drug use to dimwitted Mama, who fetched the doctor in to haul Don off to the clinic. But—"

"And we now find that, A, Don isn't really hooked on anything. Just experimenting. And staying away from the H because he knows what that can do to you. And, B, he has a rather extensive cache of the hard stuff, representing quite a little investment, stashed away at home. Would either of you take any bets—"

"Well, for God's sake, Luis," said Higgins impatiently, "we're not idiots—of course we saw that! He was likely setting up as a seller, maybe a pusher—what you got from Faulkner just underlines that—"

"*Pues sí*. And consequently, George, all things being equal—"

"Oh, my God!" said Hackett suddenly. "But what fools—I just—"

And Sergeant Lake ran in. "Threatened shooting—black-and-white on the way—the McLaren Building on Wilshire, second floor—"

They all got up in a hurry. Mendoza snatched the .38 and a box of ammo from the top drawer; they met Grace in the corridor and ran. Hackett fell into the Ferrari after Mendoza, in the lot downstairs, and Mendoza switched on ignition and siren at once. Higgins and Grace dived into Grace's little blue Elva and tailgated the Ferrari out of the lot.

That building was a good forty blocks across town, one of the modern new office buildings just beyond MacArthur Park; the Ferrari's siren clearing the way, they made it at the same moment the black-and-white zeroed in from the opposite direction.

The crowd had begun to collect in the street.

A man came running out the front entrance of the building. "Police—thank God somebody called—shots fired, a lot of shots, just now, not two minutes ago! Up there somewhere—I was just getting into the ele—"

Mendoza gestured the uniformed men to the rear of the building with one savage movement; Higgins pounded after them. The rest of them ran into the building and up the marble stairs to the right. Whoever had called had said, second floor—

Up there, the whole corridor was in an uproar. Every door was open, people out in the hall, the more timid peering from doorways, asking questions, exclaiming—a woman screaming somewhere.

"Police? Up here—" They ran for that door, halfway up the corridor from the stairs, on the left side. The man there was very badly shaken; he was a tall, thin, nice-looking Negro wearing a doctor's white smock over dark pants, and he said, "In there—I think—the shots came from in there—I haven't been in, but Mrs. Stafford said—I haven't gone in—"

"I called," said a breathless voice. "I called you—I heard him—the door was open—" She was a diminutive blonde in a nurse's white uniform. "I told Dr. Blaise and he—but then all the shots—"

They went in with guns out. But a gun had spoken in there, and there wasn't any need for more guns.

It was an expensive modern office, as all those in this building would be. The gold lettering on the corridor door said *Dr. John Harlow, M.D.* There was a waiting room, heavily carpeted in beige pile, a beige couch and chairs, a long low fruitwood coffee table spread with magazines, several lamps, ashtrays. A glass panel to the left of another door: it was open, to show the receptionist's desk beyond, and the door was open to a short hall, other doors off that and at the end an open door.

Inside the door to the hall sprawled the white-uniformed body of a woman. A young Negro woman, bloody and still, the blood still widening slowly in a little pool beyond the body. "My God—" said Hackett.

The doors on either side opened on small examining rooms with the tables, the sinks, empty and sterile. The door at the end of the hall led to the doctor's office—a desk, thick carpet, chairs, fluorescent lighting—and more death. The man lay on his back, legs twisted, grotesque, in the middle of the room: he had on light gray trousers, a white smock, and a stethoscope still dangled around his neck, the slow stream of blood still running, staining it. The woman lay nearly across the threshold of a smaller room off this: a young woman, Negro, her blood still pumping from some artery—even as they came in, that suddenly stopped, and her body quivered once and was still.

For a heartbeat, they just looked. The woman had been young, pretty, well dressed: on this hot summer day, a jersey-silk sheath, cool blue; no stockings; medium-heeled white sandals. A big white patent handbag lay a few feet away from the body. The man had been hardly older, in his thirties: a tall man with regular chocolate-brown features.

"My God," said Hackett again.

The other man came in then behind them. "I didn't like to come in—she called you, we thought— *Oh, my God!* Dr. Harlow! It's—and his nurse out there—oh, my God!"

The woman in the hall stopped screaming abruptly.

"But Dr. Harlow—" The big Negro in the white smock looked at them dumbly. "Who'd do a thing like this? Who'd—"

Hackett said automatically, "You can identify the victims? May we have your name, please."

He nodded jerkily. "Colcannon. James W. Colcannon. My office—I'm a dentist, my office is right across the hall—I heard the shots, naturally I came—but Mrs. Stafford said— It's Dr. Harlow, yes, but who would do such a—"

Mendoza turned. "What about the two women? Can you tell us who they are, Doctor?"

He shook his head blindly. "The nurse—Dr. Harlow's receptionist, I think her name's Jenkins—"

Higgins and the two uniformed men came in. "Nothing," said Higgins. "He got clean away, Luis—we were just too late. Nobody in the parking lot—we can ask if anybody saw him come out, but there's not a smell there now. No telling even which way he went after leaving the building."

But there'd be places to ask questions: all the ground-floor offices, the buildings across the street. Mendoza said, "Keep these people out, for God's sake!" and the two patrolmen went to mount guard on the door to the corridor. "Art, we'll want a lab truck and an ambulance. Ask Bainbridge to come in person—he'd better see this from the start." Hackett went out in a hurry.

"But, everybody in the office," said Grace numbly. He holstered his gun. "The doctor, the nurse, the patient—" He went over and looked at the white handbag.

"But who'd want to do this to Dr. Harlow?" said Colcannon.

"Jase—" Mendoza came up beside him.

"It'll take prints, that patent, but—" Grace bent and pushed back the flap of the bag gently with one fingertip: the clasp was unfastened. He tilted it a little and a woman's blue leather billfold slithered out; they squatted over it, and Grace coaxed it all the way out with the tip of his pen, flipped the billfold open. On the left side, a plastic slot for an I.D. card, filled out in a neat hand. *Mrs. Ann Harlow,* an address in Leimert Park, *in case of accident notify Dr. John Harlow*—

"His wife," said Grace. "Harlow's. Why—"

"But Dr. Harlow," Colcannon was repeating, "Dr. Harlow so well thought of—such a good man—did a lot of charity work, I'd heard—who'd have any reason to—"

"Luis—" Higgins beckoned him. Mendoza went halfway down the hall; Higgins had the little blonde there. "Just tell the lieutenant about it, Mrs. Stafford. Mrs. Lilian Stafford, Luis, receptionist for Dr. Blaise down the hall—"

"Orthodontia and dentures," she said. "Two-fourteen. That's right. Oh, my God, are they all *dead?* It doesn't seem possible—I was—it was my coffee break, I only took ten minutes because we

66

were busy—I went down the hall to the rest room, I was coming back, I—" She was excited, but she was a level-headed young woman and in control of herself. "I came past Dr. Harlow's office, the door was open just a crack and I heard him—a man's voice—he was saying, 'I'll kill all of you, I will too, I'll shoot you all'—and he sounded— And I ran back to the office and called the police right away and then I told Dr. Blaise and he'd started down here when there were all the shots—oh, my God, are they *dead?* I can't believe—"

"We'll want a statement from you, Mrs. Stafford." As well as from most of the other people here on this floor when it happened, and probably those on the ground floor too. This one was going to be a king-size mess to work, Mendoza foresaw.

The ambulance arrived downstairs, the interns coming in with a stretcher. "Hands off," said Mendoza. "The full treatment on this one."

People were still milling around in the corridor, the interns hanging around waiting, when Dr. Bainbridge bustled in with, coincidentally, Scarne and Duke of the lab behind him. "Give this one the eagle eye, boys," said Hackett. "Did we say business was slow, everybody waiting for the next earthquake? My God, the wholesale slaughter—"

And Scarne was aiming the camera, Duke phlegmatically dusting the desk, five minutes later, when they heard it. The little fretful whimper from somewhere—that other door off the office—beyond the woman's still body.

It was a compact little lavatory, white tile floor, commode, Pullman vanity washbasin, stall shower. It was in the stall shower that Jason Grace, rushing in just ahead of the other men, found it. Where Ann Harlow, perhaps hearing that threatening voice—*I'll shoot you all*—had hastily, fearfully, hidden her baby—before going to the door to her husband's office, where death had waited.

Grace picked it up almost reverently and said, "My God—my God, its mother must have—"

The baby had been asleep, just waked up to loneliness. As they were to find, Celia Ann Harlow, just three months old. She was fat and brown with big brown eyes and a dimple beside her rosebud mouth, and she had kicked off the pink blanket around her and she smiled up from Grace's arms and gurgled.

"My God," said Grace. "From now on I believe in the guardian angels. Everybody else in the office— But who? And why?"

# 5

"But how did we miss him?" said Higgins savagely. "You heard what that fellow said—not two minutes ago, the shots—just as we got here, Luis! How did he vanish into thin air, whether he went out the front or back? This is a big building—"

It was an eight-story building, occupying nearly a full block with its large parking lot behind and to one side. The patrolmen and Higgins, running round to the rear, had found the parking lot nearly empty, at that time of day, and not a soul to be seen. Round the other side of the building, nothing. There were pedestrians passing, on Wilshire; then, realizing that something had happened, stopping to form a little crowd. But none of them had seen a man run out of the building.

They had called up three more cars—before Mendoza had called for a lab team and Bainbridge—and made a hurried search of the first three floors. In the lobby, a door to the basement (so the sign said) to the left of the entrance was locked; that was N.G., and of course for nearly a hundred percent sure he'd left the building at once. Only a couple of people on the third floor had heard the shots: everybody on the ground floor had, but the time element was against them there too. Nearly every tenant in the building was a professional of some kind: doctors, dentists, optometrists, a couple of lawyers—more doctors than anything else—and they didn't as a rule start office hours until ten. On the ground floor, where the bank of elevators took up half the corridor, the only offices occupied, at the rear of that long hall, had been those of a lawyer and another dentist; and by the time they and their office help had got out to the hall, to the front of the building, the gunman would have had time to get out that way without being seen.

Had had, in fact. By that time they had talked to Mrs. Myrtle Boggs, whose screams had welcomed them to the second floor. Mrs. Boggs had seen him go, and a lot of use she was to them. She'd been on her way up the hall toward the office of Dr. Edward Cunningham, gynecologist; she had a ten-thirty appointment. She had passed Dr. Harlow's office and was four or five offices up the hall—by what she could tell them—when she was paralyzed at the fusillade of shots.

"And I couldn't *move,* maybe twenty seconds, I was so scared —and I screamed—and I looked back because the shots came from back there—and I *saw* him! He came out that door—yessir, the door of that doctor's office—he came out running and he ran down the stairs—the front stairs—I saw the gun in his hand—and I couldn't stop screaming—"

They had asked her questions, and she'd tried to answer them. But she couldn't tell them much. They could hope after she'd calmed down a little she might remember more; but it wasn't surprising she hadn't seen more details. These corridors were lighted, but not all that well; and she'd been startled, confused; and she'd only seen his back.

"It was so *fast*—I don't suppose I saw him more 'n five seconds, and he was gone, down the stairs—well, it was a man, but I only saw his back, and the gun in his hand—he was running, and I couldn't even guess how tall he was or what clothes he was wearing—but he was the one, I saw him run out of that door and · I saw the gun—"

Slowly, in Harlow's office, order was being brought from confusion. The baby had been taken over to Juvenile Hall pending the discovery of any relatives. Grace had gone out to the Leimert Park address to look for relatives, friends. Bainbridge had examined the bodies; photographs had been taken and, eventually, the bodies removed. The lab men were dusting everything they could see in here; the detectives kept out of their way, talking to other tenants in the building, hunting anybody who might have something relevant to tell them.

The other nurse in Dr. Blaise's office identified Harlow's receptionist: Mrs. Harriet Jenkins, and supplied an address and that of Bill Jenkins' employer. Palliser went over to break the news to him. Jenkins was a skilled mechanic, working at a big Cadillac agency on Washington; he came down to the morgue to identify the body before he broke down. "We were saving for the house—wanted to get the house all paid off, only reason she went back to work the last five years—she liked the doctor, a fine man—it was the house payments, reason she—"

The men at Homicide came up with answers most of the time; the one answer they never had was the one to that question, Why did it have to be—?

Bainbridge had said they didn't look like very big slugs, but at close range any gun was deadly; had been here. He'd try to get them out at once for Ballistics.

They got this and that, talking to the other tenants on that floor. "I knew him—just casually," said Dr. Colcannon, calmer then. "To say hello and nice morning, is all. He'd been here longer than I have. I was busy with a patient when I heard the shots—and of course I didn't think it could *be* shots—backfires or— It wasn't until, oh, five or ten seconds later I realized it was shots, and came out through my waiting room—" He hadn't seen the gunman. "Just the woman standing there and screaming—"

The tearful pretty brown girl named Mary Ellen Rosden, from Dr. Blaise's office, told them that Mrs. Jenkins had been her best friend's aunt—her best friend Carla Jenkins. It had been Mrs. Jenkins had got Mary Ellen interested in nursing. "That is, she was a graduate nurse, but she was hired just as the receptionist in Dr. Harlow's office, he had a regular nurse too, Mrs. Jenkins was just as glad to take that sort of job, not on her feet so much —she liked Dr. Harlow—but who'd do such an awful thing? When I think of that baby being there—"

The other nurse had arrived by then, to faint dead away at the news; but, revived, she couldn't tell them much either. Everybody had liked Dr. Harlow, nobody would have had any reason to—

Grace called in at twelve-thirty. "So what have you picked up, Jase?" Everything had been printed then, and the lab men were gone, leaving Mendoza and the others in occupation of Dr. Harlow's once immaculate office, now bloodstained and disordered, with a film of fingerprint powder on most surfaces, and the furniture in disarray where they'd moved it to get at awkward spots. Mendoza was sitting at Harlow's desk going over the few solid facts they had with Hackett and Higgins.

"Nothing," said Grace. "Or nothing to give us any leads at all. There aren't any relatives, period. I've got two neighbors, one on each side of the Harlow house—Mrs. Gaster and Mrs. Pine. Mrs. Pine and her husband—who's an optometrist—about the same age as the Harlows, and knew them better. In fact, well enough that she called her husband and they've offered to make funeral arrangements, there being nobody else. Both the Harlows were brought up in orphanages, there aren't any relatives at all. Harlow in a private orphanage back in Maryland, his wife in a Catholic place in San Diego. They'd been so happy about the baby, married seven years and given up hope of a family."

"Yes, Jase." And they all knew the Graces felt like that too. Mendoza lit a new cigarette. "No enemies, no recent trouble."

"Nothing. He was thirty-four, she was thirty-two, she'd taught art for a couple of years, gave it up when he'd got his practice established. He started out in general practice eight years ago, right in that same office. He had a fine reputation, everybody"—Grace sounded tired—"liked him."

"Yes. Why was Mrs. Harlow there with the baby, did anyone know?"

"Just chance," said Grace sadly. "Another random thing is all. Harlow had hospital rounds to make most mornings—he wouldn't have office patients scheduled until about eleven—"

The first appointment listed in the book had been at eleven-fifteen. "Yes. So?"

"—And Mrs. Harlow had been fussing about the baby. Mrs. Pine says, the least little thing—but you can see why she would,

72

coming so late when they hadn't hoped— Anyway, she thought the baby had a little temperature, and she called her husband's office when she knew he'd be there, about ten-fifteen. And he told her to bring the baby right down—her name's Celia Ann, by the way—for him to check. Mrs. Harlow had her own car, it'll be in the lot down there—white Chevy Corvair five years old." He added the plate number. "Just chance that she was there. The Pines were close friends and they've never heard anything about any difficulties with patients, any quarrels or threats. But—"

"Mmh?"

"Nothing," said Grace. "Really. But the name sort of rang a bell with me—I seemed to remember my father mentioning Harlow—so I called to ask him." Grace's father was on the staff at the General Hospital. "He knew him, sure. Harlow interned at the General. Dad says he was a very good man, very competent. He'd tried to persuade him to specialize—said he had the makings of a very fine surgeon—but Harlow decided on general practice."

"Well," said Mendoza. "All of which gives us no ideas at all." He brushed his moustache the wrong way and back again. "Damnation. Could it have been just a nut off the street? That random? No, damn it, he must have known who he was threatening to shoot— Well, we've done what we can here. See what the lab picks up. See what Ballistics— We're going up to Federico's for lunch."

"So, I'll see you," said Grace.

At Federico's, waiting for lunch over preliminary drinks, they came to no conclusions except that this one was going to give them a lot of work.

"Take a look at all his patients," said Palliser with a sigh. "For somebody who—what? Thought he'd used the wrong treatment or something? At everybody he knew, for any trouble or—borrowed money, lent money? Was he a gambler, maybe, reneging on a deal?"

"Was he playing around with somebody's wife?" contributed Landers.

"I should doubt that, considering what Jase got," said Mendoza. "The Harlows seem to have been a perfectly respectable couple, all wrapped up in the baby they'd never expected to have. And that wasn't any kill over a gambling debt, John. This, if you want my considered opinion, was a nut. Pure and simple."

Grace came up to the table to hear that. "And that I'll go along with, Lieutenant. Perfectly respectable you can say. It's a nice house—colonial." Leimert Park, of course, and View Park where the Graces lived, were both very superior, well-groomed city areas where a considerable number of Negro professional people lived, with a few of the formerly wealthy white residents still scattered around. "She was a gardener—always puttering around her flowers, Mrs. Pine said. They were homebodies, didn't go out much—of course he had a busy routine—a few close friends, not socializers. He'd take a highball before dinner. She was Catholic, of course, but there wasn't any argument about it, he was perfectly agreeable the baby should be brought up in her church. They were just crazy about that baby, she said."

"Respectable married couple," said Hackett. "I had a thought, but it's a dead end."

"What?" asked Palliser.

"If he had white patients as well as black. Would he, Jase?"

"I should think probably—some, anyway. These days. Why?"

"Yes, I just thought if somebody with the funny notions got the idea that the stupid nigger doctor had given somebody the wrong medicine—but of course nobody like that would be going to Harlow to start with. Or, likely, anybody in such a family."

"Dead end," agreed Higgins. "We look at his patients and everybody he knew. My God, what a job."

"It's a shame about that baby," said Landers. "Cute little thing."

"That's so, Tom," said Grace. "A shame."

They checked in at the office at a quarter of two, and as they came in Lake looked up from his paperback. "Oh, John, you're to call this number. I don't know what about—a woman."

Palliser sat down at his desk, got an outside line and dialed.

74

Presently a female voice answered, and he said, "This is Sergeant Palliser."

"Oh. This is Reba Roberts, Sergeant—you know, you're the one came to tell me—about Chris—the other day."

"Yes, Mrs. Roberts. I haven't checked, but I think the body—that is, you can probably claim it today or tom—"

"Well, I wasn't calling about that, but thank you, I guess I can make some arrangements—"

"Any funeral director will take charge for you, claim the body and so on."

"Oh. Well, what I wanted to ask was, when could I have Chris's car? I suppose you wanted to examine it and all, and of course there's no hurry, I don't drive, but—"

Palliser stared at the phone. "His *car?* He was driving—" But what idiots they had been not to ask—not to assume he had been. Practically everybody in L.A. had a car, or access to one. And Hauck, living in Hollywood, ending up at the Sheridan Hotel downtown— *Both Tom and I slipping,* thought Palliser. Tom had an excuse: he was in love. *But I'm married to the girl,* reflected Palliser with a mental groan. Supposed to be trained detectives, and a little thing like that— "We didn't know he was driving, Mrs. Roberts. We haven't got his car. Can—"

"What? Well, I certainly thought—then where is it?"

Palliser could have a good guess. It was in the possession of Linda Schnell, or Foster Sterry, or both. And they were two days late sending out a call on it. "Can you tell us the make and model, Mrs. Roberts?"

"Surely. I've got the license number too, had it written down in the phone book—mine, I mean—on account, well, you know I told you how Chris was—and if I ever had to— It's a Buick, a white sedan, he got it new six years ago. The license number is HNO 504."

"Thanks very much. I'm sorry about this, somebody should have asked you if he had a— Well, thank you."

"I'm sure I hope you find it, Sergeant. As I say, I don't drive, but I can get something for it, I suppose."

"We'll let you know," said Palliser. He then naturally sought out Landers across the room and asked him why they'd been such idiots. "We might have known he was driving. And damn it, you've got an excuse for acting like an idiot—"

"I have?"

"You're in love with that cute blonde. But I haven't—at least, I've got the girl all tied up legal—only she's off on this miserly kick. Going back to work to get the furniture paid off, damn it. I don't approve of working wives. But I can guess where Hauck's car is, can't you?"

"No," said Landers. "What I can guess is who's driving it. Seeing that it hasn't been hauled into the Traffic garage as abandoned on the street. We'd better put it on the hot list."

"I'll do it," said Palliser.

Of course there was quite a lot of the tedious routine to do on the Harlow shooting, even if no leads turned up. They had to get the formal statements typed up and signed, from everybody in that building who had told them anything pertinent; and one from Mrs. Pine, and Bill Jenkins. That would take time, but if they ever got any evidence on this killer, they had to have all that down in black and white for the D.A.

Meanwhile, of course, they had been deflected off the Logan case, off the Hauck case, the other things turning up to make more paper work if no mysteries. Palliser confessed his sin of omission to Mendoza, who told him everybody had moments of aberration. "At least you've got it on the hot list now. It may turn up your floozy and her boy-friend."

Piggott and Glasser drifted in about then and everybody asked where they'd been. "At a time when we needed every man—"

Glasser said indulgently, "Well, you have to make allowances. He's just got engaged. I was on legitimate business. Nothing much—report to type. Old lady died in her sleep, apparently, apartment over on Virgil. Jimmy said something big was up when I called in."

They all looked at Piggott, who said with dignity he'd been out buying an engagement ring. "Though with everything a cop sees, I think maybe we're fools, try for the peaceful married life,

76

maybe a family. With the devil going up and down— Well, she didn't want a diamond, I got her her birthstone—it's an amethyst, with some little diamonds each side—"

"Very nice," said Glasser benignly.

Palliser, Landers, Grace, Piggott and Glasser went back to the McLaren Building to fetch the witnesses in and get the statements typed up. "It just occurs to me," said Hackett, sitting down in the chair beside Mendoza's desk, "that when all this erupted, we were just making some educated guesses about something else."

Higgins had followed him in. He was looking grim. "I thought I'd check," he said. "I just called the hospital. On Logan. He's had a relapse. They thought he was going, about nine this morning, but he's still hanging on—just barely holding his own—he could pass out any time."

"My God," said Hackett. "When we thought—"

"So, all the more reason to catch up to the X's on that, boys. *¿Qué le parece?*" Mendoza stabbed out his cigarette. "Where were we?"

"Deducing that Don Franks was setting up as a seller. With that hoard stashed away, maybe had been set up as a seller some time. But Franks couldn't have had anything to do with beating up Logan—"

"No. But reason it out. The unnecessary violence on Logan— why? No personal grudge that anybody knew of. The only unroutine thing Logan had done lately was to offer advice to dimwitted Mama Franks. Thereby getting Donny incarcerated. Incarcerated, Donny couldn't supply the fix for any of his customers, and that must have—"

"Annoyed them," said Hackett. "How did any of his customers know that it was Logan put the finger on Donny?"

"If they did, any of them—if that's the way it went—doubtless something will emerge as you go along," said Mendoza. "You might hunt up that Bob Vandermeier. Shortcuts. They were in junior high together, Vandermeier may still attend the same school as Donny."

"That had occurred to me," said Hackett.

Before he and Higgins left the office, however, the lab report came in. The lab hadn't picked up any useful latents at the Logan house, any strange prints. They had found two kinds of bloodstains—a lot of type O, which was Logan's, and a little of type AB, which was a fairly rare type. "That's funny," said Hackett, reading the report over Mendoza's shoulder. "We said if Logan got in a couple of blows, that was all—knocked out almost right away. Of course he might have bloodied a nose—"

"Or," said Higgins, "whoever had that knife was turned on and not noticing just where he aimed it."

"And that is also a thought," said Mendoza. "Suppose you go and look, *compadres.*"

"While you do what?"

Mendoza trickled smoke through his nostrils. "I have here," he said sleepily, "Dr. Harlow's case records. They look like fairly dull reading, but one never knows when something suggestive might show, or where. It's a place to start."

"And the hunch rising up to biff you between the eyes, let us hope," said Hackett.

Which sometimes the hunches did. Mendoza was sitting on the end of his spine, hands clasped across his flat stomach, eyes closed. "Symbolic," he said. "Very symbolic. Improving my education, Alison says."

"What's symbolic?"

"Rumpelstiltskin," said Mendoza. " 'Discover my name'— Mmh, yes. Reach in blind and hope the hunch hits you. *¡Vamos!*"

Hackett found Bob Vandermeier at three forty-five, by the simple expedient of checking with Hollywood High School. Summer school was in session and a skeleton staff was there. Bob Vandermeier attended Hollywood High School, and his address was Briarcliff Road: another hillside street, a newer wealthy residential area.

Mrs. Vandermeier, small and dark, was frightened and indignant, police asking for Bob, and Hackett was patient, explaining —just questions about another boy at school—and she thawed under his big reassuring smile. "It isn't that I worry about him," she said at last, "I know Bob's all right—but dear Lord, these days can you be sure about anything? I'll get him, Sergeant—he's out back with the pup—he's starting her on her obedience lessons."

Bob Vandermeier was not a handsome boy, but he was reliable-looking: the only word for it. He had a round freckled face and steady blue eyes and close-cropped sandy hair and heavy shoulders: a big boy, mature-looking too. He sat on the couch opposite Hackett, with a leggy Great Dane pup at his feet, and listened to Hackett soberly.

"Don Franks," he said. "I'm not a pal of his anymore, Sergeant. *Sit,* Cleo. He's in trouble? I'm not surprised at that. He's really goofed off, the last couple years."

"In what line? I don't want to—" Hackett hesitated. "That is, if you feel—"

The boy smiled. "Make me rat on him? Sergeant, some of us have a little more sense than you might think. That's kid stuff, isn't it? If somebody's doing something wrong, illegal, it's only sense to see they get stopped. No, I didn't know Don was doing anything wrong, just suspected. He really got in with the wrong ones, first year in high—that was when we split up, way back there, so I couldn't tell you anything about him since, not that I know myself."

"Except that he was running with the wrong ones? Wrong which way? Who?"

"What do you think? The drug scene—the longhairs and beautiful people," said Bob. He looked down at the dog, the lines of potential grandeur blurred by puppyhood, the awkwardness of fast growth. He smiled. "It's kind of like Cleo here," he said. "Kind of. I mean, those kind, they're always talking about doing your own thing, what you want when you want, freedom, they talk about. But it's like Cleo here—just letting her do like that, she'd be the biggest nuisance you could have around, you know. All over the place— Well, you've got to teach 'em how to behave, how to handle themselves. So they're good for something, you know? That kind—I don't know how they figure—but they don't think just so logical. Besides going for the dope, which is just plain silly."

"So it is," said Hackett.

"I don't know that Don's gone in for that. But some of the kids he goes with—I could guess," said Bob. He scratched behind Cleo's ears reflectively and she grinned widely up at him. "Was he?"

"In a way," said Hackett. "Who does he run with?"

"Oh—I don't know any of them, just their names. I do know Ken Burkhart's been arrested once, something to do with drugs, I think. The others, I couldn't say. I wouldn't know all of the ones Don ran with. Jim Root, Marty Murphy, Ron Dolan, that girl—Kathy something—Cuthbert, Cathcart, something—and one they call Buck—I wouldn't know 'em all. Yes, they all go to Hollywood High—well, that is, or they did. You did know Don had dropped out, last semester? A couple of that bunch had too. At least, I had the same English class with this Murphy and the Kathy girl, and they hadn't showed up the last couple of months of the semester. And that's another thing, you know, Sergeant."

"What?"

"Well, they were both," said Bob, "so stupid in class. We're supposed to think that kind have got the answers to everything—them and their Do-your-own-thing whatever and whenever—when Murphy spells *hotel* with two *l*'s on a blackboard assignment, and doesn't know a comma from a semicolon?" Hackett laughed. "Well, I only got a B in that class," said Bob, "but I'd like to think I'm some smarter than that. It's like my granddad says—I think it's an old-country proverb—you got to learn to walk before you can run."

And it was reassuring to reflect that there were, hopefully, more teenagers like Bob Vandermeier around than the other kind. That was of no immediate help in locating these more recent pals of Don Franks's. By the time Hackett had seen Bob, the school staff had gone home. Tomorrow. . . .

Just before Mendoza left the office, the lab sent up a preliminary report on the Harlow shooting. The slugs had been examined by the Ballistics men: four in Harlow, three in Mrs. Harlow, two in Mrs. Jenkins. They had not been much damaged, and Ballistics had pinpointed the gun: a Harrington and Richardson nine-shot .22 revolver. Which was no surprise in one way: what they'd got, that X in and out fast, he wouldn't have had time to reload. A nine-shot: so, the gun emptied, the people dead, and every last thing they knew was that X was male. Seen from the back, running, gun in hand. Three people dead, why?

"It's beautiful, Matt," said Prudence.

"I suppose we've just got to have faith," said Piggott, holding her hand with the amethyst ring on it, "that there'll be ten righteous men to save the city. Satan going up and down—"

"Pessimist." She laughed at him. "There are always more good people than bad, darling."

"That is a fact," said Piggott more cheerfully.

Landers, feeling tired—thinking about that baby, and the Harlows, and Patrolman Pat Logan—God, like that time Hackett had lain between life and death—Landers took Phil O'Neill out to dinner at Frascati's. And Phil, looking impossibly cool and neat in such heat, smiled wisely at him and said she *was* making up her mind, when they'd known each other longer they could tell better if they'd get along.

"But, Phil darling—"

"Sentimental," she said. "Because I do not approve of divorce, Tom. And it's the little things that are important. Whether you're tidy or sloppy, or laugh at the same things, or—"

"We do."

"—Or believe the same things," she said vaguely. "Do you like beets?"

"No."

"That's good, I detest them. You're passing tests, don't fuss," said Phil sedately.

Palliser got home late, and over warmed-up stew regaled Roberta with the Harlow shooting. "Just nowhere to go—unless, of course, the boss has a hunch. And the cutest baby you ever saw. Jase saying, the guardian angel—maybe." He felt his shoulder. "Damn it, I've definitely done something to this shoulder—manning a shovel last week, of all—"

"I've been figuring," said Roberta inattentively. "With what I'll be earning, John—we can put all of it on the contract for the furniture and the new refrigerator—we could get the whole thing paid off in eighteen months, do you know that?"

"So all right." He looked up at her, his lovely dark gray-eyed Robin, slim and thoughtful. "We could. We said, a family—two anyway—and as far as I'm concerned—"

"Well, eighteen months isn't very long—"

"I'm not going to argue about it," said Palliser. "We don't have fights, do we?"

"No, darling. Ever. All I say—"

"Well, eighteen months," said Palliser with a sigh. "All right. Miser."

Sergeants Galeano and Schenke, on night watch, were desultorily discussing rival baseball teams when a call came through from the desk downstairs. They both went out on it. The call was clocked at ten-fifty; the black-and-white was sitting on it when they got there.

It was a mama-and-papa store, a little grocery and delicatessen, on Third Street. The ambulance came five minutes after they got there. There was a woman, elderly and fat, dead behind the counter where the cash register gaped open. And the shocked, shaken old man— "We was just about to close, we close at eleven—I'd gone into the back, we got our apartment behind the store, and Amy was just puttin' a new roll of tape in the register—I hear the bell go, customer come in, it wasn't quite eleven and— And then I hear Amy yell and the shot— But there wouldn't've been more'n fifty bucks— Amy—we was just about to close—Amy was puttin' a new tape— No sir, I didn't see anybody, time I got out—"

So there was something else for the day watch to work.

82

Mendoza was annoyed on Tuesday morning to find that new one waiting to be worked; business picking up again; and one of the petty nuisances of police work was the necessity, as new things came up, of dropping one case before it was finished to deal with another.

He handed Schenke's report to Hackett; Higgins read it over his shoulder. "So we chase off on this? I want to track down some of those punks Franks knows. Have you called the hospital —how's Logan doing?"

"Just holding his own," said Mendoza. "And damn it, that William Campden is up for arraignment today, one of you'll have to be there."

"Anything we get on this we'll get from the lab," said Hackett, dropping Schenke's report on Mendoza's desk. "I think it's more important to locate these punks."

"*Conforme*, you can go hunt the punks." It was Grace's day off; they were a man short.

"What about Harlow?" asked Higgins.

"I'm on that—if there's anywhere to go on it. Call in, and *buena suerte*." And as they turned, "Hold it, what's this?"

"Autopsy report on Hauck—just came in." Sergeant Lake handed it over.

"So, if John and Tom are in yet—"

Hackett and Higgins started out to look for the punks.

Palliser came in feeling his shoulder, with Landers behind him. "Damn it, I've pulled a muscle or something, it's been getting worse the last few days. That picket's wandering around again, did you notice?"

"*No me diga*—I didn't." Mendoza looked out the door. "Oh, Matt—good. We've got a new one overnight—here's Bob's report. As Art said, anything useful we get on it we'll get from the lab, but it won't do any harm to talk to the old man again—Jacob Durand. Wife Amy was D.O.A., single shot. Ask if they'd ever been held up before, any neighborhood punks who might be likely."

"Will do." Piggott took the report.

"Did she like the ring?"

Piggott smiled. "She did. She tells me I'm a pessimist, saying what an awful chance we're taking. Which I guess I am." He glanced at the report. "Little bit more of Satan's work, and the poor old woman— I'll see if I can pick up anything."

Mendoza sat down to read the autopsy report, handed it over to Palliser; it didn't hold any surprises. Hauck had actually died of strangulation, and of course that was a very easy way to kill somebody whether you meant to or not, in the heat of the moment. He had a few bruises making it look likely that he'd exchanged blows with somebody just before he died. And he had been well past the legal point of intoxication. Time of death estimated as between midnight and four A.M. last Friday night.

That told them nothing new. If Hauck's Buick was being driven anywhere around, it should be spotted eventually; but this was a big town with a lot of cars on the streets, and Traffic patrol was spread thin. Palliser and Landers agreed that there wouldn't be much percentage in locating more of Linda Schnell's girl-friends; they knew she'd been in that hotel room with Hauck, said Palliser, and what Marian Henry said—

"*No hay tal,*" said Mendoza. "Details, details. Marian Henry's been in the county jail for a month. She told you that about five weeks back Linda was teaming up with an old boy-friend she'd just come across again. Foster Sterry. We don't know anything about him. You've seen Linda's record. Are you seriously convinced that in five weeks she couldn't have forgotten all about Sterry and picked up with somebody else, or picked up with a dozen other boy-friends? Aside from any johns she may have rolled?"

"Well, when you put it like that," said Landers, "that's so, of course. She could have. So we'd better find some more pals of Linda's, who've seen her more recently, and ask."

"I think so," said Mendoza.

"Have you had any hunches on Harlow?" asked Palliser.

"*Nada.* Unless— Well, a couple of ideas. We'll see. . . ."

As Hackett and Higgins came up to the scarlet Barracuda in the lot, the ground shifted slightly and rolled under their feet for ten seconds. "These damn aftershocks," said Higgins. He looked up at the Police Building—and these days, of course, they were calling it Parker Center for that irascibly tough and high-minded and dedicated chief who had been largely responsible for making this the top police force anywhere—and shook his head. On this side of the big rectangular building, a crew on a scaffolding suspended from the roof was installing glass in the second-floor windows. "Well, progress. They may get to us a week from tomorrow. In this weather, my God." He got into the car.

"How's Mary?"

"Oh, fine. She says she's tired of looking like a dirigible. She looks fine," said Higgins comfortably. They did say, the older they were the harder they fell; and Higgins, fond though he was of the Dwyer kids, was looking forward to his own family. Hackett thought of Angel saying, if it turned out to be a girl, the worst spoiled brat in the country. Well, little girls—

The steering wheel of the Barracuda was almost too hot to touch.

"These punks, Art. How strong a lead is this?"

"Well, it could be a hot one, George. The way this Logan thing shapes up. God, I hope he makes it—he seems to be a good man."

"Yeah. Try the high school first for addresses."

At Hollywood High School, they got addresses for the kids Bob Vandermeier had named—Martin Murphy, Ken Burkhart, Jim Root, Ron Dolan; who Buck might be nobody knew. Hollywood High was a big school and took in kids from a wide area: the fashionable hillside places, the shabby streets of central Hollywood, and every sort of neighborhood in between. These days, it didn't seem to matter what kind of neighborhood the kids came from. The turned-on generation came from all kinds of backgrounds.

They looked for the nearest address first—Jim Root, Edgemont Avenue. It was one side of a duplex on an old block, half single houses, half rental units. The woman who answered the door stared at their badges. She was a slight woman in a drab cotton dress, brown hair going gray, a thin face, and she said, "Jim? You want to see Jim? What's he done?"

"We don't know that he's done anything, ma'am," said Higgins. "We'd just like to talk to him."

"Well, you can't because he's not here. And I don't know where he is." She put a hand to her mouth: a hand calloused with hard work. "You try," she said tiredly, "you try. He's my only one—his father walked out on me when Jim was just a baby, I had to support us. I have—I've never been on the welfare, I've taken care of myself and Jim, and I tried to bring him up right. But you see how it was. I had to work. Leave him alone. I saw he went to Sunday School—I talked to him. But a boy gets to be fourteen, fifteen, he gets away from you—it's like you don't know him at all no more. He got a job once when he was fourteen, fifteen—at a market—he never liked school much and he wanted to earn—but they wouldn't let him work, see. Said he wasn't old enough. *I* went to work awhile before I was fourteen. But—"

"I see. How long has he been gone?" asked Hackett.

She shook her head. "After that, he just seemed to—not care about anything. He was like a stranger. Saying and doing things —he wouldn't talk to me, listen to me. He'd go off a week at a time, I wouldn't know where— Only this time I guess it's for good. Like his dad walking out. Well, he's turned eighteen, you can say he's grown. He's been gone since the middle of May—I haven't laid eyes on him since. He went while I was at work—I work for the Ace Cleaning Company, they take contracts like for cleaning big buildings, offices. He took all but a few of his clothes and all the extra money I'd saved from the coffee canister, and I haven't seen him since."

"Well, thanks very much," said Hackett.

She just made a defeated gesture and shut the door. "I've just thought of another bad pun," said Higgins. "Root the rootless."

"More truth than poetry," said Hackett. "It's a sad thing to think, George, that eventually life is going to catch up to all these irresponsible louts of kids. You can't go on goofing off and getting away with it forever."

"What she said about his acting different—could be he's hooked on something."

"Or a lot of different things." They got in the car. They didn't wonder how Jim Root was managing to live. The turned-on kids, goofing off, crowded together sordidly in a rented room, relying on the petty theft, mugging, or more serious crimes for their basic necessities—which would involve a narco salesman.

The next address was for Ron Dolan, Yucca Street. It was another old place, a single house, and they waited nearly five minutes for an answer to the bell. When the door opened, they faced a little old lady, white-haired, thin and stooped, with thick-lensed spectacles riding low on her nose. She blinked up at the two big men, at their badges. "Police officers, ma'am. Does Ron Dolan live here?"

"Police—" she said. "Police? Ron? Why, what—what do you want—with Ron? He's my grandson. Ron wouldn't do anything wrong, officers. He's just a boy—he's only eighteen."

"Well, we'd like to talk with him, Mrs.—"

"Dolan, I'm Frances Dolan, I've brought Ron up and he's a good boy, officers. Why do you want to talk to him?"

"Excuse me, Mrs. Dolan, where are his parents?"

"They're dead," she said. "My only son—and his wife, they were killed in an airplane crash when Ron was five. I've brought him up and he's a good boy—"

"Well, if we could see him, please. Is he here?"

She let them in reluctantly, led them back to the kitchen, an old-fashioned square kitchen with the table in the middle. Ron

Dolan was sitting there finishing breakfast—bacon and eggs, a smell of good coffee in the air. He looked at the badges, and he said, "What you want with me? I haven't done anything."

And Hackett and Higgins recognized him instantly. They'd both seen a lot of the punks, and they came all shapes and sizes, but certain things about them never altered. Ron Dolan was tall and thin, dark, with dark shifting eyes and a narrow chin, and he was neatly enough dressed in a blue shirt and dark pants. But the automatic sullen suspicion in his eyes and voice, the quick resentment-of-cops attitude before he even knew why they were there, told the story. His hair was down past his ears—probably all the old lady, dim and vague as she might be, would let him get by with; but he had a swashbuckling pair of side-burns.

"You happen to know where Jim Root is, Ron?" asked Hackett conversationally.

"No. I don't. I haven't seen him awhile." Ron's eyes moved once; he didn't change expression, but he had answered that too quick. He had, surprisingly, been expecting that question. Hackett and Higgins shared silent curiosity.

"What about Don Franks?"

"I haven't seen him either. No."

"Think hard," said Hackett.

"I don't have to. I don't know anything about it."

"I don't understand this," said Mrs. Dolan anxiously. "What do you think Ron's done? Ron's a good boy—" And both the Homicide men could read his impatient glance at her without an interpreter. The woolly-minded old woman, never any suspicion that Ron was anything but what she expected of a grandson, clean-cut-American-boy— Quite evidently she wasn't aware that he'd dropped out of school in the middle of last semester. He'd find it easy to get away with murder in this household, help himself to her money, tell her anything; and naturally he despised her for a fool.

"Did you know Don Franks is selling the hard stuff?" asked Higgins.

"I don't know anything." But he did; they read him like a

book. This kind wasn't very smart, and all the more vulnerable because they thought they were.

And there wasn't anything they could bring him in on. Get a search warrant? On what grounds? Was he holding any dope? If he was, he'd get rid of it as soon as they were out of sight. But he knew something about Jim Root, and he knew about Franks. Did that say he was tied up to Root some way? On what?

They could go on talking to him, questioning him, for the next hour; they'd get nothing. They went out and sat in the Barracuda, aware that they were probably being watched. "He knows where Root is," said Hackett. "Doesn't he?"

"I think so. But so what, Art? That doesn't say that any of 'em has anything to do with Logan. It doesn't say that either Ron or Root was a customer of Franks's, even."

"No, it's up in the air. But if we're ever going to find out," said Hackett, "whether either of them has anything to do with Logan, it might be worth an hour's time to—er—beat the bushes to alert the hare."

"Come again?" said Higgins.

"Well, there's a Spanish proverb—*Más vale una onza de práctica que una libra de gramática*. More in one ounce of experience than a library of books. I guess you could say experience tells us this and that, George. About the ones like Ron. And whether Root, Franks or Ronny-boy had anything at all to do with Pat Logan getting jumped, Ronny-boy knows something about Root—and unless we are both woolgathering, George, it's something cops would be interested in. *¿Cómo no?*—are you with me?"

"Right behind. You want to beat some bushes?"

"Just for kicks. The punks always think they are so smart, and they so very seldom are." Hackett glanced in the rearview mirror. "About a block up, George, is a drugstore on the corner. With, I hope, a phone booth. Call Wilcox Street and get a black-and-white up here. And arrange a tail for Ronny."

Higgins grinned. "What they call a catalyst." He slid out of the car. Hackett sat there and smoked a cigarette, watching the house, until he came back. Five minutes later the black-and-white drifted up and parked ahead of the Barracuda, and Hackett and Higgins got out to confer with the two uniformed men. The usual uniformed men: trim, clean-cut, alert-looking. This the top force anywhere.

"What's up, sir? You the Central detectives—on Logan? I'm Walsh—Gonzales."

"Little playacting, boys," said Hackett. "There is a punk in that house we're hoping to scare into doing something silly."

"It doesn't take an awful lot to do it sometimes," said Gonzales. "This punk had something to do with Pat getting beat up?"

"It could be. There'll be a plainclothes tail arriving to sit on him in about fifteen minutes," said Higgins. "You just sit here till the tail takes over. The punk won't notice the tail, of course, but I hope he's feeling nervous about all of us right now." He and Hackett delivered simultaneous sinister looks at the Dolan house, very open and obvious. Ron would be watching.

"Little playacting," said Walsh. "There's just one thing."

"What's that?"

"Well—" He looked at the two senior sergeants from Homicide, burly Art Hackett, massive-shouldered Higgins. "If the pair of you didn't already scare the punk, will he scare at all?"

Mendoza had found Dr. Harlow's records extremely dull reading. Dr. Harlow had had the usual run of patients any general practitioner would have: the chronically half-ill elderly people, young mothers, children, people of all ages with the aches and pains, the need for minor or major surgery. He had had a good-sized practice, a full daily routine. There was nothing at all exotic, unusual, or suggestive in the records; no sudden hunch hit Mendoza about the run-of-the-mill general cases Dr. Harlow had handled.

They hadn't finished getting all those necessary statements down yesterday by any means; Glasser and Piggott (after he'd seen Jacob Durand) would be fetching more witnesses in today.

90

Mendoza, going out to ask about that, found Glasser just coming in with Mrs. Gladys Short.

"Good," he said. "I wanted to talk to you, Mrs. Short."

"Mr. Glasser said a statement—well, you told me yesterday—"

"Yes. You can do that later—right now I'd like to ask you some questions."

"Well, of course, if I can help any way, to find out who— It just doesn't bear thinking of," she said. "Dr. Harlow—and his wife, such a nice woman—and Harriet Jenkins. I never had such a shock in my life." She followed him into his office, sat down in the chair beside his desk; she fanned herself absently with a handkerchief. It was very hot in the office, the sun striking brightly through the glassless windows.

Gladys Short had been Dr. Harlow's other nurse: the one who actually served as a nurse. She was a plump woman, milk-chocolate color, about forty, with a normally round pleasant face now looking a little drawn, and intelligent eyes.

"Did you think," said Mendoza, "that if it had happened half an hour later, you might have got it too?"

"That was just one of the things I thought about, Lieutenant," she said quietly. "Yes. And all I can think—such a terrible thing, and just the Lord's mercy that poor sweet baby didn't get killed too—all I can think, a lunatic. Because—"

"Picking Dr. Harlow at random? You know, if you follow me," said Mendoza, "I could just buy that—if his office had been on the ground floor."

She stared at him for a minute and then said, "Oh. Oh, I see—because—he went to the trouble of—"

"Climbing the stairs. He didn't just want to shoot somebody. It was somebody specific. Had you been with Dr. Harlow long?"

"Since he opened his office. I worked at the General after I graduated, but it's a rat race like they say. It's a good hospital, with a good staff, but it's big—and always busy. We got run off our feet half the time—"

"You know a Dr. Grace there?"

"Dr. John Grace? Why, yes, sir, he's chief of gynecology—a very nice man, a good doctor. Why?"

"No reason—his son's one of our bright boys in this office. You probably met him yesterday. So—I'm going to ask you to think back and tell me anything, anything at all you can remember—"

She had, of course, denied that there *was* anything like that, anyone with a reason to have a grudge on the doctor. He laid out some persuasive charm, and she said suddenly, "Well, there had been that Ainslie man. . . . I think it was around May— it'll be in the records. But a little thing like that—! Well, if you want to hear—"

A William Ainslie, coming in with an infected hand. Said he'd cut himself accidentally trying to get something out of a garbage disposal. Two fingers had been badly mauled. Dr. Harlow had done what he could, but in the end Ainslie had lost all but partial use of two fingers on his left hand, and he had threatened to sue the doctor. "It didn't come to anything, of course, because the doctor'd done all any doctor could do, and besides it came out that Ainslie hadn't gone to a doctor right away, he'd tried to take care of it himself until it got infected."

And, under prodding, she remembered the girl. Awhile before that— "I can't think what gets into these little fools—" A girl named Karen something, that would be in the records too. She'd come to see the doctor, just a teen-age girl, a new patient they'd never seen before, and been told she was pregnant. She'd evidently been very upset and scared—"You could see that. I'd have felt sorry for her, but for what she tried. And how she ever thought she'd get away with such a thing I don't know, but she told her father the *doctor* was responsible—that she'd gone to see him and he'd attacked her or something— There was quite a scene," said Mrs. Short indignantly, "we had the man creating an uproar, calling the police and all—honestly, that girl having the gall to—. But of course Dr. Harlow could show it wasn't true. He never saw a woman patient alone—at least, more than five minutes or so. Especially young ones. Doctors aren't fools, Lieutenant."

"No. Father a fool, or did he believe that?"

"Why—I don't know. He wasn't an educated man—terribly upset about the girl—he didn't make any formal charges, no, but I don't know whether he—maybe went on believing we were all lying, just to protect the doctor. Maybe—"

"Mmh. Anything else?"

And she thought, and suddenly began to laugh, and sobered. "Oh, dear, I just remembered that. Oh, the doctor did laugh so over that! He wasn't—wasn't a *solemn* man, but he was quiet, you know—serious. But he did laugh so over that. We all did. It was a little Chinese fellow—Kun Low Soo, I couldn't forget that name! You know, Lieutenant, most Orientals here now—well, most *people*—they're smart, city-wise people—but you get all sorts, and this little fellow could hardly speak English. He was a chef at some restaurant in New Chinatown, and he came in with his wife. A pretty little woman—she was pregnant. The doctor did all the usual things, you know, ran some tests and all—I seem to remember her blood pressure was low, and he prescribed some medication for that—and she came in every month for a checkup, and finally she went into labor and it was a little girl. No complications, everything went off just as it should—of course she'd had nine other babies, in about ten years we gathered. But the little man was simply furious!" Remembering it, she laughed again. "He came to the office the next day—he said the doctor had swindled him—nine worthless daughters his wife had produced, and this time he'd taken his boss's advice and brought her to a real doctor instead of a midwife, and a real doctor should have guaranteed that it was a son—he was furious! He really believed it, you know—I've never seen the doctor laugh so—"

Mendoza grinned. *"Ridículo,* yes—you can't yet make out the order, wanted, one male, live birth—as I know to my cost—"

"Oh, do you have all girls too?"

"One of each. Twin monsters. But—when was this?"

"Oh, just last June. But, Lieutenant—"

"An ignorant man. Really believing— Well, that's interesting," said Mendoza. "And something to look at closer."

"But you can't think—that silly little man would—do *that?* Shoot the doctor, and—just for *that,* no reason at all?"

"You said to me, a lunatic," said Mendoza. "Which means, somebody irrational. I could just see Mr. Kun Low Soo qualifying as irrational, Mrs. Short."

But just occasionally—possibly an effort on the part of the guardian angels to spur them on as good cops, reassuring them that the dedicated routine did pay off—occasionally something went right by the book, smooth as cream, just the way the manual said routine should go. And that could be very gratifying.

Hackett and Higgins came in, briefed Mendoza on their beat-the-bushes operation. Ron Dolan had taken off, with the tail after him, in a ten-year-old Ford, about half an hour after the tail had got in position. They'd waited round the corner to see that much. Sooner or later they should hear more.

Palliser and Landers had found another girl-friend of Linda's and were questioning her down the hall.

And at a quarter to twelve Duke called from the lab. "Sometimes we do all your work for you."

"So you do. What have you done now?"

"This heist job last night. No witnesses, piddling take, and a D.O.A. We went over the place, of course. Four nice clear latents on the cash register. Oh, and the gun was a Colt .22 of some kind, Ballistics says an oldie and beat up."

"The latents. Identified?"

"Oh, yes. Idiots they are," said Duke. "He must know they're on file. It makes you wonder."

"Sometimes it does. I have been wondering about the small-time punks," said Mendoza, "for twenty-four years, Duke—since you were in kindergarten. I haven't reached any conclusion yet. Who is the small-time punk, ¿por favor?"

"Edward Hobart. Little pedigree, B.-and-E., petty theft, purse-snatching, attempted burglary. The usual counts, probation, et cetera. Twenty-three now, five-eleven, one-fifty, Caucasian,

94

brown and blue, no marks. Last known address, Beacon Avenue. He lives—or did live—with his mother."

"*Vaya historia*," said Mendoza. "Thank you so much."

"No trouble, we just had to look," said Duke.

Mendoza passed that on. "My God," said Hackett, "doing what comes naturally. But no record of violence before?"

"There is that." Mendoza got up and looked across the hall. "Matt? You hear anything more from Durand than what Bob and Nick got last night?"

"That poor old soul," said Piggott. He came into Mendoza's office with a report in one hand. "I was just getting it down. They'd run that store for thirty years together. Harmless old couple—no family at all. No, Durand said they'd never been held up before, never had trouble with anybody in the neighborhood. He never saw the heist-man at all, he was back in their apartment while she was closing up. He just heard her scream, I suppose when the fellow showed her the gun—and then the shot. He—"

"Mmh," said Mendoza. "And Hobart's record—the little sneak thief, trying for something a little bigger than he'd ever done before—and possibly panicking when she screamed—yes."

"Oh, have we got him?" asked Piggott.

Mendoza brushed his moustache absently. "Seeing that Hobart's last known address is some sixty blocks away from Third Street, and that ordinary customers don't have any occasion to touch the cash register, I would say we have, Matt."

Hackett got a call just then from Wilcox Street, so he and Higgins went off to hear the latest on their catalyst. Palliser and Landers emerging from the sergeants' office, Mendoza asked them what they'd turned up.

"Nothing new," said Palliser. "Girl-friend of Linda's who saw her last Thursday tells us she's still going around with Foster Sterry. We sent an inquiry to the Feds, see if they know him."

"So now you can go look for Edward Hobart," said Mendoza, and filled them in on that.

"But my God," said Landers, "you would think some rudimentary *sense*—when he knows we've got his prints—"

"The Edward Hobarts don't have rudimentary sense," said Mendoza. He sat at his desk with the cards fluttering absently in his hands—Alison and the domesticities had ruined his poker game but he still thought sharper with the cards in his hands—and there were people who said Luis Mendoza had missed his calling, should have been a pro gambler. He thought about Dr. John Harlow, and William Ainslie, and that teen-age girl, and Kun Low Soo. . . . People to look at. People, coming all sorts, and you never knew what they might do. . . .

Occasionally, it worked out just the way it should, theoretically. The lab handing them the nice evidence; the pedigree on file; the address the right one.

At the shabby apartment, Mrs. Elmira Hobart told Palliser and Landers that Eddy was looking for a job. "He's engaged to get married," she added. "A nice girl, Julia is, and Eddy wants to get a job so as to marry her. She don't know about that little trouble he's been in— Eddy don't mean anything wrong, it's just, it's hard for him to hold a job—"

A gun? Oh, Eddy didn't have a gun. Eddy wanted to get married, he wouldn't be getting into more trouble, and he'd gone up to that employment place, the state one, about an hour ago. To try to get a job. They wouldn't tell Julia about Eddy getting in that little trouble, would they?

"Really, it makes me feel tired," said Palliser. "Not two cents' worth of common sense, Tom." He felt his shoulder.

"Well, what we get paid for," said Landers philosophically. As they came back to Palliser's Rambler, suddenly the earth gave under their feet, sickeningly, and for ten seconds was unsolid. "These damn aftershocks— Where is that agency? Olive, I think—"

They found Edward Hobart sitting patiently in a line at the California Employment Agency, and brought him back to headquarters to question. Mendoza sat in on that.

"I didn't mean to!" said Hobart in a high frightened voice.

"I never meant to do such a thing! I'm awful sorry it happened —it was just—well, my God, I had to have some money, I had to—you gotta understand, I want to marry Julia, I just got engaged to Julia, and I needed some money. I wanted to buy her a nice ring and all, a wedding trip some place—"

"Where'd you get the gun, Eddy, and where is it?" asked Palliser.

"Why'd you pick the Durands' place?" asked Landers. "You couldn't have thought there'd be much loot there?"

Hobart licked his lips. He was unhealthy-looking, pasty-faced, otherwise not bad-looking. "I—I'd never tried anything like that before, a real holdup—" No, he was small-time. "I—I— I borrowed the gun—from a guy I know—I said I'd cut him in, but it was only forty-two bucks! I was—kinda nervous, try a real big place like a—a theater or a drugstore—people around—I —a little place like that, I thought easier— But when she yelled, I—I didn't mean to shoot off the gun! I don't know much about guns—it sort of went off, and—"

"So who'd you borrow the gun from?"

"I—a guy named Al. Al Koonz. I guess he's got a record. I didn't mean to—"

"But you did." The D.A. might call it manslaughter, or murder second; that wasn't up to Homicide.

"But it was just for Julia!" he said wildly. "I just wanted to get the nice things for Julia—oh, *Julia!*" He began to sob. "It was just because I love Julia so bad, I had to—have some money —and I couldn't get no job—"

"Love, in fact, in general," said Mendoza. Late home, he surveyed Alison sitting up in bed reading, the lamp turning her red head to flame; she had on a new topaz nylon nightgown. "You look very fetching, *enamorada*."

"*Gracias*. Love?" said Alison.

"Love. It is a dangerous commodity," said Mendoza, "depending on who harbors it." El Señor, annoyed at being waked, uttered a few low curses from the tangle of cats at the foot of the bed. Mendoza yawned and began unbuttoning his shirt. "And of course Kipling always had the word for it, too." His strange enthrallment to Kipling was still puzzling his household.

"Love," said Alison. "*¿Qué es esto, amante?*"

"*Too much Ego in his cosmos,*" said Mendoza. "Really what it always comes down to."

# 7

Hackett got home at six-thirty and said he hoped dinner was ready. "I've got to go back downtown—overtime. I'd have called and picked up something down there, but we have to wait for the lab to do a hurry-up job and I thought I might as well come home."

"We are flattered," said Angel. He slapped her behind and she yelped. "You don't know your own strength, Tarzan." Mark bounded up precipitately, hearing Daddy's voice, and Sheila came tottering holding up her arms.

"And how's Daddy's own Sheila?" Hackett picked her up.

"She is a nuisance," said Angel. "Been under my feet all day, and pulling the cat's tail—"

"Now, Angel—"

"Well, I have to do something to counteract your spoiling her, Art. Yes, you do. Yes, I know she's just a baby—it's the principle of the thing. Men." She smiled at him. "What's the overtime? Is that going to be a black eye?—for heaven's sake—And how's that patrolman doing?"

"Holding his own. That's the overtime—fingers crossed—I think. And if so, just for that— Well, the jungle gets junglier all the time, my Angel. George and I have been sitting on it most of the day, waiting for something to jell, and it finally did, so—the overtime."

"You've *got* them?" Angel's mountain-pool eyes sparkled with most unchristian pleasure.

"Fingers crossed," said Hackett again.

"Dinner in ten minutes—pot roast and brown potatoes, Italian beans and green salad with Roquefort—not for you—"

"I'd like some peas for a change."

"Four times the calories."

"Damn it, I know. Well—"

"How'd you drop on them, darling?"

"Well—"

They had waited round the corner, having ostensibly driven away from the Dolan house, until the tail arrived and the black-and-white departed. The tail was a nondescript, youngish man in a shabby suit, with an inconspicuous dark sedan several years old and very dusty. He got out of the car, having parked on the opposite side of the street, set a briefcase down on the grass near the curb, and got out a clipboard. He spent some time apparently checking addresses, and finally backed into the car, feet planted on the ground, door open, and industriously accomplished some paper work on what looked like order blanks. A salesman doing his tedious job, obviously.

They had hoped he wouldn't have to wait long, and he didn't. About fifteen minutes later Ron Dolan came backing out the drive in an old blue Ford. The tail finished his pen work, gathered in the briefcase, shut the door and slid under the wheel. In thirty seconds the two cars vanished, turning at the next intersection.

"And let us hope he is really good," said Higgins. And that was at eleven o'clock, or thereabouts. They kicked it around for a few minutes—it was really all up in the air, not what either of them would call a good solid lead at all—until Hackett suddenly swore.

"By God, George, we're slipping. The quake scared us out of any wits we— You know what? The Vandermeier boy said one of those, Ken Burkhart, had an arrest record."

"And we never checked it out."

In the interests of saving time—and there was no telling when the tail might report in, with what, and probably their home office could use them on some job if this one didn't pan out—they went back downtown, and called R. and I. for the record on Kenneth Burkhart.

They were just briefing Mendoza about it when the package came up—and that was a little surprise. There were two of them. Kenneth Burkhart senior, Kenneth Burkhart junior. And both had pedigrees. The one, long and bad; the other, short and suggestive.

Hackett looked at them and said, "Not exactly surprising—but what a— I wonder how the boy escaped being made a ward of the court. Some mix-up, I suppose. But what a—"

Kenneth Burkhart senior was now forty-seven years old. He had a pedigree with the LAPD, the L.A. Sheriff's Department, and the Pasadena Police Department, and it started thirty-four years ago when he was thirteen, picked up with some other kids for vandalism. It went on, attempted assault, public drunkenness, B.-and-E., attempted burglary, burglary, robbery from the person, armed robbery. He'd served time—the latest time, in Quentin for six years; he was on P.A. right now. He'd got off on other counts, technicalities, insufficient evidence; he'd only served twelve years altogether. But he was, by the record, the very typical pro hood—allergic to work, partial to the bottle, and picking up what he could how he could. The P.A. report tagged him as a widower, made no mention of the son. Some mix-up in the record?

Kenneth Burkhart junior was now eighteen. He'd first been dropped on, four years ago, for attacking a younger boy on a school playground with a knife. And who had he been living with then?—the record said, Probation to guardian. Then, attempted B.-and-E., grand theft auto, and more recently narco possession—Mary Jane.

"Such an old, old story," said Hackett. Higgins, reading, just sighed and lit a cigarette. He'd just finished looking at that record when Sergeant Lake said, "Art—Wilcox Street."

Hackett listened, said tersely, "We'll be up. Yes, O.K., I see that. . . . The tail called in. He'll be reporting to Wilcox

Street, we'd better go up and sit on it. Oh, get Burkhart's address—same as the kid's?—I just wonder—"

The tail's name was Bill Knowles and he was supposed to be good. He'd called in at one-fifty. Ron Dolan had driven around aimlessly for awhile— No, not trying to shake the tail, he hadn't a clue he was wearing one—and stopped at a MacDonald's for a coke and sandwich. He had then taken off again and ended up at a single house on Genesee Avenue. He'd rung the doorbell and gone in, and come out a few minutes later with another kid about his age, and they'd driven off—both in Dolan's car—and when Knowles called, they were sttting on a bench in the first picnic-ground area in Griffith Park up from Riverside Drive, just talking. The car parked a little way down the hill. He'd stick with them, call in when he could. . . .

"Ronny-boy scared the fuzz knows something," surmised Hackett. "Who'd he pick up?"

"By the addresses we got from the school, Martin Murphy," said Higgins.

"Well, well. It's not very far from here. Let's see if there are any more Murphys home."

It was a modest house, a California bungalow, on a quiet street in central Hollywood; the yard was well kept up, with a green lawn, flowering shrubs round the porch. The woman who answered the door was nice-looking if not young—once very pretty, brown-haired, brown-eyed, with discreet makeup, a neat housedress, a pleasant contralto voice.

"Mrs. Murphy?"

"Why, yes—" She stared at the badges, and her face whitened, and she said, "Something's happened to Jim! Oh, what—"

"Your husband? No, Mrs. Murphy, it's your son we'd like to talk to you about. Your son Martin."

"*Marty?*" she said. "*Police?* Will, this is just crazy—Marty's never been in any trouble with the— That's impossible! Marty's a well-raised boy, this is a good home, we go to church regular—"

"May we come in, Mrs. Murphy?"

She let them in reluctantly. "You aren't saying you think Marty's done anything? Anything wrong? It's just impossible, that's all—"

"Where is he, by the way, do you know?" asked Higgins in his deep voice.

She looked at him angrily. "Well, of course I know! If that isn't just like the cops, try to make out— Of course I know! He's gone somewhere with the Dolan boy—"

"The Dolan boy. You know him?"

"Well, of *course*. They've been all through school together— Ron's a nice boy, good manners, a good home. Like Marty. *What* do you think—"

"Know where they've gone? When to expect him back?" asked Hackett.

"Oh, for heaven's sake! They're not children, they're both eighteen and it's vacation—I can trust Marty—"

Which told a story, and a too familiar one to cops. Too many parents, trusting the kids, and not exactly kids, of course—you didn't check up on an eighteen-year-old the way you did on a five-year-old. Naturally.

*"What* do you think he's done? It's just silly, but—"

"We don't know that either of them has done anything, Mrs. Murphy," said Hackett. "He just—showed on the edge of something."

"Well, you can just show yourselves out of my house—trying to say Marty's in police trouble! Crazy—"

On the way back to Wilcox Street Hackett said, "But it is natural, you know—that age, they're practically grown up—or should be—and if the parents have never had any reason to suspect the dope, anything else, it wouldn't cross their minds—you don't check up on kids that age like toddlers—"

"Yes, yes," said Higgins. "Words of one syllable. And isn't that the reason the speed's so popular?" The speed—methedrine —produced a short-term high that wore off without many revealing symptoms; the kids innocently attending a record party, a picnic at the beach, and back to normal by the time they came home.

It would be quite a shock for the Murphys—as it had come as a shock to God knew how many other parents across the nation—if it turned out Marty was mixed up in something like that.

They sat in the detective bureau at the Wilcox Street precinct and waited for Knowles to call. "My God, it is *hot*," said Hackett. This was an old precinct house, and lacked air conditioning.

One of the Hollywood detectives said, "You're just spoiled, based down there at headquarters. The nice central air conditioning—"

"Not," said Higgins, "this last week. The quake broke most of our windows."

"Well, for God's sake, I hadn't heard about that. But we've been busy. Tuesday and Wednesday they had me helping the civil defense evacuate people—with nineteen things to do here and all the paper work—"

"That so? We were downtown digging up that mission for bodies—"

They were still exchanging reminiscences of the quake when Knowles called in at three forty-five. "They're back in town," he said. "They made a phone call from the park, that is, Dolan did. They're now at a bowling alley on Fairfax, just watching the play. I'm here too. . . . Oh-oh."

"What's up?"

"Nothing—one of these aftershocks, didn't you feel it? Funny. Well, I'll call in when I can."

He didn't, until four-thirty, when Hackett and Higgins were feeling as if they'd wasted the whole day. Awhile before, they had called the hospital; Logan's pulse was a little stronger, they were told, and he seemed to be getting restless. "That's a good sign," said Higgins.

"You would know?"

"I would know, boy. Since that week we spent fussing about you, assaulted just the same way and all those damn doctors saying gloomily, Even if he lives he may never recover his mind. That," said Higgins, "was quite a week, Art. What with that multiple killer running around loose, and the abortionist—"

104

"Yes, I've heard. What—"

"Well, I was just thinking," said Higgins, "we have been busier than we are now. Feeling more harried, if that's the word. Come to think, we've only got a couple of fairly tough ones to work— Of course Harlow—"

"Don't say it, don't say it," begged Hackett. "So we congratulate ourselves, only a few things on hand, just inviting the tough ones to come at us hot and heavy! What *I* remember out of the dim past is saying one morning, all in the most innocent way, that it was a little boring to have business so slow—and, wham, we got the funny king-size tough ones turning up all at once."

Higgins chuckled sleepily, loosening his tie further. "Those coffins . . . I don't think it's right, you know—keeping people jittery. All the stuff the papers are running, pressure still building on the San Andreas, we could have another one any time. . . . That picket was up by the Plaza this morning."

"Sometimes," said Hackett, "I almost agree with Matt. All we see at the bottom, George—a wonder the Lord has held His hand this long."

They were both feeling tired and useless by the time Knowles called again. The whole day wasted. This had been no kind of lead at all, and they had probably wasted their own time, and Knowles's, following it up.

And then Knowles called. "I only hope this may say something to you, Sergeant." Knowles, out on the street, driving, was very tired and hot too. "They met another kid at the bowling alley, and they've come up to an address on New Hampshire —old apartment building. They've all gone in. I don't know which apartment yet."

"¿Dónde estamos ahora?" said Hackett, surprised.

"What?"

"Excuse me—now and then I go to echoing the boss. What the hell? Wait a minute—George, what's the address on the Burkharts?"

"New Hampshire—old part of town—why?"

"Now I do wonder," said Hackett. "Thanks, Knowles, I think we'll be over."

"If you want a relief for me, you'd better set it up with Sergeant Barth—"

"We'll see," said Hackett. He relayed that to Higgins, who rubbed his jaw and thought it over.

"Ronny is worried about cops calling. He picks up Marty, they have a private talk in a private spot and make a phone call. They pick up—who? And why? And is it anything to do with us at all? Young fellows in summer vacation, just roaming around."

"Well, I wondered if that was Jim Root they picked up. Let's go see."

"But we've got nothing, Art. No reason even to ask them any questions. About what?"

"Maybe something will emerge," said Hackett vaguely.

Something did. By the time they got to the New Hampshire Street address, they found a black-and-white just pulling up to the curb, the uniformed driver getting out. As they got out of the Barracuda, Knowles came out to them from the apartment entrance—an old tan-brick apartment.

"Sergeant—there's been a fuss of some kind going on—I think it's our boys, by the voices—not a fight, just an argument of some kind—second floor up there. Neighbor across the hall has complained three times, and I guess just called the law—"

Hackett ran to catch the patrolman. "This could be our business, we'll come in with you." The patrolman looked surprised, looking at the badges, and then curious.

The argument was still going on, a blurred cacophony of raised voices, obbligato to a blaring TV, beyond the door of the second-floor apartment. A couple of neighbors in the hall, looking indignant. The patrolman pounded on the door, got no response to his announcement of police officers, so he and Hackett hit it together.

The usual shabby, shoddy living room of a cheap apartment this vintage. A paunchy middle-aged man in undershirt and shorts looked blearily up at them from where he watched the television, a can of beer in one hand. The voices came from the bedroom, only now understandable.

106

"For Jesus' sake, Ken, *listen* to me! *Do* something, Marty, he's gotta—he's the one—"

The patrolman pushed the door open. "Now break it up—quiet down—police!"

The three on their feet whirled and froze to a little tableau.

"Club meeting?" asked Hackett. "What about, boys? Do we need a password to get in?"

Ron Dolan, a hefty, redhaired kid who might be Marty Murphy, a nondescript dull-looking kid, sandy-haired, who might be Jim Root. They looked at the law breaking in on them, and just for a breath Dolan and Murphy looked very frightened, and then the heavy secret sullenness shut down on all their expressions.

"You can't do anything to us," said Dolan. "We haven't done anything. You been—*following*—that's police brutality—you can't—"

"Well, you've been creating a disturbance," said the patrolman briskly. "That'll do for a reason to look you over."

"And I think," said Higgins pleasedly, "there'll be another reason." He walked over past the three and looked at the fellow sprawled on the unmade bed.

That one looked up at him and said muzzily, "Who're you?"

"Nemesis," said Higgins, who remembered this and that from English Lit in high school. "You'll be Ken Burkhart."

"*Ken—for God's sake—*" screamed Dolan desperately.

Burkhart was feeling no pain. He was coasting now—just nicely high, not quite incapable but turned on just right, with all his inhibitions comfortably blocked off and feeling fine, just fine. He was a big fellow, dark and thick-chested, with a hairy torso visible because all he had on was a pair of shorts. He grew a heavy beard and he hadn't shaved in a few days.

He giggled up at Higgins, and he said, "Tell 'em—go 'way. Don't bother—come back t'morra. Can't be bothered now—'bout tha' cop. The pig. Beat up—on the pig, tha's good. Zowie —did a job—on tha' one."

"*Ken!*"

"Hell of a fun thing—but tell 'em—go 'way now. T'morra—talk about the pig—"

Higgins looked at Hackett; they wore identical grim smiles. "And isn't that interesting," said Knowles behind them; unconsciously he balled one fist and caressed it with his left hand.

"It looks as if we haven't wasted the day after all, Art," said Higgins.

In the course of shaking the five down before bringing them in, they had a look at the old Chevy registered to Ken Burkhart, in the garage behind the apartment; and in the trunk they found a homemade sap, the thick end of a baseball bat wound with electrician's tape. It had stains of some sort on the business end. There was also a bloodstained T-shirt and a switchblade knife, also stained.

Kenneth Burkhart senior gave them more trouble than the kids. He was half drunk and had no clear idea what cops were doing there, why, or what was going on. When they took his beer away and told him to put on his pants, a shirt, he lunged out at random and gave Hackett the makings of a nice shiner before Higgins and the patrolman got hold of him.

They filed the kids out ahead, and he blinked at them and said, "The kids—you droppin' on the kids—what the hell? Them pills, stuff—what the hell, *I* like a few drinks, what the hell if the kids take a li'l ride on—Fuzz! Ever' time a guy turns around, damn fuzz—"

"That's right," said Hackett, feeling his eye, "we're the world's worst spoilsports, always ruining somebody's good time."

At headquarters they handed the sap, the knife and the shirt to the lab and demanded a hurry-up job. The thugs who had assaulted Pat Logan they wanted to nail hard and fast, with every piece of solid evidence they could turn up.

"Amen," said Duke. "We'll get right on it. We ought to have something for you by eight o'clock, say."

Hackett found Mendoza and brought him up to date. "The luck going our way for once, Arturo, I'll sit in on this."

So they were all back there at seven o'clock, to try for a voluntary statement from one of them. They pried at Ron Dolan first: the weakest link, said Mendoza. But weak characters are also frequently very obstinate characters, and Dolan was terrified by then but he wouldn't say a word. It was probably the first time he'd ever been caught up to, to face any sort of retribution; and he didn't know how to face it except by denying that it was happening. He just went on shaking his head and saying, "No—I don't know anything about it—no—"

Ken Burkhart junior was unfit to question; he'd been sent over to Central Receiving to be sobered up from whatever he was high on.

So then, after a while, they tried Martin Murphy, and he was frightened too but he was smarter than Dolan and he wasn't parting with a thing, not even *Don't know nothing about it.* The punks—such big men until they were caught up with.

At seven-thirty Barth had called from Wilcox Street. They had, he said, the panicky parents calling, on Martin Murphy—wanted to report him missing—and before that, Dolan's grandmother. Having informed them that the boys were in custody, they now had a pair of belligerent Murphys creating a disturbance, demanding to be told chapter and verse, demanding to see the boy. Hackett relayed that to Mendoza, where Sergeant Thoms sat minding the switchboard, and Mendoza grinned, took the phone from him, and said, "Barth? Stall them half an hour longer and we'll be ready for the indignant citizens. Rescuing Junior from the stupid and/or brutal cops."

"You've seen a vision in your crystal ball?" muttered Hackett.

"I think," said Mendoza, "we pin our faith on our infallible men of science." Duke came in just then and he added, "*¡Tanto bueno por aquí!* Preserve calm, Barth—you won't get sued for false arrest this time. . . . So what have you got for us?"

"Just what you want," said Duke pleasedly. "The shirt has got blood on it, about four days old. It's type AB mostly, some type O. The knife—we can tell you the manufacturer, the retail outlets where it's sold—but more to the point it has got Ken Burkhart's prints on the handle and type O blood on the blade."

"*Muy lindo,*" said Mendoza.

"The sap has got blood on it, all type O."

"Thank you so very much, *compadre*," said Mendoza. "And now we will ask some more questions and find out just what did happen."

"You are so optimistic," said Hackett. "We know more or less what happened, Luis—but if they're not talking, is this enough for a case? A lot of people have type O blood. It's a first count on Murphy and Dolan, and nothing really ties them in—"

"We've seen Murphy and Dolan. Third boy," said Mendoza. He took the lab report from Duke.

Jim Root wasn't nearly as bright as the other two (Ken Burkhart's potential intelligence they would judge when they'd seen him minus the dope). He faced them there in the interrogation room warily; he said, "I haven't done nothing—you got no reason bring us in like this. So what if Ken was turned on? We wasn't—and—we didn't know what he was talkin' about—"

"Oh, didn't you?" Hackett stood over him and he looked nervous. Hackett might intimidate anybody by mere size: and add George Higgins alongside him, anybody might look nervous.

Mendoza, slim and dapper and elegant as always, even at this end of a day, looked at him contemptuously. "We have quite a lot of nice evidence here, Jim, even if we can't expect you to grasp just how solid it is. Laboratory evidence, if you know what that is, Jim. There was Pat Logan's blood and somebody else's on that T-shirt. The knife has Ken's fingerprints on it—you do know about fingerprints, Jim?—and Pat Logan's blood on the blade. The sap—"

And Root burst out, "That——cop! That——pig! Oh, my God, it was Ken—never 've did it except we was all turned on some and Ken said— *It was all that——cop's fault!*"

Bob Schenke took it down in shorthand as it came out of him, and he probably didn't realize it was being taken down, and he probably wouldn't have cared.

"What the hell," he said dully. "It gives you a lift. Things a real drag—no bread, always gettin' fired off any job you get—

110

Ma always at me— I get fed up. I moved in with Ken. His old man don't care— What? I only got a job part-time, that bowlin' alley, yesterday—boss at me all 's morning—"

(They were to find that when Ken Burkhart's mother died, her sister had been named guardian, Burkhart senior in Quentin then; she'd washed her hands of the pair of them and moved out six months ago.)

"What? That cop—that *pig*—Don was the seller, see? The seller we knew—he was the contact. For anything—Mary Jane, speed, barbs, whatever—I and Marty and Ken and Ron, I don't know who else bought from him— But that day, we knew about that damn cop because Ken 'd gone home with Don to make a buy, see—met him some joint in town, and he wanted some stuff—he went back to Don's place, get it—and he was still there, Don took some speed then, about all Don ever did turn on with, I guess—and he was still there, Don puttin' records on and all—when he hears the old dame—onna phone. Hears her say how that cop—that *pig*—tole her about—about—"

Pat Logan blowing the whistle on Don, and Mama calling the doctor.

"He was the seller!" blurted Root in remembered panic. "He had the stuff—for a price—we didn't know no other contact— and when you need it, you need it bad, man— Ken got out, but he saw that ambulance come—take Don off somewhere— He was the seller! That Goddamn cop—it was all his fault! If he hadn't— What?"

"You thought it over for a couple of days—without anything to turn on with—and decided to beat up on the cop in revenge?" Mendoza's tone was gentle.

"What? I—I—it was just—I don't know! That Goddamn cop —no call interfere like that—do your own thing, nothin' to do with him—Goddamn— Only Ken made another contact, he won't say who—but he got some speed— I don't know what day, Thursday, Wednesday, what's with the day—Friday, yeah, yeah —we got to thinkin' about that *cop*—no call interfere— You know something? You know something, Don he got a kick outta livin' acrost the street from a pig! A real charge he got— So we knew—

And the door wasn't locked—we just went in there. I—had—that
—sap. We made— Well, he was a real tough guy. Only, they
was four of us, see? He knocked Ken down—and he hit me,
my nose started bleedin'—that was my shirt—but— We thought
he was dead, we left him— Is he dead?"

"You had better start praying," said Higgins, "that he isn't
going to be."

"But it was all his fault! Goddamn cop, if he hadn't—"

If he hadn't, they all thought, been doing his job. The way a
trained LAPD man should.

Before he went home, Mendoza called the Logan house, and
got Royce.

"The punks," said Royce tiredly. "The junkies. For that reason—can we call it a reason, Mendoza?"

"No. *Ya lo creo. ¿Quién sabe?* We've got them. To charge,
on the evidence."

"And what will they get?" said Royce. "If Pat dies—"

"God forbid. I know. Assault with intent, and the first count
for three of them, and with one of these damn softheaded
judges— What's the hospital saying?"

"Doubletalk. His pulse is better, he's getting restless— That
is a good man, Mendoza, a good cop, and these Goddamned
irresponsible little punks—full of dope—" Royce uttered a literal
growl. "By God—"

"Doing their own thing. *Too much ego*— Well, we've got
them. The assault with intent, at least."

And he went home to Alison. Quite often he wondered just
what the hell he was doing still down here, at the thankless
dirty job, after the old man died and there'd come to light all
the gilt-edged stock and real-estate deeds. The money for the
luxuries, for Luis Mendoza and now Alison and their hostages
to fortune—

Higgins said to Mary, "Will you tell me why I picked this
job? Talk about the bottom of things—the muck in the gutter!
Those damn irresponsible lazy *louts*—"

112

"Because you're a responsible, honest, upright man," said Mary.

"Because I'm an idiot," said Higgins.

"Well, you've *got* them, at least."

"Which will be a fine consolation for Sally Logan if Pat Logan should die—or end up a permanent invalid."

"Which will *not* happen," said Mary. "Because I think there are guardian angels, George."

"I can only hope you're right."

"I'm right," said Mary serenely. "Since you got away from those thugs, George, I have all sorts of faith in the guardian angels."

**8**

On Wednesday morning, with Piggott and Glasser off and Grace back, there was still a good deal of cleaning up to do on the punks. The inevitable paper work had to be finished and sent in the right directions; and they had to bring Don Franks into it too, get a statement from him if possible.

"The punks," said Grace, hearing about that. "At least let's hope they'll be out of circulation for a while."

Mendoza called the Huntington Beach clinic and was told that Franks had been discharged. The sometime user, not a hard addict; no reason to keep him. He called the Franks's home and Mrs. Franks told him yes, Donny was there. "So," said Mendoza, "suppose you chase up and get him, Art. See what we can get out of him, anyway." Hackett and Higgins would be busy most of today finishing that one up legally.

"And what are we doing on Harlow?" asked Grace. Landers drifted in and followed him into Mendoza's office. Palliser, Sergeant Lake said, had already been in and gone, on a call from Traffic.

"I did a little legwork on that myself yesterday," said Mendoza, "with no luck at all. I didn't find anybody I wanted to see. Maybe you two will today." He told them what Mrs. Short had remembered; she had identified the names in the doctor's records, and there were addresses. "I know they're no motives at all, to the rational mind. But whoever did that wholesale shooting—"

"True," said Landers. "As you've said before, it depends who has the motive. I could just see a little thing like these triggering it—except for the Chinese fellow, which is just silly. But the only thing that does occur to me—if anything like that was going to start X shooting up the doctor's office, wouldn't it have been right then? Not a couple of months later?"

"And I'd say so too," said Grace.

"I don't know," said Mendoza, smoothing his moustache absently. "Again, it depends who. Somebody brooding over something? All I do say is, these are the first possible leads we've got on Harlow, people who had, or thought they had, some grievance on him. We'd better look at them."

"I see that." Landers got up. "So let's go do some legwork, Jase."

"And even if we didn't have to," said Grace, "we wouldn't be any more comfortable here, would we? There was a crew working on the third-floor windows when I came in." It was very hot in the office, and the occasional gust of wind sweeping around the tall building, this high up, blowing papers around, didn't improve any tempers.

"Toss you for which car," said Landers, and won the throw. "So you drive. Just as well, that thing's starting to nickel and dime me to death. New battery last year, and now it needs a lube job and a new tail pipe, and it's been eating oil— And who can afford a new car?"

"Especially if you're going to get married," said Grace. They got into the elevator.

"That's another thing. Damn it, Jase, I always thought blondes were supposed to be scatterbrained flibbertigibbets with no common sense. Common sense! That girl's got her head screwed on so tight— We haven't known each other long enough, it's better to be safe than sorry, and besides she likes her job and doesn't want to stop working— But I'll get her eventually, I swear I will. She is," said Landers, "quite a blonde."

"So I hear." Grace grinned at him. They got into the little French racer, the bright blue Elva, in the lot. The picket with his white beard and homemade sign was patrolling Temple

Street today. "Before we go looking for these people, Tom, there's something I want to check out at that office building."

"Sure. What?"

"Well—"

The call from Traffic in Hollywood had been relayed downtown just this morning. It had been called in to Wilcox Street as the Traffic shifts changed last night, before the night watch at Homicide had gone home. Chris Hauck's car had been spotted in the parking lot of a third-class nightclub on Fairfax Avenue. And Palliser, heading for Hollywood now, was cussing out loud and wondering why the hell it hadn't been staked out. The call sent out on it must contain the information that it was wanted in connection with a homicide—

Actually, he found out at Wilcox Street, it didn't. Once in a long while even the efficient LAPD goofed, and whoever Sergeant Lake had talked to in Communications had just put the plate number on the hot list, period. The patrolman who spotted it was riding a tour alone and couldn't do anything but report to the station, which he had, at twelve-thirty. And Wilcox Street had a night watch too but as it happened the call on the hot car had come in at the same time as a rather spectacular accident happened, a four-car crash on the boulevard with two dead.

"I'm sorry as hell," said Captain Garden contritely when they'd sorted it out. "Sometimes these things— And of course it might just have been abandoned there—"

"What a hope," said Palliser gloomily. He went and looked, of course, and of course this morning the nightclub's parking lot was as bare as a desert. Palliser said several other things to himself, heading back downtown.

At least his shoulder felt better. He'd stopped at First Aid before going home last night, and a nurse with hamlike hands had manipulated it and made some adjustments, it felt like, to his spinal cord; and Roberta had got out the deep-heat massager. . . . That was another thing, thought Palliser. Robin going back to work. He did not approve. They were getting by

116

all right on what he made—the house payments heavy, but they could make it, it wasn't necessary for her to go back to teaching. Get into the habit, he reflected now, feeling depressed, and she'd keep putting off any family—he could hear her—just another semester, John, until we get the furniture paid off— Women!

And where the hell were Linda Schnell and her boy-friend? The car parked in Hollywood last night, but were they still driving it? The word was out to the pigeons—maybe some time something would turn up. Of course Chris Hauck had asked for it, and probably wasn't much loss, but the case had to be worked.

"What occurred to me," said Grace, "after I thought about it, was that door. The door to the basement. Higgins and the patrolmen were searching the building—well, that is, looking around for any sight of him because it was barely minutes after the shooting, by what we heard. And that door was locked, but I wondered if it had been."

"Had— Oh," said Landers.

"If it wasn't, and just locked itself when it got slammed—I'd just like to know," said Grace, "whether it had been locked, and if there's another way out of the basement."

"As usual, having the simple mind, you think of the simplest thing."

"And that would be pretty simple."

They parked in the side lot of the McLaren Building and went in. There was a building superintendent; they'd seen him on Monday too but hadn't taken a statement because he hadn't seen or heard anything, he'd been on the top floor examining a recently vacant office for needed renovations. His name was Enoch Shepard, and he was in his office on the ground floor: a cubbyhole with a desk, a couple of chairs. He was a big broad black man about fifty, with rimless glasses, and he listened to Grace's questions and said, "I see what you're after, sir. That basement door? That hood—whoever it was—killing all those people. Terrible. I couldn't believe it, I heard about it first. But—"

"What's in the basement? Who'd go there?"

"Odds and ends. We hire a company to come and clean—floors, windows, rest rooms, all like that. But you stop to think, a big building like this, little things needing fixing all the time. Venetian-blind cords, light bulbs needing to be put in, washers in faucets, toilets getting stopped up, all sorts of little things. I hire a fellow, part-time job, to come in and do that—help me, that is. Him and me's the only ones 'd be going to the basement, we keep supplies like that there. And toilet paper and towels for the rest rooms, and so on. But I hadn't been to the basement that morning myself and Freeman hasn't got a key. Wait a minute, now, there's an extra key to that door always hangin' right here—" He pointed to the wall beside the door. "Master key for every floor, key to the basement, to the elevator housing. But Freeman isn't here, mornings—comes in at one o'clock. Dick Freeman. He's got a regular night job, likes to earn extra."

"And the basement door was locked." Grace and Landers exchanged glances. Even if X had somehow known about that key to the basement—it wouldn't have been any use to him, for the pursuit had been fairly hot, if he had detoured to get that key ten to one he'd have been collared by the patrolmen. And it was a very unlikely thing for a fleeing gunman to do, dive into the basement. It was absently that Grace asked about another door out of the basement and was told that there was a back door giving on the parking lot.

"That's N.G.," said Landers when they'd thanked Shepard and started back to the car. "But now we know, anyway. Where do we go now?"

"Looking for William Ainslie, who got a couple of fingers mashed in a garbage disposal."

They found Ainslie after some trouble. He wasn't at his apartment on Vermont, but when they checked with the manager to ask if he still lived there, he offered them a lead. "Mr. Ainslie? Oh, yes, sir, he does. But he's usually out mornings. If it's important you'll probably find him at the Whitman Recording Studio on Santa Monica."

118

"That's where he works?"

"Oh, no, but he goes there to do his practicing. We couldn't have that in the apartment, you see. He's a musician, Mr. Ainslie, plays with a very popular combo, the best nightclubs."

They found the Whitman Recording Studio, went in and asked. "I think he's here," said the improbably flaxen-blonde receptionist. "I'll ask Joe—" She got Joe on an inside line. "Oh, I thought— Well, yes, I saw Mr. Feldman come in but how'd I know—" And presently she told Grace and Landers, "He was here, he'll be back, they don't know when, but his agent came to see him and they went off somewhere— I'm sorry, I don't know exactly when he might be back."

"There are days like this," said Grace philosophically. "Now, this teen-age girl who tried to throw the doctor to the wolves to convince Daddy she hadn't either been a bad girl—"

"Karen Lightner. Down on Geraldine Street."

And that was a backwater, and what they found there might or might not be suggestive. Mrs. Carol Lightner, small and brown and meek-looking, said, "He won't like it, your coming to ask. He just don't care to talk about it. We've always been respectable folk." Reluctantly she revealed that her husband was home; he worked nights, was a night watchman at a big warehouse. "He won't like you coming," she said.

He didn't. He was a big beefy man, and when she led them out to the back yard of the little frame house, he was carefully trimming the hedge between this and the next yard. The house and the yard were small, but very neat. There was a patch of lawn here, and flower beds. And Henry Lightner didn't like their arrival at all, but he went into the house with them and answered questions.

"I'm a deacon in our church," he told them. "I always been a religious man and I respect the law, officers. We never had but the one child, and I figured we'd raised her in the right way, like the Book says. It's been a grief to us. I don't like talkin' about it."

"We understand that, Mr. Lightner," said Grace in his soft voice, "but we have to ask you a few questions. We—"

119

"Why? Has that man done somethin' else?"

"Do you mean Dr. Harlow?" He grunted. "Did you believe your daughter when she told you the doctor had—er—raped her?"

Lightner was silent, and then he said very reluctantly, "I reckon—when I heard all them others say, them nurses and— I reckon I believed her right off, but I got to say I—I just don't see how a man like that—educated and all, making' a lot of money—why he'd do such a thing—I don't know what to think, and that's all I can say."

"Henry," said his wife timidly, "you know what she said—later on—"

"I know she lied to us. She was raised to know better. She lied to us once we know, she maybe lied other times." He shook his head.

"She said—after that doctor could show it wasn't like she said—she said some boy at school had—you know. But that wasn't so either because—" She faced Grace and Landers miserably, twisting her hands together. "Because later on her friend Mona—Mona Wilson, she was just cryin' her eyes out, couldn't b'lieve it, a good girl she is—she tole us her own brother, he heard fellows talkin' at school, 'bout how Karen—Karen—oh, we couldn't b'lieve it but— How she went with a lotta different boys, and—" She began to cry.

"Mr. Lightner, where is your daughter now?" asked Grace. The episode with Dr. Harlow (and how stupid could the girl be?—she hadn't gone to him until she was pregnant, and his records would show that) had happened last January.

Lightner said heavily, "I don't care to talk about it anymore, officers. It's a shut book. I been prayin' for her, all I can do now, and I reckon my duty to do." He got up and went out of the room.

"She—she's dead," whispered the woman. "She had a miss, that time, lost the baby. But 'long last month, I guess—she found out—and she went to one o' these nasty women do such things, girls in trouble—and she got sick from it and she died. Last week over in the big hospital."

"Thanks very much, Mrs. Lightner," said Grace gently. They

120

went out to the Elva. "What do you think, Tom? That says a little to me. Last January—but just last week, the girl's death bringing it all back. He'd like to think that somebody outside was responsible for—"

"Setting Karen's feet on the downward path," said Landers thoughtfully. "Yes indeedy, Jase. There may just be something here."

"We'll lay it in front of the boss, maybe he'll see something about it in his crystal ball. Meanwhile—" It was only ten-thirty; they drove back to the Whitman Recording Studio.

This time they found their man. "Studio Three," the blonde told them, and they hunted down several corridors, found the door.

"You the cops looking for me?" He turned from the big orchestra-sized marimba: a nattily dressed young man, a little darker than Grace and clean-shaven, and obviously a successful young man. His light-gray suit was sharply tailored, his tie real silk, he wore a flashy diamond ring on his right hand and a gold watch on his left wrist. He was a good-looking man, the same lean regular features as Grace, but his eyes were restless. "Bill Ainslie—me. What do cops want with me?"

Grace introduced themselves. "So sit down—shoot," said Ainslie. He sat on the piano bench—this cluttered studio room was littered with musical instruments, music stands, tables piled with sheet music—and Grace and Landers found a couple of folding chairs.

"You went to a Dr. John Harlow," began Landers, "with an infected hand—and you—"

Ainslie looked suddenly disconcerted and concerned. He thrust his left hand into his jacket pocket. "Harlow?" he said. "Yes, that's right. This same Harlow who—" The press had had modest headlines about the wholesale shooting, and several ministers had based sermons on the theme of the miraculously preserved baby. "It *was* him?" asked Ainslie in a subdued voice. "That got— Yeah, the same address—my God, what a thing. What a thing! His wife, the nurse—and that baby—the *Herald* had a cut of her, cute little tyke. My God—" And he sat up

121

suddenly and said, "For God's sake! You—are you thinking—
*me?* Bill Ainslie? A thing like—oh, my God!"

"You—er—made a little fuss," said Grace. "Threatened to sue
the doctor—"

"Oh, my God!" said Ainslie rather wildly. "Listen, I—Well,
of course it's all *right,* I can prove where I was. When it happened. Monday morning—well, of course I was right here, and
so was Les—Les Morton, he's the bandleader, and part of the
time Lee McHugh was too—going over some new arrangements
—up to noon."

"They'll say so?"

"Sure they'll say so. But listen, I've got to tell you how it was
—I know I acted like a damn fool that time, but it was— Well,
damn it!" He took his left hand out of his pocket and held it
out. The third and fourth fingers had healed crookedly, with
visible scars on the back of the hand, the fingers obviously stiff
and useless. "You see, I'm a musician, my hands— Well, it was
a *thing.* I had to train myself—thank God I'm not a piano player
is all!" He shuddered, and shrugged. "I'm the drummer—drums,
marimba, xylophone—so it could've been worse. But—I know I
was acting like a damn fool, but I was just so mad—and I ought
to say, Harlow was nice about it. He could've been mean, but
he wasn't. And I calmed down, I apologized and—my own
damn-fool fault—"

"How come you didn't go to a doctor right off, when it happened?" asked Grace.

"Oh, for God's— Look," said Ainslie, "look. I was at this
dame's. She's married, her husband's a gorilla. And she's fixing
drinks in the kitchen when she drops her damn ring down the
garbage disposal by accident—she's not a very smart dame,
boys—and my God, I'm fishing for it when she accidentally flips
the switch—and I nearly got out in time, but—" Both Landers
and Grace were grinning. "Look, my God, I'm dancing round
the kitchen dripping blood all over like crazy, and she's having
hysterics when, my God, her husband walks in the front door!
She thought he was out of town at a match—he's a pro heavyweight. Well, I tell you, I'm long gone out the back door, hand

122

and all, so he doesn't know who was there—but he knows some-body was on account of the blood—and my God, they're always dropping in at the Kit-Kat Club, that's where we're playing right then, and if he sees me sporting a bandage—! I'm not exactly famous for being backward with the girls—" Ainslie ges-tured, and added, "It wasn't funny, boys. I could've got clobbered —that gorilla—"

"How'd you pass it off?" asked Landers amusedly.

"I told Les I had the flu. By the time I finally went to the doctor, thank God that gorilla *was* out of town. For a while. And I've had to train myself, hold the stick in three fingers. But—"

But it wasn't Ainslie, completely rational Ainslie, who had shot up Harlow's office.

*"Con qué estamos con esto,"* said Mendoza. He leaned back in his chair at the big table at Federico's and swallowed straight rye. "The autopsy report came in—on the Harlows and Jenkins. Nothing in it, of course. We know what they died of. All healthy specimens, no indication of any addiction, alcoholism, et cetera. Quite respectable corpses."

"Which we also knew," said Hackett. He and Higgins had had a busy morning on all the paper work. Grace and Landers had just come in and joined them to report their morning's labors.

Mendoza finished the rye and said thoughtfully, "that Light-ner. I just see what you mean, Jase. That's human nature—we see a lot of it. Looking for the scapegoat. Love—a dangerous commodity, yes. . . . The girl was well brought up, as the phrase goes, and shouldn't have stepped off the straight and narrow voluntarily. How much was it due to the strict upbring-ing that she did, or do any of you go along with the Freudian notions?"

"Your age is showing, Luis," said Hackett. "You don't keep up with progress and a changing world. The head doctors themselves don't go along with Freud any more, not all of 'em anyway. The puritanical upbringing maybe sends A straight into a brothel, B into a nunnery, and C to Z into perfectly normal adult lives. Human nature."

"Yes," said Mendoza. "But when Lightner found out, how tempting to think that some evil male had given her a shove. The first tale she told was the one on Harlow—and it could be that, emotionally as they say, Lightner does believe it."

"But nobody could, when you think it over," said Landers. "She didn't lay eyes on Harlow until she was pregnant—" He stopped.

"Oh, didn't she? That's not what she told Papa."

"Of course not," said Grace slowly. "Of course it wasn't. However she happened to go to Harlow—maybe picked him out of the phone book—she told Papa the reason she went to him was because he was the one *did* it, made up to her and lied about not being married and seduced her. And—"

"And then she dies just last week—post-abortion septicemia," said Landers. "Could be he started brooding on it again, convinced himself it was all Harlow's fault? It could be, but—"

"I think, just to be thorough," said Mendoza, "we look at Mr. Lightner harder and closer. He doesn't sound the type to be talking free and loud about it—could be he's a brooder. So, where was he on Monday morning? Does he own a gun or have access to one? If so, does it happen to be a Harrington and Richardson nine-shot .22?"

"We'll look," said Grace.

"There is also, of course, Kun Low Soo."

They all laughed. "Scraping the bottom of the barrel," said Higgins. "That's just stupid."

"*Alla vá*," said Mendoza. "As stupid as shooting three people to death in public."

"A way to look at it," said Grace.

Hackett sighed at the low-calorie plate as the waiter served them. "At least we're getting the paper work out of the way on these punks. That Don Franks. . . . Do you know, it hadn't struck me, but we hadn't laid eyes on him until today. Providing the leads, really the one behind the whole caper."

124

"And what kind of punk is he?" asked Landers. "Not that we can't guess."

"Too smart," said Hackett and Higgins together. "Laughing at us and saying he wasn't stewing," added Hackett, "probation all he'd get, Mama with a high-priced shyster, and what the hell, pretty soon it'd all be legalized anyway, the hard stuff too —and why not?"

Landers looked at his steak sandwich. "That picket was out again."

"I noticed him," said Mendoza. "Yes, and when that happens—¡Dios me libre!—we can all happily go mad together. . . . We'll look hard at Lightner, Jase."

"And you always say," said Higgins, "we clear up one thing, we're apt to clear up another. Things going by threes. Has—"

"You're just inviting trouble, George," said Hackett. "It also works out that you clear up one thing, right off the bat three other things show up to work."

"Don't be superstitious. Donny annoyed me," said Higgins, "is all. Because for one thing he is very probably right—Mama will retain the high-priced mouthpiece, and with all the legal double-talk—"

"Mother love," said Mendoza, "mmh. And there is the proverb, *Sin hijos y sin celos, no hay de consuelos.*"

"And that means what?" asked Higgins.

"Without children and without jealousy, no affliction. . . . Not that I'm troubled with jealousy," said Mendoza, "being sufficiently egotistic. But I began to believe that as soon as those twin monsters appeared on the scene. But maybe I am improving my education at that." He poured himself more coffee. "Human nature. . . . There's a very basic sort of symbolism there, you know. Interesting. Encouraging."

"Where?" asked Grace.

"Oh, the fairy tales. Grimm. All the fairy tales." Mendoza lit a cigarette. "The basic, primitive, bedrock convictions of mankind expressed in them—just as in the mythology. ¿Cómo no? And it's very encouraging that whatever vicissitudes occur to the heroes and heroines, in the end everything comes out all right. The wolf who ate Grandmother getting his comeuppance, and—"

"Encouraging, hell," said Hackett, "it's wishful thinking. And if I had a dime for every time I had to read that story to Mark—"

"And," said Mendoza, "the wicked stepmother and stepsisters getting their just punishment and— The twins are a little young to appreciate it, but *I* appreciate 'The Fisherman's Wife.' Basic convictions of mankind, which we can say must be rooted in experience, that in the end right triumphs and evil is punished. Mmh, yes—Rumpelstiltskin—'Discover my name—'"

"Has anybody," asked Higgins, ignoring him, "called the hospital?"

"They're sounding just slightly more hopeful," said Mendoza abstractedly.

"So, fingers crossed that we get the punks only on a charge of assault with intent."

Palliser, having a busy day, was unaware that Hackett was being an unwitting prophet about new ones coming along. He was just feeling harassed.

He'd got back to the office in time to take a new call—everybody else in was busy on the paper work, on questioning Don Franks, then—and Sergeant Lake said no, there hadn't been any pigeons calling in. Damn it, thought Palliser, Linda and her boy-friend were somewhere—with the car showing up in Hollywood last night—for ninety percent sure they were driving Hauck's car.

The new one was nothing but the promise of more paper work. The kind of thing cops in any big city saw, carbon copies whether New York or Los Angeles, Miami or Portland. The young woman dead in a third-rate hotel room, sediment in the bathroom glass, note propped on the bureau: he doesn't love me, I'll show him how much I love him, good-bye. Palliser looked at it sadly, irritably, resignedly.

The paper work, the lab work, all to add up to just another

suicide. There was identification on her, the family to contact: in this case in Des Moines, Iowa.

By the time he'd typed a report on it, it was getting on for noon. He went out for a sandwich and a malted milk (feeling momentary sympathy for Sergeant Lake whose years of sedentary labor at the desk these days had him counting calories and comparing bitter notes with Art Hackett) and came back to find that one of their pigeons had called in. In re the A.P.B. on Linda Schnell. The pigeon didn't know where she was, but passed on the information that maybe Mae Gallio might know. The address was Breed Street in Boyle Heights.

Palliser went over there to see if Mae was home. She was. He hadn't looked, but he could guess, a similar record to Linda's—frosted dark hair, lavish eye makeup, a psychedelic-print pantsuit. She was, however, clean at the moment and hadn't any objection to talking to the fuzz. And none of Linda's other pals they had talked to had been able to tell them her latest address —the Lindas moved around—but Mae Gallio could.

"A place on Darwin," she told Palliser. "Rooming house. She hadn't been having such good luck lately—it can be a drag, you know?—she was down, way down, last time I saw her. What?"

"You know Foster Sterry? Her latest boy-friend?"

"I don't know," she said. "Never heard the name. But she was moaning about all her bad luck lately. Got behind on the rent and all."

After prodding at her some more, Palliser went on to Darwin Street, which was a very tired-looking area of old L.A., and found the rooming house where Linda Schnell had had a room for, he learned, about the last three months. It was the kind of rooming house which housed a lot of the Linda Schnells. Its owner, a slatternly elderly woman, told Palliser pithily that what roomers did was their own business, she couldn't care less as long as she got the rent on time, and she couldn't say anything about Linda Schnell—she didn't pay notice to roomers coming and going, but that one, Room Four upstairs, she'd moved out last Sunday with all she had, one suitcase. She didn't know if there'd been a man with her, or if there was a car.

Palliser swore to himself. Well, the Lindas drifted.

And there was this Harlow thing—and Logan— They had been busier, but he felt a little harried. He had, from the pals of Linda's he'd talked to, the names of a few favorite hangouts of hers—the Black-and-White Bar on Fourth, the Ace-High on Grand—but where was the manpower to stake those out?

And he said to Lake, disgustedly, "Just for one like Hauck! The middle-aged Lothario who ought to have had better sense. Asking for it, picking up the floozies, flashing the roll—"

"Well, Matt would say, equal in the sight of God," said Lake seriously. And plugged in and said, "Central Homicide, Sergeant Lake . . . O.K. Oh? What's the— Got it."

"Don't tell me, something new," said Palliser.

"That's just what, John. West Kensington Avenue, up by Echo Park. A body, yes."

It was the body of a woman, in a bathtub in an elderly, neat and ordinary apartment: an eight-family unit. The body had been identified: a Mrs. Rhoda Fleming. Apparently beaten.

Her son-in-law had found her. He was a tall, thin, dark young man in his twenties, and he said to Palliser, agitatedly and volubly, what he'd been saying to the patrolmen— "Rosie couldn't raise her on the phone, she's been worried, her mother I mean, Rhoda—we always call her Rhoda, a nice woman, a respectable woman, she works of course, Rosie's father died four years ago —Rosie and I been married three years this month—Rhoda worked at this gift shop in Hollywood, a nice place on Sunset—"

Palliser called in for a lab team.

"But my God, officer, my God, how could it have happened? Is she drowned? A heart attack maybe— And my God, I've got to tell Rosie—"

## 9

Since yesterday, of course, they had had an A.P.B. out on Al Koonz, who had loaned his old Colt to Ed Hobart for a heist job. He hadn't turned up yet; when he did he'd go right back to Quentin to finish a three-to-five for armed robbery—he was out on parole.

This morning there had been a teletype from Washington; the Feds knew Foster Sterry. He hailed from Tennessee originally, and he had a long string of minor charges in a dozen states, D.-and-D., petty theft, attempted burglary, pimping. Nobody had picked him up again since he got out of jail in Alabama two years ago.

Coming back from lunch, Hackett and Higgins left the dispatching of this morning's paper work to Sergeant Lake, and went out to see Myrtle Boggs and Lilian Stafford again. Sometimes, after the initial shock was past, a witness to violence would remember more detail.

Mendoza, hearing about the new one, went up to West Kensington Avenue to see what Palliser had turned up.

"Well, not much yet," said Palliser. He looked a little tired; as usual when he was annoyed he'd been unconsciously rubbing his heavy eyebrows, and they were untidily beetling. "The names. Rhoda Fleming, fifty-three, widow, worked at this gift shop in Hollywood. Married daughter Rose Scott, husband Gavin, he's a skilled workman of some kind at Lockheed. His day off today. Daughter usually talked to Mama several times a week on the phone—they live out in Sunland, don't often get

129

in to see Mama—and she hasn't been able to raise her since Friday night, so not knowing any of the neighbors to call, she got her husband to come and look—they've got a new baby. Boom, he finds the apartment door unlocked and Rhoda dead in the bathtub."

"Drowned?"

"No—I'd have a guess, strangled, but also beaten. Naked as a jaybird. And nobody knows anything."

"As usual. Interns have any guess about the time?"

"Vaguely. She's been dead at least two days and probably longer. I've talked to a couple of neighbors—" By now the squad car had gone, but the mobile lab truck was still there in front of the apartment house and little knots of curious residents were out along the block. Past the front lobby, where Mendoza had found Palliser, the manageress was up the hall talking excitedly to a couple of ground-floor tenants. "A Mrs. Faraday, who has the apartment next to Mrs. Fleming. She says she didn't hear anything from there the last few days, no disturbance or screams. So does the woman across the hall, Miss Binder. Mrs. Faraday doesn't work—Miss Binder is a stenographer downtown. She was out Saturday night, but both of 'em home every night since, and Friday. They say, and the manageress, a Mrs. Upjohn, says, that while most of the tenants here have been here awhile—Mrs. Fleming nearly four years—they don't, well, socialize. Know each other's names, that's about all."

"So. Fleming have any men friends? Go out with friends of either sex, and where?"

"I put that to Scott," said Palliser, scratching his handsomely straight nose, "and he looked horrified. I might have suggested that she went out hustling. She was over fifty, he said, and a respectable woman. Well—"

"Así," said Mendoza amusedly. "Según y conforme. It's funny how some people—puritans?—seem to think nobody over thirty-five should be at all interested in that old devil sex."

"Anyway, he said she didn't. Said she went to work and came home. Talked to daughter on the phone. Did her own laundry and cleaning. She had a couple of women friends here—Hollywood—I've got the addresses—but she certainly didn't go out in the evening often. But the door wasn't forced, and Scott said she always kept it locked."

"So, we go the long way round," said Mendoza. "And hope the lab picks up something useful."

Scarne and Duke came down the front stairs with their bags and Scarne said, "It's all yours, Lieutenant. They're just bringing the body."

The interns came down after them, slow on the narrow staircase, with the basket swinging between them, the body covered with a plastic sheet. Mendoza stepped forward.

"Let's have a look." Sometimes something about a corpse offered suggestions.

The interns set it down and unstrapped the fastenings at one end. Mendoza turned the sheet back. Death was never pretty, minus the last-minute attentions of the mortician's art, but he looked at the upper half of Rhoda Fleming and made certain objective deductions.

She had still a good figure for a woman her age. Remnants of makeup and a curl in her hair; her hands had been manicured, nails enameled pale pink, before she'd struggled with somebody and torn a couple of them, one broken right off. She had taken care of herself. Well, she had been working, had to keep looking groomed, smart. He reached to push back the hair at one temple: hair kept in a short curly cut.

"What'd you find?" asked Palliser.

"Nothing. She kept her hair tinted," said Mendoza. The hand he had picked up, the right hand, bore a thin lighter mark on the ring finger. He stepped back. "O.K., boys, take her. Let's look at the apartment, John."

The apartment was on the second floor, a pleasant single unit —living room, kitchen with small dining area, bedroom and bath. These older places always had larger rooms, looked— and were—more substantial than the newer ones. *"Un día de estos,"* muttered Mendoza to himself, "one of these days—" Everybody saying so smugly that it proved the new high-rise buildings were safe, coming through the quake unharmed; the fact was, none of them had been anywhere near the line of the quake. Next time—

There were evidences of a struggle in the apartment. A scatter rug between living room and bedroom bunched up in a tangle: a chair overturned in the bedroom: bloodstains on the made-up bed where the bedspread was in disarray—bloodstains in the bathroom. And in the bedroom, a little heap of clothes untidily scattered on the floor. Aside from that, and the evidence of the lab men's activities, the apartment seemed to have been neat and clean. Mendoza looked at the little heap of clothes with his head cocked, and said, "Pulled off her in a struggle? I wonder if she was raped." He picked up the clothes piece by piece and put them on the bed. A white nylon brassiere, 36-B. White nylon panties. Low-heeled white sandals. A nylon-jersey tailored pantsuit, bright coral color.

"What are we looking for?" asked Palliser ten minutes later. Mendoza had been prowling around the place opening drawers and closets and muttering to himself.

"Evidence of character. So often what a person was like points a small finger in the right direction. She was—mmh—up to date," said Mendoza. "Not dowdy or old-fashioned. She had several pantsuits in her wardrobe, slacks, a couple of worn but originally very good cocktail dresses. Sheer stockings. Medium heels for work, spikes for dress-up. She smoked. Chesterfields. In a holder. She took an occasional drink—there's a bottle of Scotch and a bottle of gin in the kitchen. She didn't take a newspaper —no old ones around."

"So?"

"*No se.* She just doesn't smell to me," said Mendoza, "like quite the dull workaday woman her son-in-law described to you. More I couldn't say at the moment. We'll see what turns up. I'll go down and chase Matt up here, you'd better talk to those friends of hers and the other tenants here."

"Sure."

Mendoza left him talking to a Mrs. Halpern who lived across the hall from the manageress downstairs, and went back to his office, which he found in a state of siege. The belligerent Murphys were there, Ron Dolan's grandmother, and two lawyers. Sergeant Lake, Piggott and Glasser were trying to calm them down enough to listen, and not having much success.

"—Never believed the stories about police, but by God I do now! When Eve told me how—arresting my son! My son in your dirty jail—"

"I *told* you, Jim, how those two came—I suppose *they're* out beating up some prisoners or something—" The lawyers, to their credit, were trying to calm them down too.

Mendoza's voice cut across Murphy's incisively. "Suppose you all calm down and be quiet. I said *quiet!* That's better. Come into my office." There, he gave them chairs; Sergeant Lake brought in more, silently. "Now, Mr. Murphy—"

"Who the hell are you?"

Mendoza sat back in his desk chair, lit a cigarette with a snap of the gold desk lighter, and introduced himself coldly. Murphy eyed his dapper tailoring, gold cuff links and tie-clasp suspiciously. "We really don't do things that way these days, you know," and Mendoza's tone was gentle. "You'll have been told the charges on your son, at the jail—"

"It's crazy! Just—"

"Mr. Murphy. We have not only some scientific evidence, but a full admission from one of the other boys—if you can call eighteen-year-olds boys—that they have been using narcotics for some time, and that last Friday afternoon, while under the influence of narcotics, they deliberately assaulted an LAPD officer in his own home. We don't know if he's going to live. He was very badly beaten—skull-fractures, broken bones, internal injuries, a severed artery. If he dies the charge will be murder in the second degree, which could carry a life sentence. We have evidence, Mr. Murphy. We don't arrest people without reason."

"I don't—believe— *Marty,*" he said. "Marty." But the toughness had dropped from his voice. Suddenly his wife started to cry.

"But I don't understand what's happening," quavered Mrs. Dolan. "Ron's a good boy—I'm sure—"

Mendoza gave one look at Lake; the little show of authority

had quieted the Murphys, who'd make no more trouble. But it was a while before Lake shepherded them out, and then Mendoza had to talk to the lawyers. He was feeling hot and irritated, and sent Lake down the hall for coffee, at three-thirty when Grace and Landers came in.

"And so what have you got?" he asked.

Landers sat down in the chair beside the desk and Grace strolled over to the glassless windows. "Stay *away* from there," said Landers. "Why, we've got a big fat mystery, that's what. Lightner didn't go to brooding over his fallen offspring, and decide Harlow was to blame. He told us he was a deacon of their church—little Southern Baptist church out on Main. And on Monday morning from ten to twelve-thirty he was at the church with the minister and two other deacons, discussing some repairs it needed."

"Oh, hell," said Mendoza.

"Just what we said," said Grace. "The minister and the deacons said so too—not oh hell, but that he was there. Sometimes these awful upright churchgoers make me feel a little antireligious, you know?" He lit a cigarette and dropped the match out the window. Landers told him to come away from there.

"We even went to look for Kun Low Soo. Wasting time."

"He's got an alibi too?"

"He's not here," said Grace sadly. "He packed up his wife and ten worthless daughters and went back to Taiwan two months ago."

"Oh, hell," said Mendoza again. "Well, I never said they were likely leads, boys, but—where do we look now? Damn it, who *would* do a thing like—walk in and shoot up the whole office? Damn it—"

"Except little Celia Ann," said Grace dreamily.

"But where *do* we?" asked Landers.

Hackett and Higgins were drawing blanks too. Sometimes a witness remembered more clearly after thinking things over; but Myrtle Boggs and Lilian Stafford didn't. Of course Mrs. Boggs

134

hadn't had a chance to see much, and Mrs. Stafford hadn't heard but a few words.

They took Myrtle Boggs down to the McLaren Building, stood her where she said she'd been in the second-floor corridor, and roped in the superintendent, Dr. Colcannon, short fat Dr. Blaise, and a few other men of various sizes from offices in the building, to play X fleeing. All that emerged from that exercise was that she very hesitantly indicated Dr. Blaise as being nearest in size to the man she had seen running, holding the gun.

"It was so *fast,*" she said. "I didn't see him more'n five seconds, and he was down the stairs. I'm sorry, I'd sure like to help you—just a terrible thing—but that's all I can rightly say."

Mrs. Stafford was even more hesitant. "How do you describe a voice?" she asked helplessly. "I couldn't. In the first place, I was so surprised and—and startled, you know, by what he *said.* 'I'll kill you all,' or 'I'll shoot you all,' it was—and I simply ran back to our office to call the police. It was a man's voice, and that's all I can tell you. I can't say if it was deep or high or— Kind of, well, medium. And he didn't have an accent of any kind, it was just—just a man's voice, saying, 'I'll kill you all'— and I—"

It was discouraging, but they hadn't really hoped for anything better.

They came back to the office and asked Mendoza if the lab had sent up a report yet. "You know the lab," said Mendoza. "We can try to jigger them up." He got Scarne on the phone.

"Listen, Lieutenant, you know how many latents we picked up there? Sure, a doctor's office, nice and clean, but the ordinary dusting doesn't remove latent prints. It'll take a month of Sundays to sort 'em out, and if you want a really thorough job we'd have to find and print all his patients. I think most of 'em belong to patients, because I don't think your gunman stopped to look at magazines or turn lamps on and off, or straighten pictures, before he started shooting—or wander around feeling of things in all the examining rooms. I don't know what we've got. I don't think we're going to give you much, I'm sorry. But we did say, from all you got, it looked as if it went pretty fast —he went in, threatened to shoot, shot and got out."

"Yes," said Mendoza. "Well—"

"It is a bastard," said Higgins. "Just nothing to get hold of."

They were still sitting there talking it over when Palliser came back. He said he'd left Piggott talking to tenants and come back to get the initial report out on Fleming. So Hackett and Higgins heard about that.

And Palliser had just finished the report, separated the triplicate sheets and signed them and put them in manila envelopes, when Sergeant Lake buzzed Mendoza. "Goldberg," he said tersely.

Mendoza picked up the inside phone. "Afternoon, Saul. Have you got your new windows in yet?"

"No, damn it. It's hot as hell in here," said Lieutenant Goldberg of Robbery. But he sounded a little amused for some reason. "I'll be taking the rest of your day, Luis. Sorry. And—" He sneezed, swore, and blew his nose. "Oh, yes, the allergies are fine, thanks. —And you'll bring one of your bright young minions with you who—whom—you can spare for a day or so. He'll be taking a little trip. We have a thing here—"

"What? What for? *Qué es esto?*"

"You'd better come down and hear about it," said Goldberg. "My God, but we do get them. Sometimes we do get them. A little trip up toward Bakersfield, escorting a prisoner. He says he thinks he knows where he left it, but he doesn't know that part of the country, he couldn't be just sure. If he could sort of see the place again maybe he could tell. And of course the sheriff up there will have jurisdiction, a heavier charge than we could bring, so we may as well kill two birds with one stone and take him back, so the sheriff can lock him up when we do find it. He and your minion and the sheriff. If he did leave it, and can find it again. In any case, if it's there we would like to find it, you know."

"Find what, for God's sake?"

"Oh, a body," said Goldberg.

. . . . .

Mendoza took Palliser with him down to Goldberg's office. Palliser, he reflected, had been looking a little tired lately, a little worried about something. Spat with his wife? Landers and Grace could take over what he'd been working, and maybe a couple of days away from the routine would cheer Palliser up.

—Whatever the hell Goldberg was talking about.

As they came into the Robbery Bureau, they passed a couple sitting in chairs under Sergeant Betts's eye, and the couple looked at them with dull forlorn eyes. The other half, thought Mendoza. The girl, not more than eighteen or so, had long tangled brown hair past her shoulders, no makeup, and she was chewing gum. She wouldn't have been bad-looking if she'd combed her hair, put on some lipstick. She had on a pair of black pants and a wildly multicolor tunic top, and sandals on bare feet. The man wasn't much older; he wasn't over-tall but very stocky and hairy, dark, and looking very sorry for himself; he had on dirty plaid shorts and a dirty T-shirt and sandals, and he needed a shave.

Mendoza and Palliser went on into Goldberg's office. "And have you got new windows in yet, friends?" asked Goldberg.

"When you say that, smile. What's up, Saul?"

Goldberg's sardonic, lined dark face was lit with amusement. "Oh, the things we run into. Sergeant Palliser, you are in for a day or so of adventure. Did you notice that pair out there?"

"We did. What about them?"

"She's Wilma Schultz. He's Tim Brodie. They come from Oregon—some little farm town up there. Ran away to get married because Wilma's father doesn't like Tim. Come to the big city and make their fortunes."

"And?"

"No fortune," said Goldberg. "Tim's got a little pedigree up there—I've talked to the chief in this one-horse burg—assault, attempted rape, D.-and-D., attempted burglary. I could deduce, the quick temper. They were picked up by Traffic detail a couple of hours ago, spotted smashing windows and rifling cars in a public lot."

"Yes," said Mendoza. "And what's that got to do with—"

"Piddling little pair, small-time," said Goldberg. "Betts talked to 'em—and came rushing in to me a few minutes later. Seems all of a sudden the girl said, 'Maybe we ought to tell them about that guy, Tim—didn't mean to kill him, it was just an accident, but sort of awful—'"

"¿Cómo?"

"Yeah. So I talked to 'em. They parted right away, no trouble. Maybe they figure if they say they're sorry we won't do anything to 'em for it. They've got an old beat-up Ford, Tim's. Drove straight through, and somewhere around Fresno, they think it was, they picked up a hitchhiker. All they know about him, his name's Steve. He was heading south too. So they got to somewhere around Bakersfield, they *think* it was—this was last Sunday, by the way—and Steve starts to get a little fresh with Wilma, so Tim hauls him out of the car and biffs him, they have a fight, and all of a sudden Steve doesn't get up and Tim finds he's dead."

"¡Caramba!" said Mendoza. Palliser just shut his eyes.

"He thinks maybe Steve broke his neck, or maybe landed on a rock—he wasn't sure. Dead, he was sure he was. So they pulled the body off the road behind some bushes and drove on south. To the big city. Only they never meant to do a thing like that, and they're sorry, and Tim thinks if he could go back there and look, he could find where they put the body."

"¡Porvida! We do run into things. My God."

"Well, you see the position, Luis. It is a homicide. And I really can't spare any men right now—"

"You think we're not busy too?"

"I *apologize*," said Goldberg. "There it is. The sheriff has jurisdiction in the homicide—if you find the body—and we'll then send Wilma up to join Tim. But somebody'll have to ferry him up there officially and hunt for the body."

"Yes, yes. Do you mind the job, John?"

"Would it matter if I said yes?" said Palliser. "For God's sake, the other half we can say. So when do we go?"

"I've laid on a car and driver for seven-thirty," said Goldberg.

138

"You should be up there by ten or ten-thirty. I've talked to the sheriff—Roudebush his name is, seems like—" He sneezed explosively, swore and groped for Kleenex—"a very nice fellow. Stash Tim in jail for the night and get an early start tomorrow morning looking for the body."

"Why did I want to be a cop?" asked Palliser plaintively. "All right. I just ask you one favor, Lieutenant. It is now"—he looked at his watch—"half past five. Between now and seven-thirty will you please see that Tim is taken over to the jail and given a long hot shower and clean clothes? If I've got to ride next to him all the way up to Bakersfield—"

Goldberg laughed. "I'll do that."

"And you can hand your notes on Hauck and the new one over to Jase and Tom," said Mendoza.

Palliser had a word with Grace and Landers about the new case; Hauck they knew about. He went home to tell Roberta and pack an overnight case, after a hasty dinner. "Of *all* things," she said. "Just all casual, maybe they'd better tell—join the force and see life! The seamy side only. How long will you be gone?"

"I haven't any idea," said Palliser. "We may find the body by noon tomorrow, or never. Because it just could be that Tim was wrong, and after they'd driven off, Steve came to and got up and walked away somewhere."

"Heavens above," said his Robin. "You do run into— I won't say, have a good time, darling."

"I don't expect to," said Palliser. "And listen, don't you take advantage of my absence to decide to buy that fancy bedroom set you want—just because you can pay for it out of your earnings starting in September."

"Masculine pride," mocked Roberta. "It's silly, John—you know it'll help—"

"I'm just afraid it'll get to be a habit."

"Just until we get the furniture paid off—I promise. Let me know if you have to be gone long—and don't be, darling."

"Not more than I can help." He bent to kiss her. Well, they didn't have fights, but this working-wives bit he didn't approve of. . . .

Occasionally Mendoza brought the office home with him. He thought Alison and Máiri would appreciate Wilma and Tim. Hackett and Higgins, also on the way home, were doubtless thinking the same thing.

He was a little earlier than usual, and swore as he turned into the drive, and backed out again. The drive was cluttered with a small cement-mixing machine and bags of cement. He left the Ferrari in the street and walked up the drive, past the wide crack. The livestock was all in the back yard—four cats sitting in a row on the back porch, and Cedric the old English sheep dog barking furiously at *el pájaro,* who was shrieking raucously from the alder tree.

"*YAWK! YAWK! Yankee Doodle came to town!*" The mocking bird swooped down on Cedric, but Cedric's thick coat made him impervious to the savage pointed beak, and he just went on barking, his veil of face-hair flying up to show his one walleye. Mendoza went in the back door muttering—just how they'd come by them all was accidental, but there really was too much livestock for a city yard—to find Alison busy over dinner, the twins presumably having their baths after supper, with Máiri in charge.

"The cement man came," said Alison unnecessarily. "He couldn't actually start work—it was only an hour ago—but he left everything ready to do it tomorrow."

"So I see. Immobilizing the garage."

"Well, it'll only be a day or so. Anything new, *amado?*"

"Oh, wait till you hear." He got himself a drink; El Señor, hearing the bottle taken down, came through the cat door in a hurry demanding his share.

"Time they were in anyway." Alison went to shoo the cats in, locked the cat door and told Cedric to be quiet.

She duly appreciated Wilma and Tim. "The things you run

into . . . but I have a surprise for you, *marido*. We really have quite intelligent offspring."

"*Naturalmente.*"

"They do say, children of elderly parents are more intelligent—"

"You will go on insulting me." Mendoza finished the rye. "Come see."

Down the hall in the nursery, the twins were pinkly powdered and ready for bed, after the half hour of stories. "The lambs," said Mrs. MacTaggart benignly. Mendoza regarded the lambs warily; he had discovered in thirty-five months that a combination of McCann, Weir and Mendoza bloodlines could produce some lively characteristics.

"Now!" said Alison. "Johnny, remember what you learned today? The wolf. English."

"The wolf. English," said Johnny obediently. "*El lobo*. Spanish."

"Good. Two ways to say it."

"Two ways. *Sí*."

"Terry," said Alison. "You remember? The witch. English."

"*Sí*. English. *La bruja*, Spanish. *La bruja* get all burned down in *la estufa!* Mamacita—"

"*¡El lobo! El lobo!*" Johnny seized the battered copy of Grimm and made one leap into Mendoza's lap. "Daddy read—read *el cuento* 'bout *la cabra* 'n' *los niños! El Lobo* eat the little kids all down! *El Lobo*—"

"Johnny!" said Alison. "Now remember—we practiced to show Daddy! The oven—*la estufa*. English—Spanish."

"The oven," said Johnny disinterestedly. "Daddy read about *la cabra!*"

"Want about Jingle!" said Terry. "*El cuento* 'bout Jingle!"

"Terry! We *practiced*. Come on, now. The little girl—*la niña*. English—"

"Jingle!" said Terry. "*La bruja* turn into *el gato!* I like *la bruja*—she put *la magia mala* to *la doncella*—"

"Oh, dear," said Alison. Mendoza was laughing. "She's taken quite a fancy to that one, Jorinda and Joringel—"

"*Sí*, Jingle! *La bruja* kill ever'body *con la magia mala*," said Terry with immense satisfaction.

"No—no—*la cabra!*" shouted Johnny. "*El lobo* eat *los niños* all down!"

"Somehow I don't think you're making much impression, my love," said Mendoza.

"At least the driveway's getting repaired," said Alison resignedly.

And on Thursday morning about ten o'clock—just as Palliser, probably, was up there in the wilds hunting for a body with Tim Brodie and Sheriff Roudebush—Chris Hauck's Buick was spotted parked on Wabash Avenue in Boyle Heights. It was Palliser who had done most of the work on Hauck, though Landers had been in on the start of it; and as he'd said it was a very typical sordid little thing, and Hauck small loss. But things came up, and they were a team after all, taking the jobs as they came.

It looked as if there was just nowhere to go on the Harlow shooting; Mendoza was brooding over Harlow's records again, maybe hoping for a hunch to hit him. The four punks—Ken Burkhart, Jim Root, Marty Murphy and Ron Dolan—probably wouldn't be arraigned until Monday, now. They were all of age, and would be tried as adults; bail hadn't been granted yet, of course. Pat Logan was doing a little better, but was still unconscious.

Both Hackett and Higgins were off today. But they were both spending some thought on the Harlow thing: that shapeless, reasonless thing. Higgins mowed the lawn front and back; formerly Steve Dwyer's job, and the leg was nearly as good as new, after the hit-run, the brace and therapy, but he still favored it a little. Higgins still felt a little strange, Bert Dwyer's good kids his, Mary his, too, and now the new baby coming soon, in a couple of months.

Hackett had found a new diet and brooded over it rather gloomily, babysitting while Angel went to the market.

Landers and Piggott went to stake out Hauck's car, and at

ten minutes to twelve a man walked up to it and unlocked the driver's door, so they went up in a hurry and nabbed him.

The man was Foster Sterry, by the I.D. on him. He looked at them and said dispiritedly, "Oh, hell. Fuzz. I s'pose you want us for rollin' that drunk. Only he wasn't drunk. That was the trouble."

"All right, Sterry," said Landers, "we have to inform you of your rights—" and he read that piece off to him. "Do you understand your rights as I have—"

"Sure, sure," said Sterry. He was a tall thin fellow with a lugubrious jowled face like a bloodhound, and he said, "I s'pose you want Linda too. She's at the hotel—we got a room there—on Soto. I just come out to find Danny, he owes me a sawbuck, but woulden you know, he's down on his luck too, he can't pay up. What a drag, and now you drop on us— Hey, I s'pose it was the car, hah? I tole Linda we oughta leave it somewheres, there'd be a record who owned it—"

They found Linda Schnell at the shabby old hotel. She was doing her nails, and she wouldn't come with them until her nail polish was dry. They were accommodating: maybe she'd open up and tell them all about it. The D.A. liked voluntary statements.

And Landers said later to Grace, "Pity John had to miss it."

"Oh, yes," said Grace. "Seeing he did most of the legwork. But on the other hand, Tom, kind of run of the mill. What we get. Not like Harlow—the offbeat one. Can we say?"

"Unfortunately, yes," said Landers. And he had a date with Phil tomorrow night; she'd be interested in Harlow. She was interested in the detective work, which policewomen didn't get to do, much. But it was so seldom they ran into anything remotely approaching the exotic plots in the paperback at the drugstore. The shapeless thing, like this Harlow thing, was just maddening to work.

And Linda looked at them, in the interrogation room that Thursday afternoon, and she looked like just what her pedigree said she was—raddled and tired with the hand-to-mouth living, picking up the johns, rolling the drunks, too many bottles and

143

men and also, of course, the history of V.D. at the General Hospital. Her bleached blonde hair was lank, her skin flabby, and she looked ten years older than she was.

She said in a flat voice, "That guy. Foss said we shouldn't ought to keep the damn car. I guess that's how you dropped on us, huh? That guy—damn it, he wouldn't pass out, see? Never *saw* such a guy, I pick him up in a bar, he's riding a little high already, I think he's a good bet. He had a roll on him, I saw that. So I string him along, get him to a hotel, pretty soon he passes out and bingo, that's it. How it usually goes with a john. But damn it, he didn't pass out—just kept pourin' it down and pawin' at me—kept saying, come on, honey, have to love it up while you can—"

Hauck, who should have known better at his age.

"And so finally I get tired of it, see, and I go give Foss the sign. Sometimes the johns turn out hardheaded like that and you got to— So Foss comes in, he followed us to the hotel, been hangin' around, see, and goes to knock him out. They had a li'l fight but the guy's far enough gone then, it don't take much. So we got his roll, *and* spent it," said Linda reminiscently. "And now you damn cops—"

"Spoilsports," said Landers. "From way back, Linda. We don't like anybody to have a good time. You do know this all adds up to murder second?"

And she sat up abruptly and her voice went high and she said, "Murder? Murder? You don't tell me that guy's *dead?* Foss never meant—for God's sake—he's *dead?*"

144

# 10

Landers typed up the last report on Chris Hauck, and as an afterthought, remembering what Palliser had said about the sister, hunted in Palliser's notes for the address and called Mrs. Roberts. . . . A funeral director had claimed Hauck's body on Tuesday and there had been a funeral yesterday. Mrs. Roberts thanked him; at least, she said, those people would be in prison awhile. "But I guess we've got to realize that if Chris hadn't been the kind—" She let that trail off, thanked him again. Landers signed the triplicate reports, separated them into envelopes and sat back and yawned.

He was supposed to be off tomorrow, but unless Palliser got back, and depending on what showed today, he'd probably be coming in.

The next thing was a call from the D.A.'s office; they were trying to speed up the court procedures, and now had Ed Hobart down for arraignment tomorrow morning. Which certainly meant that Landers would be in. Sergeant Lake went to tell Mendoza about that, and found him practicing the crooked deals, a cigarette in one corner of his mouth, talking to himself.

"I do not care, Jimmy," he said, "there was a reason on Harlow. A lunatic reason, but a reason of some kind. And all we can do is go over the same ground again and get nothing. *¡Condenación!* And damn it, a big building like that—people coming and going—it was just random luck, his luck, that nobody got a good look—that he got clean away— That Boggs woman— *¡Milrayos!*"

"Natural," said Lake. "That hour in the morning, a professional building like that—annoying, but natural, Lieutenant. Are you going out for lunch at all? It's one-thirty."

"Maybe. A wholesale slaughter—" Mendoza put the cards down; he might as well have some lunch. But as he yanked down his cuffs, straightened his tie, reached for his hat, Lake, back at the switchboard, put through an inside call.

"Fletcher, Traffic," he said. Mendoza swore and sat down again.

"Now we don't think this is anything for you yet, Luis," said Fletcher. "We hope to God it isn't. But I thought you'd better be alerted. There's two kids reported missing over on Elden Avenue. Single house. We don't know much yet, but I've got four cars over there now. First report is, the grandmother's babysitting them, missed them from the back yard about half an hour ago—"

"That's early for you to be agitating about it," said Mendoza inattentively, suddenly aware that he was starving. "Hardly the place for a snatch. And kids wander."

"They do," agreed Fletcher. "But the girl's sixteen months, the boy not three yet."

"Oh. Oh, my God, I see. But they could still—"

"We're looking. They couldn't have got far under their own steam. But it just could *be* something a little more serious. I'll let you know."

"Thanks so much." The kids had wandered down the block and were playing with other kids in a strange back yard. Or— But things did happen. Not nice things, sometimes. . . . And Harlow—Mendoza took up his hat and went out. He decided he was going through Dr. Harlow's records again, slow and careful. Hoping for the belated hunch. Because there was *some* answer on the Harlow shooting, and the irrational mind which had conceived the wholesale slaughter was not, could not be cunning enough—

But, thought Mendoza sardonically, pushing the button for the elevator, as an experienced cop he ought to know better than to go woolgathering like that. The real bastards to work

146

and the cases that so frequently ended up in Pending were just the ones like the Harlow shooting. The shapeless ones with no handle to grasp, no lead pointing in any direction, nowhere to go to look for one. He hoped the Harlow shooting would not end up in Pending, but he wouldn't take any bets on it.

At one-fifty that Thursday afternoon, Patrick Henry Logan opened his eyes. He tried to turn his head, and the doctor beside the bed, holding his wrist, said quietly, "Speak to him, Mrs. Logan. His pulse is good—let's discontinue that I.V. for the moment, nurse."

"Pat? Pat darling—it's Sally, Pat, can you—"

Logan moved again weakly and got out her name on a little gasp. "Sally—"

"Oh, *Pat!*" She put down her head on the bed and began to cry.

"He'll do," said the doctor. "Keep him quiet. Please, Mrs. Logan—you're upsetting him—" Logan was trying to move, to lift his head; the nurse restrained him. Sally Logan sat up and wiped her eyes.

"I'm sorry, I'll— Pat darling, you're going to be all right—" And Royce was there, grinning down at him too. Logan's vague gaze wandered up to Royce's face and focused a little more clearly; and then, suddenly, it wasn't just a badly injured man lying in the hospital bed, but a cop—an LAPD officer.

"Royce," he said in a stronger voice. "Tell 'em—four kids— four young punks—never saw b'fore in my life—"

"We know, boy," said Royce gently. "We know. You relax and start getting well."

Landers and Piggott came back from their belated lunch at two-twenty, and found the picket drifting up Los Angeles Street just past the entrance to the parking lot.

"Children and fools," said Piggott. "Have you ever read any of Velikovsky? The *Worlds in Collision* fellow?"

"Yes, but I didn't think you would have, Matt."

"Oh, I may look dumb but sometimes I read more than *True*

*Detective,* Tom. And you just can't prove that man's wrong, about all the catastrophes that have happened. We don't know how many times we've got to the top, with all the inventions and industries and airplanes and all, only using it for evil—so the Lord brings down the destruction. And isn't he right too when he says all those verses in the Bible were meant literally, about mountains overturning and the sea rising up and so on. We think we're so smart. We don't *know.*"

"Yes, I think he's got something too. Plenty of geological evidence—" Landers put his hand on one of the double doors to the lobby, and the ground suddenly slid away under their feet and for ten seconds rolled uneasily under them. They felt the building move slightly.

"He did promise," said Piggott, "not to do it with a flood again. I don't know but what I'd prefer a flood."

They found the Homicide Bureau empty except for Lake. "Where's Jase? I haven't seen him since he fetched Linda and Sterry down to jail," said Landers.

Lake said he hadn't a clue. "The boss has vanished some place too." He was studying a paperback book, *The Doctor's Quick Weight-Loss Diet.*

"Goofing off," said Landers. "Nothing new gone down?"

"Not yet," said Lake.

There was no sign of any work crews replacing windows on this side of the building today; it was to be hoped they were on the other side, gradually working toward Homicide. Somebody had brought a thermometer into the detective office; it was on Palliser's desk, and right now it read ninety-seven. And whereas August was often a month of overcast gray skies and a little cooler air, preparing residents for the last hellish heat in September and October, this August of the earthquake was bright and sunny. The sun streamed through the glassless windows of Homicide cheerfully, and they could have done with less of it.

At three o'clock Lake buzzed them. "New one—call in from a doctor. Dr. Roger Stuyvesant. Direct to us, not Traffic—maybe he rode an ambulance awhile. He says he'll meet detectives there. It's Colyton Street over across the tracks."

They both went on it. They had a little hunt for it at that; it was a short street. It was one of the many narrow old streets down here on Central's beat, which was the oldest part of Los Angeles. The Los Angeles River meandered through part of that area, wandering into the city from the valley through a natural pass in the foothills. It was dry ten months of the year, but could be a menace in heavy rains, and the riverbed these days was encased in concrete walls forty feet high—an ugly trail through this part of town. Along the route of the riverbed ran the railroad tracks, converging on the great bare dirty expanse of the Southern Pacific yards, behind Union Station. Union Station was a handsome modern building, very clean-looking, very Californian, but away from Union Station with its tiled floors and mosaic walls there was the old and tired and shabby tangle of streets, the oldest in the city, the poorest now.

It was a street, when they found it, of little frame houses on narrow lots: houses older than the century, mostly. The one on the corner had been partly knocked down by the earthquake, and apparently abandoned. The one they wanted was in the middle of the block. No car stood before it; evidently Dr. Stuyvesant, whoever he might be, had farther to come.

It was a very shabby old house, very small, and it hadn't been painted for a long time, and what grass remained in the narrow front yard was brown. It had a narrow rickety front porch which shook under their feet, and an old-fashioned doorbell. The sagging front door was half open. Landers pushed the bell and it rang halfheartedly. He rapped on the door.

After a moment a faint quavery voice said, "Doctor—"

"Police officers, ma'am. Where—" The door opened direct on the living room, which was about ten by fourteen: a derelict sagging couch, a chair with torn upholstery, a thin strip of rug, a table with one lamp on it. There was a door opposite the front door, standing open; they went in there.

A bedroom, small and square and shabby: old brass bedstead, a straight chair, a chest of drawers, door to a tiny closet.

She was sitting in the chair beside the bed, an old woman, thin and bent, with white hair thin where pink scalp showed through. The sun streamed in a window curtained only with a torn dime-store shade.

"I called—the doctor," she said. "The doctor—at the hospital."

"He called us, ma'am. What's wrong here? You—" And then they both realized that the old man in the bed was dead. Landers went round to the other side and felt his neck; he was cold. He was a wizened, bald old man, and he wasn't wearing his false teeth, so his cheeks fell in like a death's-head. Landers looked around, saw on the makeshift bed table the old man's false teeth in a plastic dish, a used glass, a little paper box. He looked at that without touching it. It had a label: *Mrs. Mallory, 1 every 4 hours for pain.*

Behind them the door opened and footsteps sounded; they turned. "Police?" he said. "I'm Stuyvesant. In charge of the out-patient clinic at General—" He was a short, spare, competent-looking man in his fifties; right now he looked very shaken. He went across to the old woman and put his hand on her shoulder.

She had closed her eyes; at his touch she opened them and looked up at him. "Doctor," she said. "You do understand it, don't you? He was—so tired, poor Dan. The pain was so bad, Doctor. It was the last thing I could do for him, you see. The last thing. We'd been together for sixty-nine years, you see. Dan and I. I was seventeen when we were married and he was twenty."

"Mrs. Mallory—"

She reached up and laid her bony, distorted, shaking old hand over his square surgeon's hand on her shoulder. "A doctor should understand. That's a long time. I'm eighty-six, and Dan was eighty-nine, and I can remember—just as clear as anything could be—the day we were married. He had a good job on the railroad then. All his life he worked for the railroad. I don't know where the time went—I can recall so clear—but it passed by—and Dan was eighty-nine, and he was tired. You understand that, don't you?"

He freed his hand gently, came round the bed and bent over the body.

"Oh, he's gone, Doctor. I waited until I was sure. You doctors, you always fight so hard on the side of life—but there's no call be afraid of dying. Easier than living, it is, sometimes."

"He's been gone for hours," said Stuyvesant to Landers and Piggott. He picked up the glass and sniffed it.

"It's what you gave me for the pain," she said. "For the arthritis. There was a full box just yesterday, and I was almost sure it would—"

"Empirin Number Three," said Stuyvesant quietly to the Homicide men. "Codeine—not much, but enough for him, in an overdose. He had inoperable cancer—probably all through him."

"You see, Doctor, you've got to understand," she said. "Dan and I, we been helping each other for sixty-nine years—loving each other—we been together a long, long time. We hoped we'd have a family, but we never. Never any babies, and I didn't have any brothers or sisters, Dan had a brother but he died years back, and he hadn't any family either. There wasn't anybody. Just Dan and me. We were so proud when we finished paying for the house—that was thirty-nine years ago—twelve hundred dollars it cost and it took us a long time to save. But I was always a good manager. Dan earned steady—not much but steady. He always gave an honest day's work for an honest day's pay."

"Mrs. Mallory—you shouldn't stay—let me—"

"It's not much but it was ours. Only—things change. With the time going by." She looked at the dead man tenderly, smiling. "The pension wasn't much, but we made do. Dan went on the pension twenty-four years back. We made do. But since the arthritis got so bad, it's hard to do things, just get up a meal, wash the dishes. Dan helped me—we always helped each other, we never asked help from anybody else, never been on welfare. But it was hard. And Dan—was so—tired."

"Yes," he said steadily, gently. "I know he was."

151

"He begged me to help him. He said he was just so tired, and the pain so bad. Ellen, help me, he said. Help me to go. And it was the last thing I could do for him—I thought those pills would do it. I gave them all to him, and—I waited—until I was sure—before I called you, Doctor." She swayed a little.

"My God, my God," said the doctor. He turned to Landers. "We'll want an ambulance—there's no phone here, if you'd— My God. She's not fit to be alone, and"—he gestured helplessly —"to *prosecute* her—for— My good God."

And Piggott said softly, unexpectedly, *"For love is strong as death,* doesn't it say."

"I remember so clear," she said. "So clear. The minister said, *in sickness and in health. Cleaving only to one another—* And I just don't know how the time slipped by. But Dan—I'd always do whatever I could to help Dan, whatever he asked me to—and it was the last way I could help him. He was so tired—"

Landers didn't know where the nearest phone might be. He went out—have to go back to the office, or—and as luck had it, a black-and-white was just cruising past the corner up there; he shouted, and it came bucketing up. He had his badge in his hand, and reached in for the mike.

At about the same moment, John Palliser was standing by the side of a very empty road fifteen miles outside of Bakersfield, with Tim Brodie and burly, genial Sheriff Roudebush and a couple of deputies with the unlikely names of Forbear and Clearwater.

"Well, gee, it sort of looks like the place," said Brodie, "but I ain't just sure—"

"It's not," said Clearwater, and spat aside. "No body. Are you sure it *was* a body?"

"Oh, he was dead. He was dead, sure. That I do know, I was awful surprised—I didn't go to kill him, I was just mad because he'd been pawing at Wilma. I just hit him a couple times, and he hit me, and then I hit him and he fell down and— Oh, he was dead. I guess he hit his head on a rock when he fell down—it felt funny, all soft. He was dead. But this isn't the place, come to think, because there was a steeper shoulder on the road—I nearly slipped, gettin' him down it—"

Palliser and Roudebush looked at each other. They had been driving all around the roads outside of town since eight o'clock this morning, and this was the twentieth spot Brodie had said looked something like the place they had left Steve's body.

Roudebush, who somewhat resembled a large and amiable Saint Bernard, dropped his cigarette and stepped on it. "Now think, Tim," he said patiently. "You said it wasn't the main highway."

"No, on account of I got lost. We stopped at a place for hamburgers, and then I got lost—I don't know this part of the country, never been here before."

"All right. You don't remember any signs? Road signs? You don't remember the name of the place you stopped to eat?"

Tim thought. "It was just a little place along the road. It had a long counter, and stools. No booths. The hamburgers were fifty-five cents, and Wilma wanted a malt too, but we only had just forty dollars and I told her—"

Roudebush scratched his cheek. "No booths. Well, a lot of places like that—you drove through town first? Bakersfield?"

"Yessir, I see the sign—Now ENTERING BAKERSFIELD. We were through town and there was just a couple real-estate places and billboards and then Wilma said she was hungry and pretty soon we come to this place, it said EATS on a big sign. Oh, and the waitress had red hair," said Tim. "I remember that."

Roudebush said to Palliser, "Marge Leatherhead at Barney's place. Possibly. We can go and ask if she remembers him."

They got into the car again. "I'm sorry," said Tim. "I never been in this part of the country before."

Palliser wondered how the boys were doing down at home, on what. If Hauck's car had turned up, and Linda and Sterry. If anything new had turned up. If they'd got any leads on Harlow. Well, that sort of shapeless thing so often did wind up in Pending. . . .

"Little change for you, Sergeant," said Roudebush as he shifted into high.

"Oh, that you can say, Sheriff. Out in the wilds, wandering around hunting a body. And if this was the place they stopped for hamburgers, does it help pinpoint the body at all?"

"How about it?" asked Forbear in the back seat with Clearwater and Brodie. "How long after the hamburgers did you have your fight with Steve?"

"Oh, gee, I don't know. A while. About half an hour, little longer maybe. See, I was driving, it wasn't till Wilma said, Make him stop doing that, I saw what he was up to—"

"We've got," said Roudebush to Palliser, "quite a lot of country up here to look at."

"I see you have. We've seen quite a lot of it already. I just wish," said Palliser, "we could be sure there *is* a body to find. Because—"

"Oh, he was dead, sir," said Brodie. "Listen, I used to help butcher—I'd know. He was dead. I was so *surprised* he was. Oh, I just remembered, there was some bushes around there—it wasn't farm land, just empty land, wild, you know, and there was these bushes with a lot of yellow flowers on them."

"About two feet high?" said Clearwater.

"Yeah, about—"

"Wild mustard," said Roudebush. "There's quite a lot of it around, wild on uncultivated land."

Palliser began to wonder when he'd see L.A. again. And Roberta. Well, at least up here he wasn't feeling the aftershocks and wondering when the next big quake was coming.

He wondered if Homicide had got new windows installed yet.

Grace came into the office as Landers and Piggott arrived back from the General Hospital. "And where have you been?" asked Landers.

"None of your business," said Grace amiably. He was looking pleased with himself. "Anything new?"

Piggott said, "The lieutenant talking about love, the other day. A dangerous commodity, he said. Those two poor old

154

souls—there but for the grace of God, do we say? I'll do the report, Tom. You look shook."

Landers was feeling that way. And he thought suddenly, he must tell Phil about this one, tomorrow night. A thing like that made you think. And just as suddenly he remembered another quote from Holy Writ—*man not meant to live alone.* . . .

"A thing, Jase," he said soberly. "One of the things we see that makes you think, that's all." Stuyvesant had taken charge, bundled the old lady off to the hospital, sent the body to the morgue; he said he'd be in to make the necessary statement. Stuyvesant had been shook too. Landers started to tell Grace about it, and Grace listened, brushing his moustache absently.

"And you can't feel the old lady'll come in for the Lord's displeasure, Tom," he said gently. "What do we do about it?"

"What the hell, Jase? I don't know. Ask the lieutenant. The D.A. The old lady living on borrowed time—the arthritis—do we charge her with murder second and trust she'll live to stand trial?" Landers made an angry gesture.

"I don't somehow think so, Tom. I kind of think," said Grace, still absently, "I'd like to call my wife. . . ." He went to his desk, swiveled around in the chair so his back was to them, and dialed. Piggott was busy over the report, and Landers didn't try to hear what Grace was saying in his soft voice.

"Well, they were a little surprised, but I was persistent, and—"
"Did they *say*—"
"Well, you know how cautious those people are, hon. All the red tape. The rules and regulations."
"But, Jase, did they *say* it might be?"
"Mostly the doubletalk. But I went on prodding at them, and by what I got, it's possible—if we keep right after it. I called Dad—he'd know something about how the rules work—and he's all for it. He said if he could help any way he will. What I gather, we might have an edge—after all I am a very upright fellow, Ginny, LAPD officer with a clean record—and when we can show, or rather they can prove, there aren't any—"
"Oh, Jase! Oh, if it does work out—" Virginia was excited.

"You hold your horses, it might take a while, all the red tape—"

"But if we *can!* Oh, Jase, it's got to work out! After the way you said, the guardian angel—"

"We'll have a hell of a good try, Ginny," said Grace. "We will."

Mrs. Candace Pine looked at Mendoza with a troubled expression. She wasn't a pretty woman, but kind-faced and friendly, a dark-brown woman with a round undistinguished face, a figure a little too plump, a warm deep voice. Her living room in the house beside the colonial house the Harlows had lived in was well furnished in early American, and Mrs. Pine was modestly clad in a long blue cotton housecoat.

She apologized again for not being dressed; she had been about to wash her hair. "I wish I could think of a thing to tell you, Lieutenant, but I just can't. Anything more. I see what you mean, about whoever did it having *some* sort of reason, just a crazy one but a reason. . . . It's just a thing you can't believe, somebody killing John and Ann and John's nurse— I'd never met her, of course—but I see that, when you say it. Only there couldn't be any reason—even for a crazy man!"

"It could be—probably was," said Mendoza, "something very trivial. Something nobody else thought twice about. Just think, Mrs. Pine. Anything, anything at all, Mrs. Harlow having an argument with someone—or Dr. Harlow—"

She was shaking her head. "They were a nice quiet couple. There wasn't anything like— And that poor baby! They'd just been in seventh heaven about that baby, Lieutenant—married so long, and not really hoping any more, and then the baby. And my husband and I—well, we talked about it, but we've got our own four and we just couldn't afford—we can hope, maybe some nice people—"

Mendoza offered her a cigarette and she said she didn't smoke. "But you go right ahead—I'll get you an ashtray—" Evidently the husband didn't smoke either; the ashtray was about two inches square, dime-store variety.

"Anything," he said. "Anything, however trivial, an argument about wrong change, about—"

And she started to shake her head again, and said, "Well, my goodness, I just thought of *that!* And it sounds just silly to tell you—but you saying— Well, they'd just, I mean Ann had just fired the gardener they had. Just last week."

"*Hagar sus apuntas,*" said Mendoza softly. "Stakes down and wait for the throw. . . . She had?"

"But a gardener—just silly. They just hired him to cut the lawn once a week, do the weeding—Ann did all the rest, she loved gardening, I told the other officer, always out fussing round her flowers. Feeding and mulching and all that— What? No, I don't know his name. My husband cuts our lawn on Sundays, and we haven't much planting to take care of, just the shrubs in front. Ann told me he turned up that day—he came on Tuesdays—drunk as a lord, and used, you know, offensive language—so she told him— Well, I think the Ashmans down the street hire him too. They might know—"

Jackpot? Mendoza wondered. It was very likely some slight motive behind the Harlow shooting, they'd thought that from the start, by experience.

He found Mrs. Ashman home and she told him they hadn't heard about Mrs. Harlow firing the gardener. They'd been terribly shocked by the Harlows' murder; hadn't known them except by name, but they'd seemed like nice people. Her husband was a physical therapist at the French Hospital. They'd employed the gardener—she thought he had several jobs right around here, coming once a week to cut lawns—ever since they'd lived here, seven years. His name—they paid him by check—was Sam Oliver, and she had his phone number, not his address. He had his own pickup truck, with his name and *Gardening Service* on it, so it was his regular job.

Heading back to the office at four-forty, Mendoza idly noted the headlines, stopped at a traffic light: *Aftershocks Number Hundreds, Greatest 4.3 on Richter Scale.*

He hoped to God they'd get new windows soon. And their air conditioning turned on.

In the Homicide Bureau he found Landers, Piggott and Grace exchanging small talk, and got on the phone to Information. Within ten minutes he got Sam Oliver's address—Bonsallo Avenue—and went across to the detective office.

"Goofing off," he said. "We've got a new lead on Harlow—a very small lead, but we never do know what might show up. Let's go and ask questions." He told them about the gardener.

"But my God, a little thing like that," said Landers. "And if he is a drunk, well, whoever shot up that office was shooting straight enough—"

"Even habitual drunks," said Mendoza, "are not drunk twenty-four hours a day. And in confined quarters such as Harlow's office, even the .22 can be lethal in amateur hands. As this one was, drunk or amateur or whatever."

"Oh, it's a lead," agreed Landers. He looked at his watch. Leave it for the night watch? The inside phone rang on Hackett's empty desk and Mendoza picked it up.

"Mendoza."

"Fletcher. I said I'd let you know. Now we know. Incredible as it is. The missing kids."

"Yes?" Fletcher's voice held some indefinable emotion.

"Gary Hildebrand, thirty-three months. Stella Hildebrand, sixteen months. Mother Alice works as a waitress, cafeteria downtown. They live with her mother—Alice is divorced, mother takes care of the kids. The kids went missing from the back yard about two-thirty, nearest we can pin it down."

"So?"

"So—" Fletcher uttered a little incredulous growl. "We've had patrolmen out looking. That area, no swimming pools, but empty garages and so on— But we just found them. And it's your baby, Luis."

"*¿Cómo dice?* You don't mean—"

"Behind a billboard in an empty lot about six blocks from the house. Both strangled. No evidence of sexual interference— just strangled, and left."

"*¡Diez demonios desde el infierno!*" said Mendoza.

158

**11**

They all went out on that, and Mendoza called Hackett and Higgins in. Dr. Bainbridge came out to look at this one from the start, and the same thought was in the mind of every man there, looking at the two small bodies in the tangled growth of weeds behind the billboard. It wouldn't have taken much —the little pressure, the little strength put out—to snuff out those little lives. Lives hardly begun, so very fragile.

Bainbridge looked sick as he stood up. "Just strangled," he said, and then put their thoughts in words. "It wouldn't take much—and no evidence of any molestation—"

This was a thing to get on, and the kind of thing that made legwork. Mendoza, Hackett and Higgins went to the house on Elden Avenue to get some background. They knew approximately when the children were discovered missing, and what they'd been wearing; the rest of them started to ring doorbells and question neighbors.

At the Elden Avenue house they found that the grandmother, Mrs. Ella Pace, had broken down and been given a sedative; but the Traffic men had the gist of her statements earlier this afternoon. "Says she checked on them often, kids that young, but they were good about staying in the yard. Besides, it's fenced—" This was an old frame bungalow, but well enough kept up, trim newly painted; and there was a three-foot-high redwood fence completely enclosing the back yard. "And the latch is stiff, she doesn't think the boy could have unfastened it. Certainly the baby couldn't. She told us the longest time she left them without checking was just before she missed them—maybe half an hour between two and two-thirty. She was making a pie or something."

Now they knew the children had been taken away. The house was on a corner, the sandbox the children had been playing in at the end of the yard; it would have been relatively easy for anybody to call the children over, lift them over the fence. Why, and who?

"The nut," said Hackett angrily, unconsciously balling his fists. "The violent nut. But a *sixteen*-month-old, Luis, for God's sake—" Hackett's own Sheila wasn't much older. And Higgins said the same thing.

"It's early to say," said Mendoza. "I want some background."

They found the mother, Alice Hildebrand, perhaps still numb and not quite believing, queerly calm and readily answering questions. "I don't suppose I've taken it in yet," she told them. She was in her late twenties, a nice-looking young woman if not exactly pretty, with ash-brown hair and blue eyes; she wore glasses and kept pushing them up on her nose in habitual gesture. "I just can't realize—Mother's always good and careful with them—I have to work, you see, I work downtown—Mother's just got Dad's pension and of course the children—"

"Your husband, Mrs. Hildebrand?" asked Mendoza.

"He's—we're divorced. I didn't like to do that, I don't—don't approve of divorce, I put up with him a long time, but I couldn't —never holding a job long and drinking and all—I finally divorced him— What?" She turned unfocused eyes on Hackett.

"Do you think he could have anything to do with this?"

"Henry? Oh, of course not. He didn't—he hardly knew the children were *there*. He didn't care about them—any way. No, that's—"

"But does he live here in town?"

"I don't know where he is. I divorced him last May. I don't know if he's here. The judge said, child support, but he never—"

"I realize the children were young, too young maybe to recognize—but did the boy ever report some adult speaking to him over the fence, or—"

She shook her head blindly. "I don't know. He isn't three yet, he wouldn't—and it'd go right out of his head if anybody had, he wouldn't—"

"Can you think of anyone, Mrs. Hildebrand, anyone who might want to harm you or the children for any reason?"

She shook her head again. "That's silly—I'm sorry, but it is. Who would? I'm—an ordinary person, we're ordinary people. *Enemies*—silly. And to hurt the *children*—I go to work and back, I don't have trouble with people, get along with everybody all right—the biggest trouble I ever had my whole life was with Henry, and I've been upset about that yet—I didn't like to divorce him, but I could see it was no good going on. I never thought I'd be divorcing my own husband, but I guess, well, I just didn't know him good enough when I married him. How he was. He left me when he knew I was pregnant again, you know—he's never seen Stella at all. I been living here with Mother ever since, two years about."

"Do you have any men friends, Mrs. Hildebrand, who would know the children?" Mendoza was watching her.

She blew her nose. "Not to—no, not really. There's Frank Fosser where I work, he's the chef—a nice fellow, I guess, he's always been respectful, treated me like a lady—he's asked me to go out with him and I did once. And Burt Fowler, he lives up the block, I've known him years, and he's asked me to marry him. But I couldn't decide anything like that yet, I was still all upside-down in my mind like about divorcing Henry. I got to where I wasn't sleeping, the doctor gave me some pills—it just upset me so, I don't approve of divorce. I guess Burt's all right —I used to go with him some, we went to high school together, he's got a good job with the telephone company—but I been still so all which way about the divorce, I couldn't think of that. Anybody else. And besides, nobody we *know* would do such a thing—such an awful—" Suddenly she put her hands to her face and began to cry.

"The hunch hit you out of the blue?" asked Higgins on the

sidewalk outside the house. "You asking about the husband, boy-friends? Ten to one it's the random pervert, Luis. Coming by, spotting the kids. We know that kind don't always go in for the sexual hijinks—sometimes the act of killing is enough."

"*Sí*," said Mendoza, brushing his moustache back and forth. "In broad daylight, George, on a residential street? I don't know if it's a hunch, but I think—just as I've been saying on Harlow— the victims were picked *as* victims. Why—" He shrugged.

In any case, there was only one way to go at it. They started ringing doorbells. Had anybody seen the children that afternoon? With or without an adult? Had any stranger been seen in the neighborhood, acting peculiarly or not? All the indicated questions, and not only around the Elden Avenue neighborhood but six blocks away, around the empty lot where the children had been found. It was an area to cover; they wouldn't finish it tonight.

Higgins, ringing doorbells, was over on Magnolia, the next street behind Elden; he looked at his watch as he rang the doorbell of the house that backed up to Mrs. Pace's house. Mendoza had said, work it until ten; this was a working-class neighborhood and people waked from bed wouldn't feel cooperative toward cops. This would be his last call.

Their name was Fanchon, and like everybody else the Homicide men had talked to tonight, they were horrified about the children and eager to try to help. But they hadn't seen anything —both the younger Fanchons worked and Mrs. Fanchon's mother, who lived with them— "I wonder if she noticed anything, Bob. But I don't suppose—she left this afternoon, Sergeant, she's going to visit her sister in San Diego over the weekend. She was taking the Greyhound at three o'clock, from downtown—"

"Then she'd probably left before the children were missing. Well, thanks," said Higgins.

Schenke and Galeano had turned out too; and they all forgathered back at the office to sort out what they had. "Not a Goddamned thing!" said Hackett savagely. He looked rather sinister, the black eye just nicely developed. Both Higgins and Mendoza needed a shave, and Landers didn't look quite so boyish as usual, his eyes blistered and tired. Jason Grace was furiously brushing his moustache. "Nobody saw the kids—nobody noticed anything or anybody near the house—nobody—"

"There's the car," said Landers. "The car noticed parked—evidently not for long—in the street right by that lot. The retired postman noticed it, from the house the other side of the lot. Noticed it because it's illegal to park there, and it wasn't there long. A white car like a Dodge or a Buick."

"All *right*," said Higgins. "Absolutely nothing says it had one damned thing to do with— And how the hell do we look for it?"

"*Paciencia*," said Mendoza. "It's a first little something. Go home to bed, boys—we'll see what turns up tomorrow. Which is also a day." He got up wearily.

"Nothing," said Hackett. "Nothing will—it's another shapeless, handleless thing like Harlow—another lunatic—"

"*No sé*," said Mendoza. "Go home. There were people not home we didn't talk to. The witness may turn up yet. I'll see you in the morning."

He went home, and the garage and house lights were on for him, and the mockingbird produced a sleepy *Yankee Doodle came* before going back to sleep. In the kitchen, Mrs. MacTaggart inquired severely if he'd had dinner at all, and Alison came, hastily tying a robe.

"We heard it on the news, Luis—what an *awful*—you can't believe a thing like that. Did you find—"

"*Nada*," said Mendoza, kissing her. "I had a sandwich, Máiri. I'm O.K. Maybe tomorrow we'll get a lead." Cedric came up waggling his hind end in greeting.

"You'll be having a dram and another sandwich before you go to your bed," said Mrs. MacTaggart determinedly. And El Señor was officially retired with his mother and sisters at the foot of the king-size bed, but he could hear any word pertaining to whiskey through the walls, and appeared shortly demanding his share.

Mendoza said, "I won't say no to either," and stripped off his jacket.

.   .   .   .

Hackett went home and before answering Angel's questions went to look at Sheila, pinkly asleep in her crib. She was going to have a hint of red in her hair, like his mother, and a good thing she'd got Angel's eyes. . . . "Sixteen months!" he said to Angel. "What kind of a— And Luis's got a bee in his bonnet. The personal motive. I ask you—impossible enough to imagine even the random pervert, but—"

"He feels things," said Angel thoughtfully. She was sitting up in bed, the big smoke-silver Persian curled asleep on Hackett's side. "Does he think that? Queer—but he does feel things, Art. What's the family like? Those poor little things—and what the mother—"

Hackett told her all they knew while he undressed.

Higgins went home and found Mary reading a detective novel. "Did you find anything? That terrible— Well, it's a lot neater in books," she said wryly, putting the book down. "A lot less— But who would do such a—"

"Babies," said Higgins. "My God, just babies, Mary. And Luis had a damned senseless hunch. Something personal—somebody they know. With all the perverts around, we need to get as offbeat as that?"

"Did he? Well, he gets the hunches, you say," said Mary. "Wait to see, George." She sighed, and looking down at herself added, "Babies . . . I'm getting a little tired of this one where it is. And all my size-fourteen clothes gathering dust. . . . You're shook on account of the baby, George."

"This thing is enough to shake anybody," said Higgins.

On Friday morning there was more of the legwork to do on that, and other things as well. There was Rhoda Fleming; there was Hobart's arraignment; and an initial report had to be written on the Hildebrand case. Higgins stayed to do that, and pick up Hobart for his court appearance at ten o'clock. Piggott and Landers took over the Fleming case, and all the rest of them went out to finish up the legwork on the Hildebrand thing.

Landers had called Stuyvesant, who had yet to make a statement on the Mallory case yesterday; he could come by and dictate it to Lake. He told them that Mrs. Mallory had had a massive stroke in the ambulance and wasn't expected to live. They started out for Sunland in Piggott's Chevy feeling rather depressed about things in general.

"Of course it's just as well, poor old soul," said Piggott. And Landers, agreeing, didn't say anything else because he was feeling depressed. He'd been surprised that Piggott had read Velikovsky, and some other time he'd like to exchange more opinions with him; this morning, thinking about those kids, about the Mallorys, he felt a little gloomy and untalkative.

Nobody had yet talked to Rose Scott, Rhoda Fleming's daughter. They found the house, a modern split-level in the hills, and introduced themselves. "Oh—" she said, and began to cry. "Ab-about Mother—oh, I'm sorry, I'll try to—" She hiccuped, wiped her eyes, and added unnecessarily, "There's the baby— excuse me—sit down, I'll—"

They waited in the neat, conventionally furnished modern living room. They had both seen Palliser's notes incorporating Mendoza's little ideas on this. Piggott said, "She seems to be a nice girl."

"Um-hum," said Landers. "Everybody said Mama was too. But the lieutenant does see things, Matt."

"No denying."

She came back with the baby, quite a new baby, silent now, bald and pink in a blue blanket. "I'm sorry—I know there are questions you want to ask, Gavin said—" She sat down opposite them. "But I can't tell you anything. It must have been a burglar —breaking in and—"

"Well, the door wasn't forced, Mrs. Scott," said Landers.

"But nobody Mother *knew* would do such a thing!" She looked at them wildly, automatically jiggling the baby. She was a pretty dark girl, not more than twenty-three or -four, fresh complexion and big dark eyes, a nice figure in a bare-shouldered yellow sundress. "And—and she didn't know many people—she—"

"Just tell us about that, Mrs. Scott," said Piggott persuasively.

"About, say, your mother's routine. She worked at this shop in Hollywood—"

"That's right. Daddy left her some stock, but not an awful lot to live on, the way prices—well, she could live on it but she was—she was still well and she liked to be busy, she liked the job— What? I don't know about Mrs. Elsberry, she owns the shop, Mother just said she was nice—I think she knew the other woman there better, Mrs. Weems."

"Weems?"

"Yes, it's a funny name, but she was about Mother's age and they were friendly. Just casual, I guess. Well, Mother'd be at the shop nine to five every day, and then she'd—well, go home. The apartment. I—we didn't get in to see her often, I was sorry, but living up here—I didn't think, I guess, when we moved up here. It's nearer for Gavin to drive to work. But he gets some overtime, and on Sunday there's the yard to take care of—and Mother didn't drive, you know. Ab-about once a month or so we'd try to drive in, take her to dinner or—but with the baby—" She blinked wetly at them. "Oh, I knew she was lonely—I should have tried to make time, see her oftener—"

"It's easy to blame yourself after something like this happens, Mrs. Scott," said Landers.

"But I should have! Daddy's been dead four years—they used to go out a lot, you see. They liked the theater, and dancing sometimes, and nice restaurants—of course there was more money then too, for things like that. I didn't *think,* and I should have—how lonely it was for her, with me married to Gavin and away up here— Of course there were people, other couples, they'd known, but a woman alone doesn't get invited out much, and with her not driving—"

"Mrs. Scott, did your mother wear a ring on her right hand usually?"

"Why, yes. Her big diamond. Daddy gave it to her on their twentieth anniversary. Describe— Well, it's got quite a big diamond in the middle, a little over a carat, I think, and two smaller ones each side. It's yellow gold, fourteen karat. I wouldn't know what it'd be worth, why, is it— It's *gone?* Well, that's what I said—a burglar breaking in and—"

"Maybe and maybe not," said Landers.

There was also, of course, the gardener—Sam Oliver on Bonsallo Avenue. Fired by Mrs. Harlow last week. Things came along in a spate sometimes; they'd get to Sam Oliver eventually.

Today they were looking for leads to the X who had strangled the children. They didn't find any. Except for the very nebulous white car parked briefly alongside that empty lot. Nobody they talked to had seen anything to indicate a lead. It might have been a ghost who had taken the Hildebrand children away and strangled them. But the Homicide men didn't believe in that kind of ghost, and they went on asking their questions doggedly.

They were, of course, a man short, because Palliser was still up there in the wilds.

Marge Leatherhead at Barney's place didn't remember if Tim Brodie had been in or not. "You don't notice faces unless they're people you know," she said. Barney's place was on a secondary road about eighteen miles out of town, and most of the people coming in were locals. She couldn't say one way or the other about Tim.

He said he was sure this was the place, all right. He remembered her, the redhaired waitress. He thought he'd started down this same road, after they'd had the hamburgers, but then he'd got lost. . . . "See, I was lookin' for some sign, tell me where we was, reason I didn't wake up to what Steve was up to right off—him and Wilma was in the back seat—till Wilma yelled. I think I turned off somewhere, off that road, before—it sort of curved and I thought it was the same road but awhile later it's narrower and, you know, not a main drag, so—"

Palliser and Roudebush sighed. Unusually for August, it was overcast and gray today, the sky even promising showers; once in a long while Southern California got showers in August; up here, this much farther north, it wouldn't be as unusual. They

167

were now driving slowly along a narrow country blacktop road with wild land on one side and a fine crop of sugar beets in the fields on the other, and Clearwater asked patiently, "This look familiar?"

"Well, kinda," said Brodie, "but, gee, a lot of places around here look the same. Just fields, and empty land, and trees and road. It mighta been this road—but before I had the fight with Steve I'd turned back on a better road, you know—a cement road."

"Right or left?"

Brodie thought and finally decided. "Left."

"Take the next cutoff toward Caliente," said Sheriff Roudebush. "We're showing you a lot of country, Sergeant."

"And I've got to agree with Tim," said Palliser. "It all looks an awful lot alike, Sheriff."

Before they got to the little town of Caliente it began to rain in a halfhearted sort of way. Roudebush parked on the one main street and said, "Jim, you can drive awhile." He got into the back seat with Brodie. "You go through any towns after you left Bakersfield?"

"No, sir. No, I'm sure of that. I got off the main road some way, I was lookin' for some sign to say where I was, and then I found one some better but still not a main drag—"

Roudebush grunted and opened the map, passing it over the seat to Palliser. There were plenty of little towns around Bakersfield, some on the main highway, some not; and enough secondary roads wandering around.

"Damn it, it's annoying, but you can't blame him," said Palliser, and looking out at the dispirited gray landscape added, "A lot of places we've tried do look the hell of a lot alike—to anybody there just once."

"Granted," said Roudebush. "Jim, head southwest out of town and let's try that secondary road toward Arvin. There's a blacktop cuts into it somewhere, past the Youngblood ranch, I think."

With a martyred sigh Clearwater started the engine.

"But, gee, it all looks different in the rain," said Brodie. "It was a nice sunny day last Sunday—I wouldn't say I *would* know the place, all gray and foggy—"

"Now, Jim," said Roudebush, "that kind of language I don't like."

"That's a pity, Sheriff," said Palliser. "I could think of something even stronger."

The legwork, on a thing like the Hildebrand case, took time. Time and patience. They had to go back to find people not home the first time; they had to listen to a lot of irrelevant comment and speculation before they got answers. But by four o'clock on Friday Grace had covered his stint at that legwork, and ran out of doorbells to ring. He went back to thinking about the Harlow shooting.

He used the rest of the day to look at Sam Oliver, the gardener.

Sam Oliver he ran to earth at a gardening job in Hollywood, trudging back and forth behind a power mower. The pickup truck sat at the curb. He was a broad, very black man about thirty, and he eyed Grace belligerently and snarled at the badge.

"Fuzz!" he said, and spat. "What you want, pig?"

Grace, who had a well-developed sense of humor, reflected pleasedly on those enterprising cops in Inglewood—of course others elsewhere promoting it, it was spreading nationwide—who had had the inspiration to capitalize on that. It was, of course, the best way to neutralize the not-so-subtle attack, turn it into a joke. The T-shirts for off-duty wear, with the fat pink pig and *Pigs is Beautiful* legend; the cuff links with the handsome gold pig, the tie-clasps, and the watches with the pig in blue uniform, arms pointing the hour, and that very appropriate legend PRIDE INTEGRITY GUTS—Virginia had got him one for his birthday and he was, in fact, wearing it now. Make a joke of it, and more power to the inspired cops earning a little extra money on the side wholesaling all that. He touched the watch on his wrist, and he thought, *sticks and stones*— And that newer motto made even more sense, *pride integrity*—

"Now, Sam," he said gently, "just a few answers."

Oliver supplied them sullenly. Yeah, he had a lot of jobs

169

like that, come once a week, cut the lawn, weed the beds—an hour or so each place, twenty bucks a month. Maybe six, eight places a day, it added up. So it did. To, Grace reflected, a lot of drinking money—only Oliver wouldn't hold the jobs long if he showed up drunk.

He was truculent about Mrs. Harlow. "She didn't have no call to fire me! I'd had a few, sure, O.K., I had, that day. It was—lessee—it was a week ago Tuesday, I'm due their place about two but I—" He looked at Grace from under heavy brows. "I, uh, been to a li'l party, thass all. Over lunch. See, this pal o' mine, Eddy Starr, he—his woman just had a kid, he's like celebratin'. Invite ever'body drop in, have a drink, like. So all right—I wasn't exactly *drunk*, she hadn't no call—look down her nose at me like she's a queen or somethin', sayin' *disgraceful*— Listen, she's black too, ain't she? She got no call do that—"

"So, let's hear about last Monday, Sam," said Grace. So convenient, he thought, if you could put people into slots like that. Unfortunately, human nature—both the good and the bad about it—didn't fit into the slots. Colorwise or any other way.

"Jeez sake, I don't hafta tell you—Goddamn pig! What about las' Monday—"

Grace persevered and got answers. He went out to check them; and at ten past six he caught Mendoza just leaving the office and presented his findings.

"¿Cómo?" said Mendoza. "Now that sounds interesting, Jase." He put down his hat and sat down again. "Details, *por favor*."

"Some interesting details," said Grace. "Sam Oliver has a regular job cutting the lawn, weeding the flower beds, once a week on Mondays, at the Starks' house in Hollywood. Raeburn Way. He usually gets there about nine o'clock Monday mornings, is there about an hour. He then usually goes to the Petersens' house on Shadow Lawn Avenue, also Hollywood, from ten to eleven or so. Only last Monday he was late to the Petersens'. Didn't get there until around noon. Mrs. Petersen was sure, because it was the day he got paid, and she waited to give him his check—it delayed her shopping trip." Grace contemplated his cigarette.

"¡Qué mono!" said Mendoza. "Isn't that pretty."

"I kind of thought so. We might look at him a little closer, you think?"

"Such as does he have access to a Harrington and Richardson nine-shot .22? Yes. Yes, indeed," said Mendoza. "When you consider it, that is exactly the kind of irrational slight motive— On the other hand, there is the fact that it was Mrs. Harlow who fired him. The doctor wouldn't have been home."

"What?—oh," said Grace. "Oh."

"Whoever perpetrated the wholesale slaughter, it was at Harlow's office. The fact that Mrs. Harlow—and the baby—were there at the time was unplanned, fortuitous, and couldn't have been known to X beforehand. Sam Oliver, if he was nourishing a grudge, was doing so on Ann Harlow. If he got to feeling vengeful enough to go out with a gun, wouldn't it have been to the Harlow house, not the doctor's office?"

"I wonder," said Grace. "That kind—there is a kind of prejudice in reverse, can we call it. Resentment, on the part of the ones like Oliver, against the people like the Harlows—educated, successful people with the nice house and— I don't know. I just thought it was suggestive."

"In spades," said Mendoza. "I think we get a search warrant, just for fun, and look harder at Oliver. And this damned Hildebrand thing—just nothing showing. *Nada absolutamente*. You would think—in broad daylight—"

"So you would," said Grace. "And we've covered about every place in both neighborhoods."

"Tomorrow—"

But as they started for the door—Sergeant Lake already departed, this phone recirculated to the desk downstairs until the night watch came on—Landers and Piggott erupted through it, and Landers said, "Oh, you're still here—and you'll never *believe* this one, *I* don't believe it—but it came up, and we were interested enough to go look, and—"

"Satan converting whom he can," said Piggott. "The things we see. And that poor innocent daughter in for quite a shock."

They had been deflected off the Fleming case when they

checked back with the office, by a hit-run out on Beverly, and then a call from a pigeon on that Al Koonz. The A.P.B. out on Koonz hadn't turned up a smell yet. The pigeon said he was at a pool hall on Third Street right now, so Piggott and Landers went to pick him up. He made a little trouble, and Landers was now sporting the beginning of a fine shiner. They'd brought him in and questioned him, and he had reluctantly agreed that he had loaned Eddy Hobart the gun—well, he knew he wasn't supposed to have a gun, on P.A., but this other pal of his had been holding it for him, and—

They had got his statement after lunch, and then taken him over to the jail on Alameda. He'd go right back to Quentin to finish out his sentence, but in the meantime of course there was that gun, the beat-up old Colt. So they had gone looking for Koonz's other pal, whose name also appeared in their records, and finally found him in the tenth bar they'd tried within a radius of his rented room. They had got the Colt. Landers had typed a report on all that; it was a minor charge, but a charge all the same and had to be followed up. And then they had gone back to the apartment building where Mrs. Fleming had lived.

"There were a few tenants who hadn't been questioned yet, you know," said Landers. (He'd enjoy telling Phil about this—he glanced at his watch—have to hurry, shower and shave again before picking her up; but she'd understand if he was late. A fellow officer—the endless human nature they ran into, she'd laugh over this one.) "We talked to this Mrs. McCloskey just an hour ago—I swear to God, *people!* The daughter gave us the clue, if we'd been bright enough to pick it up. Mama must have been lonely. But I swear, you'd think anybody would have better sense. The people where she worked, the gift shop, didn't know her well—said, ordinary nice woman, to work and home, the quiet life—"

"Until we came to Mrs. McCloskey," said Piggott. "And there'll be some more legwork tomorrow—"

"*¡Dios me libre!*" said Mendoza. "What showed?"

Mrs. McCloskey lived in the apartment across from the manageress, on the ground floor. She hadn't been home when detectives came before, questioning tenants. She apologized; she was a masseuse, taking private appointments, and her hours were irregular. She was a massive female with large square hands and a contralto voice and piercing dark eyes, and on her well-developed bosom hung a large gold cross and on her living-room wall a large religious painting.

"I didn't know her at all," she told Landers and Piggott.

"Even by sight?"

"Oh, by sight—I knew who she was, of course, that she lived upstairs."

"Did you ever see her with another person? Ever exchange any words with her, hello, nice day, like that?"

"Not at all," said Mrs. McCloskey regally. "Of course I don't like to say anything derogatory about anybody—I don't suppose she deserved to be *murdered*—and a murder, *here*—a nice quiet place, I've lived here for nineteen years and never the whisper of any scandal—and I would have thought that the manageress would be more particular whom she rented to, but I expect the woman put up a ladylike front—"

"What do you—Mrs. Fleming?" asked Landers.

"Oh, yes. She *drank*, you know. I had encountered her just a few times when I had late appointments—coming in. Quite obviously—er—under the influence. Just last week I came in about twelve-thirty and she was in the lobby, positively *reeling*, and wearing pink trousers—I was intending to speak to the manageress—"

## 12

"You don't mean it?" said Phil. "The respectable widow?"

"And what a shock it's going to be to her daughter," said Landers. "We only went to one place asking—Matt was going out on it again—but they knew her. We figured as she didn't drive, and wasn't going out *with* anybody apparently, it'd be the nearest bars up on Echo Park or Sunset, and the only one we tried, they knew her. We'd found some snapshots in the apartment, manageress pointed out one of her—"

"But why all of a sudden?" said Phil, wrinkling her freckled nose.

"She was lonely, we can have a guess," said Landers, swallowing Scotch and water. It wasn't beginning to cool off much, but it was nice out here on the terrace at Frascati's, Phil across from him at one of the patio tables. "Didn't drive, didn't get invited out much, it wasn't an interesting job. And we can guess too, a woman who didn't get much out of reading, out of watching TV. Liked people around—and probably found the few highballs cheered her up. You can read it. But—"

"Poor thing," said Phil, looking at the last of her martini. "But also stupid."

"Which is also human nature. But isn't it somewhere in the Bible, *man not meant to live alone—*"

Phil glanced sideways at him; his very darling—but intensely practical—Phil who worked the computer down in R. and I. and liked her job—and said, "You're hinting again, Tom."

"Well, damn it—"

She laughed. "Never mind. As I told you, you're passing tests. You don't use cologne, for one thing—I detest cologne on men. And you remember which jokes you've told me, which I think must be one of the more important attributes in a husband."

"You'll end up like Mrs. Fleming. Lonely spinster taking to drink because you were too damn particular." But looking at her neat blonde head and the spattering of freckles across her nose, he knew he wouldn't want Phil any other way: she was herself.

Piggott called Prudence and said he'd be a little late; but they hadn't been going out anywhere so it didn't matter. Prudence lived with her mother, whom Piggott liked, in Hollywood; and it was with the comfortable expectation of seeing them presently —his soon-to-be real family—that Piggott, that strict teetotaler, went into the Pink Pussycat Bar and Grill on Sunset Boulevard at eight-thirty.

"Have you ever seen this woman in here?" he asked the bartender, bringing out the badge and the snapshot at once. It was a good clear snapshot, showing Rhoda Fleming fullface, and seeing it at first Piggott had thought about Mendoza's deductions. The lieutenant did feel things. She hadn't looked her age, and she'd been a nice-looking woman, attractive. You could see that left alone, the daughter married, husband dead, she'd been lonely. And maybe, with the advent of the grandchild, resenting the implication that life was all over for her, any fun to life. But—

"Her?" The bartender looked at the snapshot, holding it to the light. "Yeah, I think I have, a couple times. No, I don't know her name, why? What? No, I couldn't say if she was with anybody, but I think I seen her here. You might ask Madge—" He beckoned the cocktail waitress over. "Cops. Askin' about this dame."

The waitress, a buxom blonde, looked at the snapshot and said, "Oh, *her*." She looked at Piggott. "You a cop? What's she done?"

"She's dead," said Piggott.

"Dead! Well, I'll be— She is? She looked healthy enough—

Well, I'll be darned. She was one of the loners—I felt sorry for her, sort of. See, she wouldn't come in here"—this was the bar, dark and gloomy, redolent of whiskey and this early very quiet —"she came in the lounge." Through a door opposite the bar, and at right angles to it, was the neon sign, *Cocktail Lounge.* "It looks nicer for a woman alone, you can see."

"How often did she come in, Miss—"

"Mrs. Mrs. Martino—this big punk's my old man." She indicated the bartender, who looked sheepish and flattered at once; he'd be a good fifteen years older than she was. "Well, lately she'd been coming in almost every night. A loner like I say. The first times she came in—oh, about a year ago, I'd say—she'd order a club sandwich or something, like she really wanted a snack, but lately she didn't bother. She came in for the drinks and company. I'd have a guess maybe she'd been other places around, but she came here mostly because we've got a piano player, and customers—you know—sort of socialize. Get talking to each other, not just the ones they came with."

Which was just about how Landers had figured. But you'd have thought, thought Piggott, that the woman could have found some decent outlet for loneliness in joining a church, or doing charity work, or— But human nature was always in the picture. And the devil's busy hands.

"When was she in last?"

Madge reflected. "She hasn't been in the last few nights, I missed her—casual like the way you do. Her being pretty regular. It was either Saturday or—no, it was Sunday, I remember for sure because we had a nut in, I remember seeing her laughin' with some of the others when the nut raised the row. One of these squares—I'd never seen him before."

"A nut?" said Piggott, thinking about Rhoda Fleming beaten and probably strangled.

"Yeah. A creep. He made a big fuss on account of Jerry—he's the piano player—did a swing job on some old hymn, 'Rock of Ages,' something—the nut said it was sacrilegious, and on Sunday too, and he stamped out without payin'." She shrugged.

176

Piggott reminded himself that a good detective was supposed to remain objective. "Did she ever pick up anybody in here?"

"No," she said hurriedly. "Not like what you mean. Like I say, the customers get friendly, talking, sometimes. If they want to introduce themselves to each other, what's it matter? Their business. I can't say I ever saw her leave with anybody, no."

"Well, thanks," said Piggott. He had been to four other places within three blocks; this one seemed to have been her favorite hangout. "You have many regulars coming in? Most nights, a few nights a week?"

"Some," she said reluctantly. "You cops goin' to be hangin' round bothering customers? They couldn't tell you nothing—"

"Well, that we don't know until we ask, do we?" said Piggott mildly.

Duty done, he set off for Hollywood and Prudence.

Mendoza had just sat down and opened Grimm, at seven o'clock, when everything loose in the house began rattling, the windowpanes clattered in their frames, the floor tilted and slithered uneasily, and the house shook convulsively. There was a low rumble, the furniture moved, and the floor seemed to rise in little rolling waves. Alison tottered to the doorway, obeying one of the few rules there are about earthquakes. Sixty seconds, and everything stopped and was solid again.

"*¡Caramba!*" said Mendoza. "That was nearly as big as the first one."

"About five on the scale, I'd say," said Alison, letting go of the doorpost. "Are you all right, Máiri? I wonder if we lost any china this time—"

"And I wouldna have set foot in a thousand miles o' the place did I know about the earthquakes—guidness to *mercy*—Janet bein' here or no, my own sister not having the guid sense, comin' to such a place—" Mrs. MacTaggart, accustomed to the uncompromising solidity of the Scottish Highlands, did not like earthquakes. Alison hurried to reassure her.

The twins, on the other hand, much appreciated the novelty.

177

"Hooooo!" shouted Johnny, bouncing. "See-Saw Margery Daw! ¡*Bueno!* Do again!"

Terry squealed, "¡*La magia* make everything go to *danzar!*"

"Do again!" demanded Johnny.

"You flatter me, *hijo,*" said Mendoza. "I am not omniscient. If that's the word I want. I didn't do it."

Unfortunately he had no sooner said it than the walls shook and the floor rolled again in a milder aftershock. "See-Saw Margery Daw!" said the twins together, happily.

Alison came back and said, "What do you want to bet that ruined all our nice new cement in the drive? And you should see the china cabinet. Máiri's keening over it in Gaelic. We may lose her over this, Luis—her first one, and she doesn't like it at all."

"Heaven forbid."

"Do again!" said Johnny.

"Your father was not responsible," said Alison, and stopped, and added, "unless Detective Piggott is right and the Lord is warning of just destruction for past sins. You must have added considerably to the amount of sin piling up to earth's account, before you got domesticated."

"Insulting me in front of the offspring now—"

The picket with his sign warning of doom to come was leaning on a palm tree outside the entrance to the parking lot when Mendoza got to the office on Saturday morning. The desk sergeant said, "That was quite a shake last night."

"Did we lose any new windows? That'd be adding insult to injury."

"Not that I heard."

"Grateful for small favors," said Mendoza. Upstairs in Homicide Sergeant Farrell greeted him, sitting in for Lake, and asked him how he'd liked the shake last night. Quite something, Mendoza agreed, and went on into the detective office, where Hackett asked him the same thing.

"It enhanced my parental role," said Mendoza. "Johnny thinks I did it."

"Families," said Higgins. "You know, I think the kids actually enjoyed it—of course nothing got broken, but—and Mary saying, Fate."

But that earthquake was over and mercifully nobody could yet predict when another might occur, and there was business for Homicide to work. Mendoza phoned in a request for the search warrant on Sam Oliver's property, and listened to what Piggott had turned up at that bar. Landers, listening too, said, "Stake it out? Overtime? See if any of the regulars knew her, maybe saw her pick somebody up?"

"*Obvio.* Very possible you'll get a lead there. But I doubt very much whether it'd have been a pickup in the crude sense." Mendoza sat back and sent a stream of smoke ceilingward, reflectively. "She was a lady. It wasn't that old devil sex she was looking for so much as simple companionship—people around, friendly, talking to her. Unfortunately, of course, after she'd had a few drinks her judgment wouldn't be working so well, and it's possible she—mmh—accepted the offer of a ride home, something like that. Yes, stake it out and see what shows."

"And meanwhile, where do we go on Hildebrand?" asked Higgins. "As if I didn't know."

"Records," said Hackett. "We've done all the asking around both neighborhoods. Now we do some real legwork—collect all the known perverts in Records, go find them and lean on them."

"And I still think you'll be wasting your time," said Mendoza. "But it's the next thing to do. We have to go by the book."

Glasser phoned in just then to report sadly that the apartment garage had fallen on his car last night; he'd be late getting in. Earthquakes did unpredictable things. They offered commiseration to Glasser, who probably wouldn't collect insurance; earthquakes are regarded by insurance companies as Acts of God.

Hackett and Higgins, Landers and Piggott went off to start the routine on the perverts out of Records. Grace hung around waiting for that search warrant. Mendoza, after rumination, went down to the lot for the Ferrari and drove out to Elden Avenue to talk to the Hildebrand children's grandmother, Mrs. Pace. He hadn't seen her before.

He heard all over just what she'd told the Traffic men. She seemed to be a sensible, practical woman, grieved and incredulous now but in control of herself. When she said she'd checked on the children frequently he believed her. And he heard again how upset Alice had been over the divorce—"Not what she was brought up to, and I doubt she'll want to marry again, after such a bad experience with Henry—" But she couldn't think of anyone who would want to hurt Alice, the children—she looked at him in disbelief. Nobody but a *monster* would—

"*¿Para qué?*" said Mendoza to himself, getting back into the car. And he was the lieutenant—he was supposed to keep tabs on every piece of business, keep the strings separated. He went back to the office.

There, he found Jason Grace poring over Dr. Harlow's records. "Any hunches, Jase?"

"Nary a hunch. Ordinary patients—not a lunatic in the lot that shows." Grace put out his cigarette, getting up to drift aimlessly around the office, lighting another cigarette immediately. "Funny. We felt the big one, but nothing got broken. Last night, half the chinaware. Virginia was still moaning about it when I left."

"Mmh. So did we. And that damned crack in the drive—they just patched it up yesterday, and all the new cement came apart. My wife's—mmh—one-half Scots has come to the fore, and she's going to make the company do it over for free or else."

"Hot again. It's always hot when we get the quakes—" Grace's voice trailed off. After a little silence he said, "I might be asking you for a reference."

"*¿Qué ocurre?* Thinking of switching to an easier job?"

"Nope. We're sort of hoping we might get the Harlows' baby. Celia Ann. I've been prodding at the County Adoption people, and of course they'll look for blood relatives but what we heard of the Harlows' background— I don't think there'll be any trouble, we can show there aren't any. Keep your fingers crossed, anyhow."

"That'd be fine, Jase. Good luck on it. Only—it's a project to embark on. Hostages to fortune."

"They occur to a lot of people who don't really care one way or the other. I figure—"

"Oh, yes. That too. It suddenly occurs to me," said Mendoza, "that the time will inevitably come when my offspring will realize I'm not an all-powerful godlike personage causing earthquakes. A pity. However—"

"Here's that warrant you asked for, Lieutenant," said Farrell, looking in.

"Ah. So now we do some work, Jase."

Glasser trudged in as they were leaving and said dispiritedly the whole damn front end of his Ford had been demolished, he probably wouldn't get any insurance, and the agency said he'd better junk it. "Act of God!" he said. "What reason has God got to be mean to me? I try to live a reasonably useful life. At least it was paid for. But why should God go out of His way to wreck my Ford?"

"Take the larger view, Henry," said Grace. "Rain falling on the just and unjust. And there were all those bodies out in the valley—"

"Oh, my God, I know, it could have been a lot worse. But it's annoying. Have you got any jobs for me?"

"You can come along and help execute a search warrant."

Sam Oliver wasn't at home at the cheap rented house on Bonsallo Avenue. His wife, a silent, meek-looking woman, looked at the warrant, at cops on the doorstep, and said Sam wouldn't like it. But she let them in. She looked frightened to death, but she struck them all as a woman who'd be frightened of a lot of things, including cops—maybe of Sam Oliver too. There was a solemn brown little girl about three, with her hair in pigtails and red ribbons, and a baby about six months old.

The house was old, and it needed paint inside and out, and plumbing repairs, and one of the front windows was cracked, but it was clean enough if untidy. Not much furniture, and that old and shaky. Not many clothes in the bedroom closet. Not much food in the old refrigerator.

After a once-over-lightly, they asked her some questions. She was too frightened of Authority to try to lie; she answered in a faint voice. No, her husband didn't have no gun. She'd never seen him with a gun.

"He earns pretty good money, doesn't he?" asked Grace.

"I dunno," she said, "sir. I dunno how much, he don't tell me." They knew: he had somewhere around thirty jobs, gardening for people up in Hollywood, an hour or two once a week each place, and on the average he got twenty a month for each job, some of the jobs paying thirty or more. Grace told her that, and she was silent.

"He doesn't give you much of it to make do with?" She shook her head. "What does he do with it?" She shook her head again, and then she gave a little gasp and put a hand to her mouth.

"I dasn't—he knock me around, I complain any—but he gamble away ennathing he get his hands on—" And she shut up, looking terrified.

No gun in the house. She said he'd likely be home at noon, so Grace and Glasser came back then and found him there, and searched the pickup. No gun.

Oliver was furious and frightened. He started out blustering. "What call you got, come here look at all my stuff? You Goddamn pigs—"

"All right, Sam," said Grace. They sat him down in the bare living room. "Last Monday morning, you didn't show at the Petersens' when you usually did. Where were you between ten A.M. and noon last Monday?"

"Why I tell you that, big man?"

"Because I'm asking, Sam," said Grace coldly. "Have you ever owned a gun?"

"A g— No, I never. What for I need a gun? I don' go shootin' people like the damn fuzz do—"

Both the Homicide men thought rather tiredly of all the red tape, the formal hearing that had to be held every time an LAPD man fired off a gun on duty. The hearing to determine whether

182

it had been justifiable to do so. But Sam Oliver wouldn't know about that. "Where were you?" asked Grace again.

"Why? Bust in here, you pigs, an' try to—"

"Because last Monday morning, Sam, three people were shot to death, and two of them were people you didn't like, and we've been wondering if it was you shot them," said Grace. "Was it you?"

"Me? Shoot— Who you talkin' about? What the hell you mean, people I—"

"Dr. Harlow and his wife—you don't look at the papers, Sam?"

Suddenly Oliver went gray with fright. "A *murder?* You think I done a *murder?* That guy, that dame that— Oh, man, you way off base—I wouldn't do no— What did you say, what time?"

"Ten A.M. to noon, Sam. Last Monday."

"Oh. Oh. I was—well, it was a hot day, I just—sorta knocked off after my first job, 'at day," said Oliver nervously. "I just— well, I just went down this place on Vermont, the Criss-Cross Club, see. Sat around 'n' had a few beers, is all. I guess the bar-keep could say I was there O.K. Oh, man, you way off— Me, a murder—you go ask, he'll say I was there—"

And how much that was worth they'd guess after they'd checked the alibi. He could have got rid of the gun.

They went up to Federico's for lunch and met Mendoza and Hackett just going in. Hackett was complaining about the tedious routine: but it usually did get them where they wanted to go. Sometimes it didn't.

After lunch they checked back with the office, and a new call had come in: probable suicide, a rooming house over by the yards. Glasser went out on it and Grace roped Landers in. They drove up to the Criss-Cross Club on South Vermont. Landers was as pleased to get out of the other routine, hunting the perverts. Once the computer had efficiently ground out the list of perverts from their records, no excuse for a Homicide man to stay down there ogling little blonde Phil O'Neill, of course.

"Let's have a look before we ask questions," said Grace.

"Sure." They went in. It was an old building in a block of

183

solid buildings, and a shabby place inside, smelling of whiskey and perspiration and dust. They weren't six feet inside the door when a slim white-aproned man stepped up to bar them. "I'm sorry, sir," he said softly, "we don't serve whites here."

Grace looked amused. "So I'll see you back at the car, Tom."

Landers went back to the car, reflecting on the peculiar notions some people had about the so-called racists. He'd smoked two cigarettes when Grace came up and slid behind the wheel. "You disadvantaged Caucasians," he said, and Landers laughed, and asked him what the setup looked like. "You want to have a bet?"

"I'm saving my money," said Landers, "hoping to get married."

"Well, I might make a little bet with you that there's the game going in the back room of that place. With the password to get let in. And maybe the pro gamblers holding the bank."

"Oh, really?" said Landers, surprised. "Oh, I see. Sam Oliver—"

"The gambling man. I think we'd better tell University division about it and see if they'd like to look into it."

"I think so too." They drove down to that precinct house and saw a Sergeant Adamski, who was mildly interested. "And what's Central's interest in a South Vermont bar for colored only?"

"We're trying," said Grace plaintively, "to check an alibi."

"Hope springs eternal," said Adamski.

"For a murder."

"Well, we'll let you know what transpires."

Even as Grace had guessed, University division broke up the illegal gambling in the back room of the Criss-Cross Club. The owner, the bartender, and four patrons swore in a body that Sam Oliver had been sitting in a crap game last Monday morning from about nine-forty to noon. The joker was that all of them had minor pedigrees and were friends of Sam's, more or less.

"On the other hand, Jase," said Mendoza, "they came out with the times voluntarily."

"So they did. We didn't have a tail on Oliver. He could have seen them before the raid."

"Being psychic and knowing which individuals the unexpected raid would nab? *Pues no.*"

"Well, he could have told the barkeep, the owner."

"It could be. But I don't think we've got there yet, on the Harlows." Mendoza looked at Dr. Harlow's records, in their neat file boxes, stacked on one side of his desk, and sighed. "I had another small idea—"

This floor was still without windows, and it was still hot; the thermometer on Palliser's desk said it was ninety-eight today.

Palliser phoned Mendoza just before six o'clock. "This God-damned thing is a waste of time," he said, "and you can pass that on to Goldberg. There isn't any body. Brodie dreamed it. We've driven hundreds of miles all round every road there is up here, and we haven't found a damned thing. Even the sheriff is getting annoyed, and the deputies are fit to be tied. I never saw so much wild land in my life, and I'm homesick for town—earthquakes and all. Hear you had another one, by the way."

"Oh, quite a respectable one," said Mendoza. "You're shutting down the hunt?"

"Well, damn it, Brodie sounds so positive," said Palliser. "He's had experience butchering, he says, and he knows the guy was dead. And I am bound to say that this wild country looks an awful lot alike, wherever you go—I can see where he'd be confused. The sheriff says, give it another day. It's stopped raining, at least."

"So you'll be home Monday? With Brodie for Goldberg to charge with petty theft?"

"I suppose. That's the program now, unless of course we do find a body."

"Always a possibility. A lot of inaccessible empty space up there where a body could lie for years."

"You can say it again," said Palliser. "Have we got our windows back yet?"

"No windows. I'd take no bets," said Mendoza, "that they get replaced and then we have another one to knock them all out again."

"Look," said Palliser, "I'm the one feeling pessimistic. And I'll put in a voucher for this call—official business—I'm running out of money. You might call Robin and tell her."

"I'll do that. Good luck—you may hit pay dirt yet."

"No bets," said Palliser grumpily.

Mendoza cocked his head at the phone. Palliser having a spat with his wife? Pity. Unusual for Palliser, that even-tempered man. Mendoza got up, took down his hat, and started home for Alison and their assorted livestock.

Landers and Piggott, doing the overtime, staked out the Pink Pussycat that night. Landers could order a highball and nurse it along indefinitely—places like this got about fifty highballs out of a fifth anyway; but Piggott the teetotaler sat over a cup of coffee.

They had asked Madge Martino to point out the regular patrons to them, and reluctantly she agreed. Her husband owned this place, and a liquor license cost in California.

On Saturday night, probably most of the regulars would be in. And most of the people, regulars or not, patronizing this place would be ordinary people, neighborhood people, who'd buy two or three drinks, listening to the piano player. Not drunks; not bums.

Madge pointed out a dozen people, mostly couples, a few men alone, and they talked to them, showing the badges, asking the questions, showing the snapshot of Rhoda Fleming. Most of the people remembered her vaguely. Recognized her as another regular in here. Some of them had talked with her casually —about the piano player, about the weather, about the head-lines—last week, about the earthquake. But nobody remembered her being with any particular man, or picking up a man, until they came to Mr. and Mrs. Orlando Frazier, just as they'd been thinking of knocking off for the night, at ten-thirty.

Mr. and Mrs. Frazier operated a dry-cleaning shop a couple of blocks away, lived in an apartment over it. They were a self-

186

satisfied, very ordinary couple in their thirties, lacking much imagination, but they were honest people willing to help out the cops, and they looked at the snapshot and said, Why, yes, they'd seen her here.

"Last Sunday night?" asked Landers. The autopsy report had come in this morning; Rhoda Fleming had been beaten and strangled, but—not raped. Time of death estimated to be between six A.M. last Sunday and six A.M. Monday. The length of time before the body was found, Dr. Bainbridge couldn't be more specific.

"Sunday—yeah, we were here Sunday. And Saturday. There was a little fuss when this nut—" They heard all about that, the piano player playing fast and loose with "Rock of Ages," and Landers asked if Mrs. Fleming had been here then.

"We didn't know her name. That woman. Yes, she was. With anybody? Well, about then—it was when that guy came in, wasn't it, May? That blond guy?"

"About then," she agreed. "He'd been in a couple of nights before too. But I guess it was that night—Sunday—this woman you're asking about, she sort of hung around with him."

"Picked him up?" asked Landers.

"Oh, well, I wouldn't like to say that," said plump blonde May uncomfortably. "I mean, this is a respectable place. But she was always alone, it looked like, and she'd talk to different people— well, I couldn't say about that, if she always bought her own drinks, I wouldn't know. We never saw her exactly *drunk*—just, you know, happy. But that night, she got talking with this fellow, and I know they were at the same table quite awhile—"

Landers and Piggott exchanged glances. "Any idea who he is? A regular in here? Could you describe him for us?"

They looked at each other—nice honest rather dull citizens, willing to help but inarticulate. "No, I hadn't seen him in here before last week. He was, well, maybe about thirty," said Frazier. "Blond like I said. About, oh, five-ten or six feet, not fat but— Well, he had on slacks, a sports shirt, blue—" He looked at his wife.

"You could ask the piano player," she said brightly. "He knew him—he went up and talked to him between numbers, I mean like they were friends, not asking for a number or like that—"

They talked to the piano player after he'd finished a mean rendition of "Rhapsody in Blue." His name was Jerry Hoffman; he was about thirty, with an engaging pug-dog face and bright blue eyes and a crooked smile. "Cops?" he said, looking at the badges. "What'd I do?"

They asked him about the blond fellow. About Rhoda Fleming. He shrugged. "The female loners coming in—any place like this—I wouldn't know. I'm hired to play the box. Period. What? A blond— Last Sunday night?"

"And a couple of nights before," said Landers. "About five-ten, six feet, sports clothes, around thirty—"

"Hey," said Hoffman, "hey. You don't mean Howie?"

"I don't know. Who's Howie?"

"Howie Engel. He's a mean man on a horn—or used to be. Sax mostly. We played in a combo together once, a couple of years back. Howie's O.K., only—"

"What?" said Piggott as Hoffman paused.

"Well, he's got the little problem," said Hoffman with a grimace. "Me, I may not be so smart but I'm smarter than that. If you get me. To get hooked."

"On what? Just the Mary Jane?"

Hoffman shrugged. "I wouldn't know. To start, I guess. Maybe the hard stuff later. I hadn't seen him since he got fired off that job—goofing off, you know, not showing up. He came in here last week, first time I've seen him since. I greet him—a guy I knew—he's a good musician if he hadn't been damn fool enough to get the habit. He showed up a few nights, that's all. I didn't have much talk with him, why should I?"

"Last Sunday night," said Landers, "did you notice him with this woman?"

"Well, yeah, I did," said Hoffman. "That's right. I don't know if she made a play for him or the other way—but she's no chicken if she wasn't bad-looking, I'd guess it was her went after

188

him. They were at the same table awhile. No, I got no idea where he's living, how should I? He never said about a job, no."

But that was a strong lead, of course.

"Has he been back here since Sunday?"

Hoffman said, "Sure. Tuesday and just last night, he was here. Over a couple drinks, about an hour. Sure, alone."

So, go on staking out the Pink Pussycat. Wait for Engel, hopefully, to show.

On Sunday they went on looking for the perverts out of Records, fetching them in when they could find them. Mendoza said, a waste of time.

"You saw a vision in your crystal ball," said Hackett.

"Just a feeling," said Mendoza obscurely. "Just a little feeling, Arturo."

And at five-fifty on Sunday afternoon, Palliser called. From the wilds. "We've found the damned body," he said. "We'll be busy on it awhile. Well, I don't know when I'll be back. But you can tell Goldberg to send the girl up. I may get back tomorrow—"

# 13

They had found the body within half an hour of the time Palliser and the sheriff had decided to quit looking. When Tim Brodie suddenly exclaimed from the back seat, "Hey, this is it! That's the place right there—" They looked at him, and at each other. Forbear put his foot on the brake resignedly.

"We've been past this point several times, Brodie," said Sheriff Roudebush. "If this is it, why didn't you—"

"Well, this is all strange country to me, but just all of a sudden I reckanized that tree, the shape of it—it's right down the shoulder, behind some bushes—"

Surprisingly, it was. The week-old corpse of a young man in old and dirty clothes, a canvas flight bag beside it. "I didn't take his stuff," said Brodie. "I was just so *surprised,* find he's dead—"

They'd let the coroner decide how. Palliser rode back to town with the deputy and called Mendoza while they routed out the coroner and an ambulance. They couldn't do much out there. The coroner said, skull-fracture, and pointed out several rocks that could have been responsible, up on the road where Tim said they'd had the fight.

There was nothing in the flight bag or on the corpse to provide a name for him, and they coaxed Tim patiently to remember—had he said his last name, where he was from? They drew blank. He'd just said Steve—and he was heading for L.A., said Tim. They took his fingerprints for relaying to Washington.

Palliser hung around on Monday until an LAPD policewoman arrived with Wilma Schultz. A couple of reporters, looking for

190

rural news, showed up and Wilma asked if this would be in the papers. "Gee, my dad don't know where we went, but if he sees about it in the papers and comes down here—he don't like Tim nohow—" It would penetrate her mind later that they'd be safe from Papa in jail.

The LAPD car which had ferried them up here was, of course, back in L.A. now. Palliser consulted a bus schedule and found he could get a bus at three-fifty which would get him into L.A. by eight-fifteen, with stops along the way. The sheriff thanked him, shaking hands, and Palliser said he didn't know what for. He felt he'd wasted the last three days.

He called Roberta to tell her when he'd be home. "Good," she said. "I've missed you, darling. And you won't have a chance for dinner—you'll be starving. I'll have something waiting. Oh, John—"

"Mmhm?"

"You'll be relieved to know you aren't going to have a working wife."

"What?"

"Well, no. A little joke on me. I'll have to call the principal and explain. The fact is," said Roberta, sounding amused and pleased and still a little surprised, "I'd been wondering, the day you left—and I saw the doctor, and he's just confirmed it this afternoon—I'm pregnant. So, no working wife—"

Palliser began to laugh. He laughed so hard he couldn't get out a word, and he hung up still laughing.

Monday morning, and the routine still going on. The routine often broke cases, but in a thing like the Hildebrand kill it was largely futile. The perverts were loners: haul them in out of Records, they could seldom produce an alibi, and that left it all still up in the air.

The Pink Pussycat was closed on Mondays, so Landers and Piggott would start staking it out, hoping Howie Engel would show, tomorrow night.

"And where the hell to go on Harlow?" said Hackett in exasperation. "Nothing solid on it in a week, and now no leads at all. A lunatic shooting three people—"

"But not quite at random," said Mendoza. "He knew who he was shooting at, Art."

"I'm not even sure of that now. It could have been very much at random for all we know. And don't say to me, he climbed the stairs. There he was on the second floor, just by chance, when the urge hit him—he goes in the nearest door and bang."

Mendoza said, "No. I know it can happen that way, but it didn't here. Those records—damn it, there's something trying to get through to me about those records—" He shook his head. "Wait for it."

They spent Monday morning looking up the known perverts. It was frustrating; they didn't find half of them, moved away or away from home, and those they found gave them nothing solid at all. And Mendoza, looking at a shot glass of rye at Federico's at a quarter to one, was still saying it was a waste of time.

"If he'd just suggest where else to look," said Hackett to Higgins, "he might be some use." The black eye had faded by now and he looked less sinister.

"I just have the feeling—impossible as it seems—" Mendoza swallowed rye and looked at Landers as he came up to join them. "What have you got?"

"Nothing!" said Landers. "What should I have? There was a hit-run called in just as we got back, Matt went out on it, said he'd pick up lunch later. Just the usual—a kid running into the street after a ball." Mendoza asked abstractly if there was any make on the car, and Landers just looked at him.

"It must be his age," said Hackett.

After lunch, Mendoza went back to the windowless office, where it was still very hot, and fidgeted around smoking too much. Lake, coming in with the autopsy report on the Hildebrand children, found him standing in front of a window and told him for God's sake to get away from there. "What with all these aftershocks—" The Lakes lived in the valley, but fortunately not in the area where the big one had hit; they'd lost part of a

192

fence and a raised flower bed. But Lake, native Californian though he was, was nervous about earthquakes.

The autopsy report, of course, gave them nothing new. The lab report, arriving a little later, added up to nothing.

Hackett and Higgins had just come back with another known pervert out on P.A. when Sergeant Lake looked in and said, "Two agitated female citizens, with information. So they say. A Mrs. Fanchon and a Mrs. Burnett."

"So, shove them in," said Mendoza. "Information we can always use."

"Fanchon? I saw them," said Higgins. "They live in the house that backs up to Mrs. Pace's, on the next street. The back yards are right together. I wonder—"

Mendoza lit a cigarette. "So, sit in on it. So do I."

Both the women were excited. The younger one burst out, seeing Higgins, "Oh, I told you—you came to ask if we'd seen anything and we hadn't, but I told you about Mother leaving that day to visit Auntie in San Diego—excuse me, this is my mother, Mrs. Burnett, you said Sergeant—"

"Higgins. Lieutenant Mendoza. Sergeant Hackett."

"—And she did see something! She just got home an hour ago, and when I told her—and asked—so we came right away, because such an awful—"

"I haven't had my hat off," said Mrs. Burnett, who was a tall grenadier of a woman with a hawk's nose and shrewd eyes. "When Della told me—my heavens above, two babies like that— I couldn't believe it could be him, not that we know them but they've lived there years—they used to have a dog that wandered, he'd come looking for it—"

"Who?" asked Hackett and Higgins together.

"I didn't think anything about it at the time," said Mrs. Burnett, "because I know he knows Alice. We know the children, of course—often see them in the back yard. And I was just leaving to get the bus downtown, that afternoon, when I saw him with the Hildebrand children, walking down the street. Burton Fowler."

.   .   .

He worked for the telephone company as a lineman; but today was his day off. He lived with his mother on Elden Avenue a block or so up from the Pace house.

When they got there, they found Mrs. Pace standing on the front porch talking with fat, gray-haired Mrs. Fowler. "Oh," she said, looking at the two big men, the slender dapper Mendoza between them, "were you looking for me? Something else you wanted to— Alice is at work. They told us—I just came up to tell Mrs. Fowler, she's an old friend, you see—we can arrange for the—the funeral now. I—"

"Mrs. Fowler," said Mendoza, "is your son Burton at home?"

"Why, yes. It's his day off. Why? Are you *detectives?* What—"

"We'd like to talk to him," said Hackett easily. Ask him to come in for questioning, all polite. And didn't their Luis have the hunches indeed—but, thought Hackett, why? Why the hell? A neighborhood friend—a man who'd asked Alice Hildebrand to marry him. Just suddenly gone off his rocker in that direction? He didn't have any record at all; they had looked.

Both the women were staring at them. "Burt?" said Mrs. Fowler. "Why, what on earth do you think he could know about this terrible— Well, of course if you think he can tell you anything, I'll— He's just watching an old movie on TV—" She turned back into the house.

"Why do you think Burt knows anything about this monster?" asked Mrs. Pace curiously. They didn't answer her. But monsters, thought Hackett, were in the mind; anybody might say, a monster, doing such a thing. And never thinking that the monster (maybe the primitive monster in most men, buried deep, but with most deep enough) lived next door to somebody, watched TV like other people, worked a job like other people . . . looking like the monster only after he was identified and caught.

He was, coming up to the screen door with his mother, not looking like a monster at all. He wasn't handsome, he wasn't ugly, he was—colorless. A neat sandy young man about Alice Hildebrand's age, clean-shaven, with pale-blue eyes. He came out to the porch, beside the detectives, and looked at them in

194

silence as they looked at him. His ears stuck out a little; he looked more shy and awkward than anything else.

"Fowler—" began Mendoza, but Fowler opened his mouth at the same time.

"You're police officers," he said. "I—I guess you've found out about it, haven't you? Somehow. That—that was me. Did that. I don't guess I was sort of thinking straight—but—but that was me did it. I guess—"

"*Burt!*" gasped his mother, and tried to scream, and went over in a dead faint. Mrs. Pace began to scream hysterically.

"*You don't mean—*"

"Oh, hell," said Mendoza. "Get some females up here, Art— the phone—"

Both the women were taken down to Central Receiving in shock. Mendoza, finding Grace in the office when they towed Fowler in, said with relief, "Our sweet talker. Go talk to Alice Hildebrand, Jase. She'll be at work. Break the news—" He outlined the situation, and Grace looked at Fowler incredulously.

"I will be damned. All right—save the nicest jobs for me, don't you? But I'll be interested in what you get out of him."

They took Fowler into an interrogation room and read him the piece all about his rights. "Do you understand that, Fowler? Do you want to waive your right to remain silent?"

He blinked up at them. Higgins offered him a cigarette and he said he didn't smoke. "You mean, do I want to tell you about it? How it happened? I *want* to tell about it. Because ever since —ever since I did it, it's been in my mind it was the wrong way to think. I been all confused. It seemed so plain to me and then —and then—after, it wasn't."

"How do you mean, plain?" asked Hackett.

"Well, Alice was feeling so terrible about divorcing that guy. You got to understand, Alice and I went to high school together, I always wanted Alice to marry me, but she picked him instead. And then when she divorced him, well, ever since she came back to live here, she was feeling so bad about it—right down sick, she was doctoring for it, and I felt bad too because I still wanted

195

her to marry me. I'd never treat Alice the way he—I just wanted to take care of her, so she wouldn't have to work, or get sick or be hurt— But she wouldn't marry me, and it was all on account of the bad time she had with that guy." He looked at them anxiously to see if they were following him.

"So?" said Hackett.

Fowler heaved a sigh. "It came into my mind," he said, "because it was just on account of the time she'd had with that guy, the time she was married to him, that she wouldn't marry me— and it came to me all of a sudden that if the kids—if the kids weren't there, it'd be like she never was married to him. To anybody. I thought with the kids gone, it'd be like it was before, her living down the block with her mother—and—I'd take her out on dates, like we did in high school—and—then maybe she'd marry me. You see how I figured? It seemed as plain as day right then. As plain as day. Without the kids, it'd be like it was— And—"

They looked at each other. "Go on, Fowler," said Higgins.

"Well, I—it was all that morning I was thinking about it. It seemed so plain—such a good idea. My car was in the garage, a lube job, and I parked the truck—I was out on the job, of course —round the corner, and got my car when it was ready and drove it back and parked on Twelfth, just round the corner from the house. And then I walked back to the truck, and I got sent on a job, repair a line over on Normandie, and I called in and said it'd take a while. It didn't really. I went back—I knew the kids of course, knew they'd be right in the back yard—and there wasn't any trouble, I just—took them. I—just—well, you know what I did. I took 'em in my car, I did it in the car before I put them—there, that place. It just seemed so plain to me, if they weren't there, it'd all be just like it was before Alice married that guy—and then she'd—"

Higgins had been taking it down in shorthand. When Fowler didn't say anything more, after a long silence Higgins asked, "Will you sign that as a statement, Fowler, if we get it typed up?"

"What? Sure. But you see—" He looked at them painfully, earnestly. "Ever since, I been feeling all confused about it. It seemed plain as could be, but it's been in my mind ever since it *wasn't* the way to do it—and nothing's like what it was before, and Alice isn't like what she used to—still feeling just terrible about things—and I been *confused*. Now, I just don't know— about anything. I just don't know."

"You just wait here for a little while, we'll have this statement for you to sign," said Higgins.

But when they had got him to sign it, and booked him in at the jail on Alameda, Hackett said, "My God, Luis, but he's nutty as a fruitcake. Schizo? Belatedly showing up? The D.A. won't even think about a trial—"

"So he won't," said Mendoza. "After what the head doctors will probably say. At least, be grateful for small favors, he'll get stashed away at Atascadero with the criminal insane. And anybody there who suddenly—according to the head doctors—regains his sanity, still has to stand trial for what he got there for. But—"

"But," said Higgins, "my God, what a thing. Those two babies —he thought if they weren't there— Christ. The things we see—"

"The dirt at the bottom of things, George. The mud we're paid to wallow in. I've stopped asking myself why I'm still down here when I don't have to be." Mendoza lit a cigarette and watched the smoke drift ceilingward; and the building moved like an uneasy sleeper and swayed a little; everything loose clattered.

"Damn aftershocks," muttered Higgins.

The outside phone shrilled on Mendoza's desk and he picked it up. "Mendoza, Central Homicide."

"Royce. Just thought you'd like to know that Pat's doing fine. The doctors say it'll be a little while, but eventually he'll be quite O.K. They let him sit up a few minutes today, and he passed on a message for you boys."

"That's good news—"

"Said to tell you he appreciates your getting right on it and catching up to those—"

"Now, Captain," said Mendoza. "He did not. He'd know we

would get on it, whoever he was—and the old reliable LAPD usually does catch up."

Royce laughed. "I was being polite. What he said was, he'd never realized before—until those punks jumped him—how the citizen feels when something happens—never a cop around when you need one."

Mendoza laughed. "Well, give him our best wishes." And that was another thing—those four young punks were scheduled for arraignment tomorrow.

Dr. Stuyvesant came in hastily just before six, to make that statement. He apologized; nothing urgent about the statement, and he'd been kept busy. Piggott, coming in with Landers just then, asked about old Mrs. Mallory.

"She died. Never regained consciousness," said Stuyvesant shortly.

Palliser, arriving home at the forty-thousand-dollar house on Hillside Avenue, swung Roberta off her feet and kissed her soundly. "I've got dinner hot for you," she said breathlessly.

"Darling love, you aren't sorry, are you?"

"Of course not, idiot. I think I'm a little relieved." Roberta laughed. "Ever since I signed up, I've been thinking about dealing with the little monsters en masse again and getting cold feet. Do you care which it is?"

"Whatever you produce will be fine with me," said Palliser.

"And I've been thinking about names—well, we figure it should be around the last week of April," said Roberta. "Of course we've got plenty of time to decide, but I rather thought of your middle name—Andrew John for a boy—or possibly David for my father—"

"Right now I'm more interested in food," said Palliser. "We'll argue that one later, Robin."

They all went home and told their wives about Fowler, and Alison and Angel and Mary said much the same things. Occa-

198

sionally the offbeat one did turn up: the thing the rational mind could hardly accept.

And Mendoza's subconscious mind was still trying to tell him something about Dr. Harlow's records. Leave it, he thought out of experience; stop trying to think what it was, it might emerge.

And the routine went on forever: they had now the Fleming thing still on hand, but other things would be turning up to work —maybe another puzzler, more likely the spate of routine violent death in the city, for any city is death-prone—the little things making more paper work, more legwork.

Palliser came back on Tuesday, to balance Grace being off, and told them all about the joke on his Robin, which was appreciated. "I never did like the idea of her going back to work, and now— Well, the doctor said about the last of April."

"And we can all keep fingers crossed for Jase," said Mendoza, grinning. "I take it he meant me to pass it on—they're hoping to adopt the Harlow baby."

"Good luck to that," said Hackett. "Cutest little thing I ever saw, that one—and we can guess, some pretty good genes there, judging by the parents. There'll be miles of red tape to unwind, that County Adoption Agency—"

"Yes, they know that. But in the end—" Sergeant Lake looked in and Mendoza sighed. "Here we go again, boys."

"Yeah, there's a new one gone down, but also—" A man in a tan jump suit came in past him, frowning at papers on a clipboard.

"Is this the Homicide place? Fourth on the list, this floor. You got, lessee, nine windows here some place, three eight by four, vertical, six three by eight, horizontal. That right?"

"Welcome, friend!" said Hackett fervently. "We could kiss you. You've got our new windows?"

"This afternoon, we're scheduled to install 'em. Have to ask you to keep out of the way."

"That's all right." The interrogation rooms were minus windows—and if the window installers delayed a few reports getting

199

typed up, it was worth it. Presumably once the windows were in, they'd get the refrigerated air conditioning turned back on.

"What's the new one, Jimmy?"

"Address over on San Marino—suicide," said Lake.

"I'll take it." Palliser got up.

It was just more paper work, of course, but—thinking of Robin, and the baby—he looked at it feeling a little angry. Which was senseless.

"He wasn't worth it," sobbed the live young woman. "A dirty bum he was—been in jail and all—she was a fool over him! I told her—time and again I told her—but Jeanie never would listen—over a bum like that—"

Palliser looked at the dead young woman, the note trembling in her sister's hand, and he felt angry because some people had so few guts. And he thought how senseless it was to feel that way—human nature—and unexpectedly he thought, *Men have died and worms have eaten them, but not for love. . . .*

"I'm sorry to have to bother you at a time like this," he said automatically, "but I'll have to ask you some questions—"

And the criminals, pro or amateur, were often stupid; but they couldn't count on that. It was entirely possible that Howie Engel wouldn't show at the Pink Pussycat again. On Saturday Landers and Piggott had found the Scotts at Rhoda Fleming's apartment, sorting through her belongings, and asked them to come in for a session with a police artist to give a description of that diamond ring so he could draw as accurate a picture of it as possible. Apparently it was a custom design.

They hadn't said anything to the Scotts about Rhoda's bar hopping. Time enough for them to get that shock later.

They'd sent copies of the drawing to all the local pawnbrokers and the press. Only the *Herald* had seen fit to run it. They thought the pawnbrokers were more likely to be seeing the ring itself than the citizenry, anyway.

On Tuesday night they sat at a table at the Pink Pussycat for three hours, Landers nursing a highball and Piggott bored over

200

coffee. Howie Engel didn't show; the piano player had agreed to point him out if he did.

They had looked for him in Records. He wasn't in theirs, but he showed up twice as dropped on by the sheriff's boys: both times, possession of narcotics.

The new calls came in. The new windows got installed, and everybody heaved a sigh of relief when the air conditioning came back on. And Mendoza, sitting brooding at his desk, still felt there was something he should remember about Dr. Harlow's records—something very simple, and yet possibly significant—

On Wednesday night Piggott and Landers staked out the Pink Pussycat. Engel didn't show.

On Thursday morning, with Hackett and Higgins off, a couple of new calls had just got sent up by Traffic—an accident down at the Stack where all the freeways came together in a glorious jumble, one D.O.A., and another body in an alley over on the Row—when a neatly-tailored man came in and told Sergeant Lake the desk sergeant had said this was where he should come. "About this drawing," he said, and showed Lake the artist's sketch of Rhoda Fleming's diamond ring. "I have a pawnshop on Ninth Street, and—"

"Yes, sir. Tom—Matt! Hold it, you got something."

Landers and Piggott had just been leaving to look at the body on the Row. They let Glasser go instead and listened to Mr. Theodore Eisenstadt.

"This ring," he said. "A custom piece, I think. I know something about stones, of course. As soon as I see this sketch I realize, I got it. I took it in. I apologize, gentlemen, for the delay—I've just lost my older brother, he lived up in Carmel, I close the shop and go up for the funeral, naturally. I only got back to the city today, and of course I find this notice from the police, this drawing. And so—" He sighed. "I bring you the ring." He laid it on Landers' desk between them.

Rhoda Fleming's ring, all right, by the description and sketch. "When did you take it in, sir?" asked Landers. "Who pawned it?"

"Tuesday," said Eisenstadt. "No, no, I mean a week ago last

Tuesday." Two days after Rhoda Fleming had died. "I have copied out the record from my books for you. His name was Harold Edwards." The old initials bit, thought Landers and Piggott. "I gave him three-fifty for it."

"What's it worth actually?"

Eisenstadt shrugged. "Fifteen hundred. Yes, he gave an address—Virgil Avenue. I write that down for you too. You think he's the one murdered this poor woman?"

"Could be. What did he look like?" asked Piggott. "You remember?"

"Oh, perhaps thirty—fair hair, six feet high, sports clothes—informal like you say."

Howie Engel. "Well, thank you very much," said Piggott.

"So what happens to my three-fifty? Stolen property," said Eisenstadt sadly. "I got to give it back. If you put out the notice sooner, I'd have spotted it then, made the excuse, call you and stall him. And I'd still have three-fifty I don't have now."

"We're very sorry," said Landers, "but we didn't hear about it until some time later, you see."

"Well, it's the way the cards go down," said Eisenstadt.

They went to the address on Virgil and it was an empty lot.

On Thursday night they staked out the Pink Pussycat again and at seven-forty the piano player caught Landers' eye and pointed to the bar. A tall blond fellow in navy slacks and blue shirt stood there, drinking a highball. Landers and Piggott went over and got him between them. "Mr. Engel?"

"Yeah, that's—" They showed him the badges and he looked nervous, tried to back away. "Hey, what you want with—"

"Just a few questions." Outside, they recited the piece about his rights to him and he said yeah, yeah, he understood that. They took him back to the office; it being a quiet night, both Schenke and Galeano sat in on the questioning.

He started out denying everything; never saw that dame, never had nothing to do with— "Then how did you happen to have her diamond ring?" asked Landers. "The daughter has identified it. The pawnbroker will identify you as the man who pawned it. For three hundred and fifty bucks. Where did you get it?"

"Oh, hell," said Engel unhappily. "Hell and damnation. All right. I got it off her. Off that dame."

"So, would you like to tell us about it? How you beat her and strangled her? Did you rape her too?"

"Who, me? Hell, no—I wouldn't do a— *That* dame? Listen, she was— Well, all right, I got to tell you how it happened, so you get it straight. You could say it was all her own damn fault, she was makin' up to me at that place that night. Makin' a play for me, yeah. I bought her a couple drinks, I think she's a neat enough little chick, and she asks me to take her home—so I— but, Jesus," said Engel, "we get there, I see her in good light, she's a bag!—an old bag, maybe forty-five, fifty, old enough be my— Well, I was kind of insulted, you get me, her thinkin' I'd— I laughed at her, what the hell an old bag like her expect, I'm interested lay a dame that old?—and she got mad, she hit me, and I— What? No, she wasn't drunk, she'd only had a couple before she got me to take her—" Of course that would have showed up in the autopsy. "And *I* got mad—what the hell, a beat-up old dame like— Well, you know that dim light in bars, it wasn't till I saw her plain— So then I, well, I guess I belted her—"

"You'd had a fix that day?" asked Piggott. "Are you on the hard stuff, Engel?"

"What the *hell?* How the hell you know— No. No. I'm not—" But then, of course, with the voluntary statement, they could search him. And in his jacket pocket they found a little pillbox with a screwed-up paper packet of heroin in it.

"All right," he said, goaded. "All right. I'd had a fix—that afternoon. I'm not on it regular. Just off and on. Not like I got to have it—"

"Not yet," said Landers. "So then you found she was dead. Why the bathtub, Howie?"

"Oh, hell. Well, damn it, I never meant her to be dead, my God, and I just thought—take her clothes off, put her in the bathtub, everybody think she fell and killed herself, see—I just—and it wasn't till then I spotted that ring, so I--"

Schenke was taking it down in shorthand. They got him to sign it, and booked him into the jail on Alameda.

"Satan," said Piggott, "going up and down."

Landers thought it was even simpler: human nature doing what comes naturally.

"Oh, yes," said Mendoza on Friday morning, hearing the account of that from Landers while Piggott typed the final report. Hackett and Higgins were back, there too because for the moment nothing new had come in. "Oh, yes. Maybe, just lately, Rhoda had been thinking about that old devil sex. Making up to Howie—asking him to take her home. And not drunk, even halfway. Mmh, yes." He laughed. "Can't we guess what the head doctors would say? Resentful of turning into a grandmother, the well-preserved, still female woman, wanting the reassurance that she's still attractive to the opposite sex— ¡Oye, no vale nada!"

"I don't know, Luis," said Hackett. "A little something in that maybe."

Mendoza laughed cynically. "The head doctors sometimes sound like the puritans, Arturo. Nobody over fifty remotely interested— ¡Qué disparate! It's the individual thing—some people yes, some people no. The individual human nature. Fatal for Rhoda Fleming."

Palliser had come in to hear that, and he said then, seriously, "That's funny. Your saying that. That suicide on Tuesday—a stupid thing, but most suicides are—I don't know what put it in my head—Men have died and worms have eaten them, but—"

"Not for love," said Mendoza. "No, not for love. Self-love—he'll be sorry when I—oh, yes. Pues sí. Life—love, and death. And death." He put out his cigarette; his tone was vague. "But not for love. What the hell am I thinking—something trying to—Harlow—"

"Harlow?" Jason Grace came in. "That call on Figueroa just gives us more paper work. Looks like a coronary. Senior citizen, I.D. tags him as belonging to a rest home on Alvarado. Anybody's guess how he got so far downtown, or why."

"Yes," said Mendoza meaninglessly, his gaze unfocused.

"*Quieto,*" said Hackett interestedly. "He's having a hunch."

"Love, and death—" said Mendoza. Quite suddenly he sat up and said, "*Muerte?*" His eyes focused on Hackett. "A hunch? Well, Arturo, for what it's worth my subconscious just came through. And why it didn't come to me before—but what the hell it might be worth—love, and death—"

"You turning into a philosopher now?"

"*No hay tal.* You can come along if you like, and see what the hell it *is* worth. Probably just another wild-goose chase—"

"Your wild-goose chases are sometimes interesting," said Hackett.

## 14

Mendoza said, "Give me five minutes to find out where we're going," and shut the office door on them. Sergeant Lake was on the phone, and held up a beckoning hand. Something new.

"So, have fun with the wild goose," said Grace; he and Palliser went over to Lake and on out. Three minutes later Mendoza came out of his office with his hat in hand and crooked a finger at his two senior sergeants.

Downstairs, they got into the Ferrari, Higgins squeezing into the jump seat behind, and Mendoza turned up to Grand and then to Wilshire. At the McLaren Building, the lot was not half full; they parked, and Mendoza led them up to the second floor.

"He's going to reenact the crime, just like the Paris *flics*," said Hackett.

"*Insolencia.*" Mendoza led them down to the door still inscribed in gold *Dr. John Harlow, M.D.*, and opened it; they went into the waiting room. The glass window where the receptionist kept an eye on patients was open; lamps were on; there was someone here. The furniture was dusty, and past the open door to the hall they could see still a few faint marks where chalk had outlined the body of Harriet Jenkins. For a breath they all remembered the first time they'd seen this place, minutes after violent death had struck, and the screams and blood.

"I should think—" began Hackett, and steps sounded in the hall.

"Your husband told me you'd be here, Mrs. Short," said Mendoza.

206

"Oh, Lieutenant—you startled me." She was in an ordinary cotton dress, not nurse's uniform; her kind-eyed plump face wore a troubled look, and she looked down at the professional-man's bag she was carrying. "Yes, the lawyer asked if I'd do it, you see, as I'd be familiar with things. There's nobody else to see to things, and this has all got to be sorted out and cleared away. The office was on lease—the lawyer'll see to that, I suppose, whatever they do in a case like this. And some friends of the Harlows out where they lived, he said, they'd offered to see to the house, clean out the refrigerator and sort out clothes for the salvage people—they took all the baby's things down to wherever you people took her. That poor mite— You know, Lieutenant, I often think one of the worst things about people dying—for those left—is having to sort through all the odds and ends left."

"It can be. There'll be quite a lot to do here?"

She nodded. "It's a puzzle to me to know *what* to do with some of it—I'll ask the lawyer. The—"

"Who's the lawyer?"

"He gave me a card when he came to ask me—" She put down the bag and produced it from her purse; Mendoza copied the name and address. Grace would probably want to see the lawyer.

"I suppose some young doctor just starting out would be glad of his instruments, and the lawyer could advertise—all the equipment worth something, the sterilizers and examining tables and the new massager—but some of it's a downright puzzle. All the sample medicines, hundreds of boxes—and cotton and sterile bandage and tongue depressors and adhesive—I don't like to throw it away. I thought maybe some of the other doctors here could just take it. Use it. I asked Dr. Colcannon across the hall—" She shook her head. "All his regular patients, Dr. Harlow's I mean, are getting transferred to either Dr. Weaver or Dr. Tansey, they're both in this building and have all their own office equipment, they wouldn't be needing—and by the way, Lieutenant, we'll have to have his records back, I hope you—"

"Yes, of course, they're quite safe," said Mendoza. "I—"

"You don't realize what a place like this accumulates," said

Mrs. Short. "All the odds and ends. And there's their house too—The lawyer said there was a will, but it just left everything to his wife. I didn't like to bother him, he's a busy man, but I wonder what will happen about that—"

Mendoza lit a cigarette. "A lot of red tape. In the end, everything going—after the lawyers have squabbled over it God knows how long—the property probably held in trust for the child, with an officer of the court as trustee. That is, if there's anything left after the lawyers are finished with it. Of course, if the child's adopted—"

"I do hope some nice people will take her, poor little thing. They were only paying for the house, of course. Well, it's a real headache to clear up this place, I've been at it for three days and it seems I've hardly made a dent yet. There were some personal things in Harriet Jenkins' desk and I couldn't locate her husband—" She sighed, and looked at them with more attention, and said, "But here I am chattering on, and I guess you'll have a reason for coming to see me, Lieutenant. Have you found out who—"

"Not yet. Can we sit down?"

"Surely." They all sat down in the waiting room, which oddly still had a professional feel to it. They felt that any minute a nurse might look out the inner door to summon a patient.

"I brooded over those records," said Mendoza, "and this idea and that came to me—nothing remotely plausible. But just lately, my subconscious has been nudging me—something about those records—but I couldn't think what it was until—mmh—about half an hour ago somebody said something to me about death, and the bell rang. Loud and clear. Those records, Mrs. Short—all those case histories of patients—"

"Yes, sir, what about them?"

"There were a lot of patients. And the records you handed me cover the last three years or so. But there's not one recorded death in them."

"No, of course not—"

"Of course? I know he was in general practice, but surely any doctor loses a patient now and then—"

208

"Of course. But when a patient died, his records would be transferred to the Deceased file. I don't know about other doctors, Dr. Harlow was the only one I worked for privately, but he kept a Deceased file for reference, like. For comparing, oh, new medications out for the same thing the person had died of, and like that."

"I see. Did he lose many patients, on the average?"

"Well, general practitioners—no more than any doctor. Why?"

"Just offhand, before we have a look at that Deceased file," said Mendoza, "how many in, say, the last six months?"

"Let me think back," said Mrs. Short. "Any doctor's apt to have a few elderly patients and they're most likely to go, of course. There was old Mr. Lord—that was around last February. He had rheumatoid arthritis—it was an embolism took him off. A blood clot on the lung, you know. It's more apt to hit sedentary, bedridden people. He was seventy-four. His wife was still coming to the doctor—high blood pressure and colonic trouble. Let's see. Then there was Mrs. Snaith. She'd already had two heart attacks. He'd ordered her into the hospital for some tests, and she went all of a sudden with another one. She was in her sixties. Oh, and one child—that was a tragic thing, but sometimes—the little Bohlen boy. Leukemia. He was only six—"

"Parents seem to feel any—mmh—resentment against the doctor?"

She stared. "Why, no, of course not. They were just all broken up—he was an only child. And leukemia—well, everybody knows—"

"Sí. Any more come to you?"

"Mr. Lawrence," she said obediently. "He was a new patient —the doctor he'd been going to died, Dr. Wrather, and some of his patients were transferred to Dr. Harlow. Mr. Lawrence was only in his fifties, but he was an asthmatic—rheumatic fever as a child, and his heart wasn't strong. He'd been a semi-invalid for years—his wife used to come with him, he couldn't drive. What are you driving at, Lieutenant? When anybody dies, you don't blame the doctor, for goodness' sake. Any doctor's done all he can to stop people dying, but—"

"*Pues sí*. No rational person blames the doctor. Mr. Lawrence. And?"

"Well, for goodness' sake," she said thoughtfully. "But, Lieutenant—anybody like that, lunatic enough to think it had been the doctor's fault, wouldn't he have said so, and maybe made threats, right then—so we'd have known and I'd have told you—"

"Not necessarily. Lawrence. Carry on."

"Well, really—there was that Squires thing." Mrs. Short looked suddenly excited. "Oh, that could have—but thinking back, I don't really— Well, what happened, it was a patient of the doctor's, a Mrs. Squires, she brought her stepdaughter in. Her husband's first wife was dead, there was this girl, and she brought her to the doctor because she suspected the girl was using dope. Which it turned out she was—heroin—there was quite a scene in the office, I remember—the doctor called the police. And she was put in jail, or Juvenile Hall or somewhere, because they found some in her possession, but of course she got out on bail and ran away. She was only fifteen or sixteen. And some time later she was picked up dead—an overdose."

Mendoza looked interested. "Father resentful of stepmother —mmh—precipitating that?"

"I don't know. I don't think so—" She looked doubtful. "He was an educated man, a salesman of some kind, not the doctor's patient. But I know he came to see the doctor, with Mrs. Squires, and talked to him quite a time—like so many people he didn't really know much about narcotics."

"But—with the girl dead—" That one they could look up in their own records. Have a look around, how Squires might be feeling about that now—and about his wife—and about the doctor who, in the course of duty, had uncovered the girl's addiction and in a way precipitated her death.

"Well, I don't know. There was Mrs. Lessing. But heaven knows nobody could blame Dr. Harlow for that—her husband brought her in, last April it was—he was a regular patient—she didn't want to come, kept saying there wasn't anything wrong with her. But Mr. Lessing—" Mrs. Short chuckled, remembered where she was and sobered. "He was worried because she always seemed so dizzy and weak in the evenings when he got home—"

"Little too much *vino* inside?" grinned Mendoza.

"That's just what—only it was vodka. Mr. Lessing never suspected a thing. Well, the doctor suspected it, and even went to the trouble of dropping into the house unexpectedly to satisfy himself. But Mr. Lessing wouldn't believe it. He's an abstainer himself, and he thought she was. He—"

"Felt the doctor was insulting his wife?"

"Well, I guess he did, then. But the poor man had it proved to him awhile later because she drank herself to death. Dr. Harlow knew the police surgeon who saw her, he told Dr. Harlow she must have killed a fifth of vodka, and naturally she passed right out."

"Mmh. Lessing could," said Mendoza, "have been brooding on that all right. But I don't see any way he could hold Harlow responsible—"

"I think this plot moves a little slow, Luis," said Hackett. "Your wild geese sound pretty tame to me."

"So, any more?" asked Mendoza, ignoring him.

"Well, let's see. It wasn't very often we did lose a patient, but sometimes the circumstances—there wouldn't be much he could do, you know. Did you ever read that old book about the Jukes and the Kallikaks? Genes—we had one new patient in just last month, he's in the General now, hereditary T.B. and syphilis, one lung collapsed, first stages of dementia praecox, and he had scurvy when he came in. Scurvy!—in this day and age—you could hardly believe it. But— Oh, I just remembered that."

"What?"

"Talking about genes reminded me. That poor young thing. I can't think of her last name, it'll come to me in a minute, her first name was Sue-Ellen. She was only twenty-three or so, and of course she hadn't any business getting pregnant in the first place. She wasn't, well, built for it at all, and besides that she had a congenital heart weakness and a history of pernicious anemia. When we took her history, it seemed her mother had died of dementia praecox, and her father was a complete invalid, premature senility and riddled with V.D.—he's in the General. Well, the doctor did what he could for her— What? Oh, yes, she was married, she was quite a nice young thing if not an educated girl—but the doctor said to me, a fifty-fifty chance if the baby did live it'd be a borderline idiot, physically defective, and if he had his way people with heredities like that 'd be sterilized. But he did what he could. Her blood count was way down, and she didn't respond to any treatment—he just couldn't get the red-corpuscle count up, at the last he was ordering a blood test every day—"

"She died?" asked Mendoza.

"Yes, she did. And the baby. The doctor said from the first it'd have to be a Caesarean, and when she was about at term, he did that. She was already in the hospital, for all the tests. But pernicious anemia— Well, the baby was dead when he took it, and she died on the table."

"Husband?" asked Mendoza lazily. Hackett shifted and sighed, bored.

"Oh, he carried on like a wild thing, the doctor said, weeping and wailing all over the place—I wasn't there, of course, the doctor told us about it. But there really wasn't anything the doctor could have—than he did. Freeman!" she said suddenly. "I knew it'd come to me. Sue-Ellen Freeman. And now I come to think, the doctor said her husband—"

"¿Qué demonio—? ¡Diez millones de demonios desde el infierno!" said Mendoza. He sat up with a jerk. "Freeman? Freeman? My God—"

"This says something to you?" asked Higgins.

"Because I've seen the reports." Mendoza got up. "Which you haven't. Come on. Mrs. Short, thanks very much. Art—George —¡vamos! We may just have got there."

In his cubbyhole of an office downstairs, the superintendent Enoch Shepard told them Dick Freeman didn't come in until one o'clock. Yes, he had his address, of course. Fifty-second Street.

But when they got there he wasn't home. It was one unit in a very ancient unkempt court, and just as they gave up ringing the doorbell the front door of the unit across the center walk opened and a woman came out. She was a rather handsome slatternly-looking female with a red turban wound around her head.

"You lookin' for Dick Freeman?"

"Do you know where he is?" asked Mendoza.

"You're fuzz. He in some kinda trouble? Thass a pity, but it don't supprise me none. Ever since his wife died, poor thing, he ain't been up to much. Ain't been home much either. He took off from work a couple weeks after, can't seem to get over it no-how."

"When did his wife die, Mrs.—?" They hadn't heard that.

"Thompson. She died, lessee, about a month ago, a bit less 'n that. But—"

"Thanks so much," said Mendoza. So, they thought, the day Dr. Harlow and his wife and receptionist had been shot was very likely the first day Dick Freeman had returned to work at the McLaren Building, after a couple of weeks off after losing his wife.

They went back there to talk to the superintendent again. He was down in the basement—and it was in the basement that they found Dick Freeman. He had made a little screened-off hiding place for himself in a dark corner, with propped-up boards and an old cot, and they heard him sobbing quietly to himself and went to look.

"He's acted sort of funny lately," said Shepard, "but I made allowances, knew he'd just lost his wife. She was a lot younger than him, and he just thought the world of her." He was looking shocked, looking down at Freeman on the cot. "But holing up here—I never suspected—"

And Freeman rolled over on the cot and said drearily, "I jus' couldn' go back that house, Mr. Shepard—where Sue-Ellen 'n' I were happy—I jus' kept seein' her there—"

"And thinking about the doctor, Freeman?" asked Mendoza.

"The doctor who didn't save her from dying?" Shepard had switched on a main light in this part of the dingy basement, and Freeman blinked in the sudden glare.

"Who're you?"

And Shepard said in a horrified tone, "Dr. *Harlow?* You saying *Dick—*"

"How about it, Freeman?"

He raised a ravaged face to them. He was a stocky black man about forty, with a big chest and a few pockmarks of some old skin disease. His woolly hair was getting thin, and he had big square hands now fastened together tight in a kind of anguished silent gesture. "The doctor, Freeman," said Mendoza. "The doctor who let Sue-Ellen die."

"He did! He did so—she *shouldn't've* died—my Sue-Ellen—"

"Oh, my God!" said Shepard. "But, my God, it was me told him to take his wife there! It was me advised him—good doctor like—oh, my God!"

"They know things, doctors—they got that great big hospital —needles in her an' medicine an' her goin' see him all the time, an' he say—she hafta tell me how he mean, some way take the baby before— She *shouldn't've* gone 'n' died! That doctor—he could've stopped her dyin'! Only—only—he *wouldn't.* I heard him, I heard him my own self, I heard him one time I take Sue-Ellen there—he's talkin' to somebody, 'n' that window thing was open, I heard—my Sue-Ellen! Say, that doctor, how people with —I dunno how t' say it, but he meant like, sickness in the fambly like—hered-something—but Sue-Ellen tole me what it meant, how they ought not *have* babies— He *wanted* her to die, 'n' the baby too! All I ever had—my Sue-Ellen—"

"Oh, my God," said Shepard. He backed away.

"I thought about it—all the while I thought about it. After the funeral. Funeral—put my Sue-Ellen in the ground, an' the little baby too—we been so happy about the baby—I thought about *that doctor.* Look down his nose at people like us, ordinary folk —high 'n' mighty sayin'— I thought *good.* An' the Bible say, eye for eye, life for life. An' I took all I'd saved up—an' I went an' bought that gun—an' I—"

214

"Where's the gun now, Freeman?" asked Hackett gently.

And Freeman fumbled with the thin blanket spread on the cot and produced it meekly. Hackett took it and broke it; it was empty.

"I didn't have—no call for a gun—after that. I th'ew away the rest o' the bullets in the box. Mr. Shepard don't know—I been comin' here, know where the key is so I get 'nother one made, get in here. I was here—that day, before I— 'N' I don't care what you do to me," mumbled Freeman. "It don't matter. I teach *that* doctor—eye for an eye—"

They brought him in and booked him. "The vision in your crystal ball," said Hackett.

"Crystal ball hell, once my subconscious got through to me about there being no deaths listed—pure logical deduction," said Mendoza.

"Any bets on where he'll end up?" asked Higgins.

"He can't afford the tricky lawyer," said Mendoza cynically, "to claim temporary insanity, pull all the other dodges. He knew what he was doing." Freeman was just barely literate, and had signed a statement. "I'll guess life—and they'll keep him. Nobody's going to be that interested, to help him get parole when he's eligible." The joker was, of course, that in this state a lifer was eligible for parole after seven years. Of late, a few judges with some common sense had been handing down life terms with a rider, no possibility of parole; and seeing that Freeman had wantonly killed three people, he might get that rider.

At least they knew who, on the Harlow shooting. They sent the Harrington and Richardson nine-shot to Ballistics, just to get more evidence for the D.A.

Jason Grace took the name of Harlow's lawyer with thanks. "He may be persuaded to jump in on our side, who knows? Anyway, he'll know the right legal steps to take. Red tape—but she'd be worth it, you know." Grace grinned. "They finally let us see her yesterday, just for a minute."

"And good luck on it, Jase."

"Which I have the feeling we'll need. Adoption agencies—oh, well, never say die."

"I do hope they'll get her eventually," said Roberta. "You'd think even an adoption agency would have the sense to see it'd be a good home, and—"

"Yes, come to think it's a lot less trouble to produce your own," said Palliser. "My God, that Freeman—of course he's uneducated, ignorant, but essentially that couldn't matter less. When the incipient violence is in him— Well, at least he's stashed away. . . . Oh, and I forgot to tell you, Robin—"

Sheriff Roudebush had called the Homicide office on Saturday and asked for Palliser. "I just thought you'd be interested to know that we finally identified Steve. The Feds didn't know him, but they passed his prints to Interpol and they made him. He was a Canadian citizen, Steven Cockburn. Native of Vancouver. He had a little pedigree with the Vancouver police—petty theft, shoplifting, vagrancy, vandalism. Twenty-three. Raised in an orphanage there, so there's nobody to mourn him."

"And he doesn't sound like much loss to the world," said Palliser.

"I don't suppose," agreed the sheriff. "We'll probably try Brodie and the girl next month."

"Involuntary manslaughter, and Brodie'll get a year. Accessory to, the girl let off on probation."

"Oh, yes. We now have Papa Schultz," said the sheriff, "breathing fire at us. The girl's out on bail and wishing she was back in jail."

Palliser laughed. "Well, let them sort it out. The Tims and Wilmas usually in trouble of some sort."

"Any more earthquakes down there?"

"Not to speak of," said Palliser.

Landers took Phil O'Neill to dinner that night, and looking at her across the table, on the patio of Frascati's where it was just starting to cool off a little, he said, "You know, the things we

216

see— Well, the lieutenant said the other day, it's a dangerous commodity."

"Your brilliant lieutenant with the crystal ball. What is?"

"Love," said Landers. "In"—he grinned at her—"the wrong hands, so to speak. Listen, how long are you going to play hard to get?"

*"Me?"* said Phil. She looked very delectable, his diminutive freckled Phil, in a narrow-strapped blue sundress and the high-heeled sandals that still brought her blonde head only up to his chest. "Me, playing— I told you, I'm only being sensible, Tom. We *haven't* known each other very long. And—"

"Don't con me," he said, reaching for her hand. "When you spent nearly your whole vacation chasing around playing detective to get me off the hook, back in June—well, you've got a sort of vested interest."

"And also some common sense. You got off the subject, you were telling me how your brilliant lieutenant came up with the X on the Harlow shooting. Go on. He wondered about deaths, so—?" She sipped her martini.

"It's my own fault for falling for a policewoman, I admit it. Too many brains," said Landers. "Which reminds me, what did your I.Q. test show, when you joined up?"

"What? Oh, a hundred and twenty."

"Well, by God, that settles it," said Landers pleasantly. "Soon or late, I'll overpower you, lady—you and your common sense. Mine came out a hundred and thirty-three."

"We'll hold some good thoughts for the Graces and that baby," said Angel Hackett, adding a dash of pepper to the pot she was stirring. "It'd be wonderful if they could have her."

"Jase can be persistent," said Hackett. "That Freeman—it makes you wonder."

"Genes," said Angel vaguely, tasting the contents of the pot. "Have you weighed today?"

"I'm down to two hundred and twelve," said Hackett with dignity. "And—" Mark, belatedly discovering that he was home, came shouting, and Sheila tottered up with arms upheld.

Hackett picked one up in each arm, fondly. "So how are my two nuisances?" And, well, they were, at times, but love, thought Hackett suddenly and vaguely, was a funny thing. . . .

Higgins went home, and wanting to tell Mary about the Graces and their campaign to get Celia Ann Harlow, was pounced on by Steve and Laura Dwyer. They had a library book all about earthquakes and what caused them and where they were likely to occur, and photographs of past destructions by earthquakes.

"There was one in nineteen thirty-three and it knocked down all the schools, George—it was just lucky there wasn't anybody in them when it happened—"

"And it says one can happen any time, just like the paper said —and wouldn't it be exciting if—"

Higgins didn't think it would be exactly exciting, if. Personally he could do without earthquakes. But of course he had all the seniority built up, in earthquake country.

Mary, exchanging a private grin with him, announced dinner. She was, these days, rather enormous around the middle— but she looked, thought Higgins, just fine.

Mendoza came home a little late that Saturday night. The driveway, as he turned in, was flat and smooth: the cement company had argued, and even mentioned Acts of God, but had proved no match for a redhaired Scots-Irish girl; they had repaired the drive the second time without charge.

It was getting dark, but the mockingbird in the alder tree, hearing the car, uttered a sleepy *YAWK* and a token *Yankee Doodle*. Mendoza went in the back door and found Mrs. Mac-Taggart just taking a pan of her special scones out of the oven. "You'll be wanting a dram," she told him. El Señor arrived posthaste as he heard the bottle taken down, and leaped to the counter top for his half ounce in a saucer.

"Ought to join A.A.," said Mendoza, and strolled down to the nursery. In the doorway he surveyed his various hostages to fortune, acquired in a somewhat helter-skelter manner over

218

a period of time—the other cats, Bast, Sheba and Nefertite, would be having a dignified nap after dinner, elsewhere; but Cedric, their accidentally acquired shaggy dog, came to greet him amiably, shaking his face veil to show his wild walleye and offering a large paw. *"Bufón ridículo,"* said Mendoza, accepting it.

"Oh, *amado,* you're home," said Alison over the welcoming shouts of the offspring. "Now listen—I *am* getting somewhere, you know. Come on, Johnny, say it—the way we've been practicing. The wolf, English. *El lobo,* Spanish. Two ways to say it."

*"Sí,"* said Johnny obligingly. "The wolf, English. *El lobo,* Spanish. Two ways. Daddy—Daddy—read *el cuento* 'bout *la cabra y los niños*—the little kids, *el lobo* eat all down! An' they fill up *el lobo con* stones, an' *el lobo—*"

"Jingle!" said Terry. "Jingle! *La bruja* make *la magia*— I *like la bruja, I* like make *la magia*—like Daddy do, See-Saw Margery Daw—an' ever'thing go to *danzar!"*

Reminded of this interesting happenstance, Johnny instantly demanded, "Do again! Make all go to *danzar,* Daddy—"

Mendoza burst out laughing and Alison said crossly, *"¡Por Dios!* Just as I think I'm accomplishing— And it's a great help for you to find it amusing, I must say! If you'd try to *cooperate* a little—"

"A losing battle," said Mendoza. "As they mature, *enamorada,* they'll sort out the problem for themselves. I hope."

"And your father," said Alison to the twins, "may be the brilliant guiding light of LAPD Homicide, but he does not bring about earthquakes—"

It was, of course, unfortunate that just then there was a slight aftershock, and everything rattled and trembled for twenty seconds.

"Honestly!" said Alison. "I just can't win. Honestly!"

And of course, whatever cases they cleared away, filed final reports on, handed over to the D.A.'s office, the inevitable routine went on for Central Homicide. The new calls, the new bodies making more paper work, if seldom the mysteries posed in the paperbacks at the corner drugstore.

That Sunday, they had another body on the Row—probably natural death: the inevitable new suicide, and yesterday's traffic accident, one D.O.A., to finish the paper work on. Mendoza was reading the autopsy report on a body from two days back, without much interest, when Hackett looked into his office and said, "New one just gone down."

"*¿Qué?* Anything interesting?"

"Well, you might think so. Body just found up by the Dodger Stadium—I talked to the Traffic man. Young fellow, no immediate cause evident, no I.D., not a mark on him. And he's wearing a false beard and moustache."

"*¿Cómo? ¡Parece mentira!* What the hell— I think I'll come with you, take a look—"

"I thought you might," said Hackett. "A little offbeat, it sounds."

Downstairs, as they got into the Ferrari, there was no sign of the picket with his doom-predicting sign. "Maybe he's decided the doom isn't so imminent after all," said Mendoza. It was a warm sunny day, clear blue sky, and the aftershocks were gradually diminishing. But of course now they had to look forward to the worst of the summer heat in Southern California.

"Imminent hell, who knows?" said Hackett. "Another article in the *Herald* last night, we could have another big one any time, pressure building on the San Andreas—"

"Don't borrow trouble, Arturo," said Mendoza cheerfully. "Sufficient is the evil— And this new one looks a little interesting. . . ."